I have edited Clive Gilson's books for over a decade now – he's prolific and can turn his hand to many genres. poetry, short fiction, contemporary novels, folklore, and science fiction – and the common theme is that none of them ever fails to take my breath away. There's something in each story that is either memorably poignant, hauntingly unnerving, or sidesplittingly funny - *Lorna Howarth, The Write Factor*

Ragged A**** Ruffian reviewed on Amazon in the United Kingdom on 27 January 2021 - A truly heartwarming, interesting, story with a wonderful narrative. Unquestionably a splendid read

A Solitude of Stars: With deft turns of phrase and an imagination that would make Philip K. Dick jealous, Gilson foresees a dystopian future, the seeds of which are definitely being sown right now. The story is a chilling glimpse of what may come to pass, warmed by a thread of love that raises the narrative beyond despair. I found the stories disturbing and breathtaking in equal measure. The Apparat and Dirigiste tribes are ranging across our solar system seeking peace by waging war, raising the question; is humanity actually capable of peace? A riveting read. - *Rob Swan, The Write Factor*

Songs of Bliss gripped me from the start - I had to read right to the end. Loved the humour. Impressed by the surprising empathy that I felt for rather - on the face of it - unlikeable characters. Look forward to seeing it in print. - *Maighdean-Mhara, commenting on Authonomy*

I just wanted to thank you once more for your help acquiring this beautiful collection. It's found a new home at the top of my library. I've already stumbled onto some wonderful stories in a couple of the collections, and I can't wait to get more. Have a wonderful holiday and a great new year... - *Richer Daniel Laporte, California, December 2021*

Melodies In Black Ink

A collection of darkly captivating short tales,
each inspired by the melodies that move us,
the lyrics that linger, and the stories hidden
between the notes

Melodies In Black Ink

www.clivegilson.com

First print edition © 2025, Clive Gilson

Printed by IngramSpark

ISBN: 978-1-915081-33-9

Table of Contents

Author's Note

The stories that you're about to read are inspired by songs that have resonated deeply with me in recent years, songs that evoke powerful emotions and create a sense of place and time. While these stories draw from the spirit of the featured songs, they are my own fictional inventions and shouldn't be taken as attempts to interpret or second-guess the original composers' intentions. Instead, think of them as a kind of homage, or, for want of a better phrase, a collection of fan fiction pieces. Each story is a tribute to the artistry and emotion in these songs, hopefully capturing how they've inspired my imagination.

Given the nature of the original inspiration, the following stories do not fit into any particular genre or style, so you'll come across a range of settings and themes. There's the odd piece of science fiction, a little gothic horror, some psychological tales, and more.

You'll find one or two characters appearing in more than one tale, which is often something of a theme in my short stories. I like to create links that allow the stories to develop as I write them. The "*Rose Trilogy*", is a good example of this process, the stories rather taking on a life of their own when *Horizon* was first written – again, one of the things that I love about

1

shorter fiction, where you're not bound by the same rules of plotting that you need to consider in longer work.

One thing that strikes me as I look at the collection is how far this set of stories and tracks is from what I would call my "Desert Island Disks" There are a lot of my favourite artists who have not made this cut, but the bottom line is that not every song, no matter how brilliant the track might be, inspires a narrative that I have wanted to work up into something that I hope you find interesting. Where, for example are the two artists that have provided a soundtrack to my life for the last few decades; P J Harvey and Billy Bragg? Oh well, maybe there's more to come one day…

Writing these pieces has been a joy as a creative exercise in exploring the echoes of other works and transforming them into something new. I hope you enjoy reading them as much as I have enjoyed writing them, and that you'll not only feel the same love and respect for the original works that sparked these tales, but maybe you'll let your own imagination run free too.

Clive

Bath, 2025

Heaven

A memory. The golden light of the setting sun didn't just filter through the trees; it flowed down in delicate streams, painting the world in hues of amber and honey. The leaves seemed to shimmer in the late-afternoon glow, each one catching the light and holding it for just a moment before releasing it.

The winding curves of a narrow, grass-fringed path lead Rose through a magical landscape towards a secret place that she shared with the earth beneath her feet and the boy that she loved. Every step she took on the gravel sent a soft, familiar crunch through the quiet air. The sounds of the wider world seemed muted, softened by the thick, lazy warmth of the summer evening, which wrapped creation in a soothing sense of peace.

Rose slowed her pace even more, deliberately savouring the sensation of time stretching out in front of her. She felt as though she had stumbled upon a perfect pocket of eternity. There was no need to rush. Nothing demanded her attention. Her thoughts wandered, untethered, floating on the gentle rhythm of her footsteps. Memories surfaced of childhood summers spent here, her small hands clasped in her father's great paw as they wandered the same path, his deep voice recounting stories she could barely remember now. With those

3

memories came a brief moment of sadness. Her father died when she was thirteen, leaving her to traverse puberty under the woeful guidance of a neglectful mother.

Rose banished these intrusive thoughts. There was something magical about this time of day. The golden hour, they called it, when the world seemed to hold its breath. For Rose, it was more than just a pretty phrase. This was a moment in which she was suspended between reality and dreams. She could imagine whole lives playing out in the soft, dappled light. She could picture lovers meeting by the river, of children laughing as they raced through the trees, of someone waiting just beyond the bend, their face hidden in shadow.

She stopped for a moment, looking up at the sky, where the sun was lazily sinking toward the horizon, casting the world in that perfect, fleeting glow. A soft breeze whispered through the trees, lifting strands of her hair and carrying with it the faintest scent of pine and fresh water. It was a gentle reminder of the river, just out of sight but close enough that she could hear the faint gurgle of the current as it wound its way through the landscape.

Rose felt weightless, as if she were no longer walking through the world but floating above it, unbound by time and untouched by anything but the warmth of the evening sun. There was a serenity here, an unspoken promise in the air, and she wished she could hold onto it forever. She wished this moment could last, stretching out endlessly like the shadows cast by the trees, until there was nothing left but the light and the quiet and the memory of a world that felt too soft to be real.

But, in Rose's experience, perfect moments were always compromised. The sun would dip lower, the light would dim, and the warmth would give way to the coolness of night. And yet, as she took another step, Rose knew that even when the sun finally disappeared beyond the horizon, this memory, this golden, quiet, sun-dappled moment, would stay with her, always lingering at the edges of her mind, like a softly spoken promise.

As she reached the riverbank, she spotted him. Jack was sitting on a wooden jetty, legs dangling over the edge, his bare feet skimming the water. The sun reflected off the surface in bright streaks. He looked up as she approached, a smile breaking across his face.

"You came," he said, his voice quiet but brimming with possibility.

"Of course," Rose replied, taking a seat beside him, their shoulders touching. The warmth of his skin against hers sent a shiver down her spine, a stirring of something long buried, something neither of them had dared to acknowledge before. They had known each other for years and shared so many moments, stories, and secrets, but this summer… this summer was different. There was an unspoken energy in the air, a quiet charge between them that seemed to hang in every glance and every brush of their fingertips. She wasn't sure when it started, this shift, but she could feel it now, as palpable as the summer heat rising all around them.

They sat together on the dock under the shade of an old oak tree, the thick canopy above shielding them from the fading sun. His arm rested lazily beside hers, their skin touching lightly, almost innocently, except that it didn't feel innocent anymore. Each point of contact sent tiny sparks through her, a soft thrill that made her heart skip just a little faster. It was as if the space between them had tightened, the air thickening with a powerful expectation.

She glanced at him, wondering if he felt it too, this strange, magnetic attraction. Jack's eyes were focused on the river, but there was a stillness in his expression, as though he was listening to something. The sunlight caught in his hair, turning it gold at the fringes, and she had to resist the sudden urge to reach out and run her fingers through it. She swallowed, her throat dry, her thoughts tumbling over each other in a rush.

There was something between them now, something fragile and new, but also inevitable, like the still moment before a storm breaks. They were balancing on the edge of it, teetering on the precipice of change, and she didn't know if she wanted to take that leap or hold back. Her chest tightened with the suspense of not knowing. Part of her wanted to reach out, to ask him what this was, what it meant. She wanted to know if he felt the same force of nature that was drawing her toward him, or if it was just some dream that she had woven out of their years of friendship, but she couldn't ask the question. The fear of shattering this delicate moment, of exposing the fragile thing growing between them to the harshness of daylight, held her back.

And so she sat, her heart fluttering in her chest, her skin tingling where it touched his, and she let the silence stretch out between them. It wasn't an uncomfortable silence. These moments, these pauses had never been uncomfortable with Jack, but now, they felt charged. Rose thought that as each second passed between them when they didn't speak, so the air around them condensed, swirling with possibilities and questions. What if they crossed the line? What if this thing between them, this attraction, was real? Would it change everything? Would it unravel the years they'd spent building this safe and comfortable friendship?

The sun dipped lower, casting long shadows across the fields by the far riverbank, and Rose felt a pang of regret, knowing that time was slipping away. Summer would end. These days of quiet intimacy would fade, and they'd return to their regular lives, but the attraction wasn't something that would just disappear. It would linger, unspoken, a soft ache that she would carry with her, wondering what might have been if she'd had the courage to name it.

Jack shifted beside her, his hand brushing hers, and for a brief, heart-stopping moment, she thought he might say something, but he only smiled, a soft, almost wistful smile, and then he looked away again, the moment slipping through their fingers like dry sand. They sat like that until the sun dipped below the horizon, both of them caught in the quiet tension of this embryonic love. As the stars blinked in the darkening sky, she knew this summer, this moment, would haunt her like an unfinished sentence in an incomplete story. They sat in silence for a while longer, the river flowing lazily below them. Rose let herself lean into the moment, into the easy stillness of the evening, and into Jack's quiet presence beside her. She felt as if this must be what heaven would be like.

As the tide of evening came in, she felt herself slipping into something deeper. Now I'm sliding, she thought, intrigued by the sensation, by this slow, inevitable drift toward the young man sitting quietly next to her. She was young, yes, but a teenager's life spent with a jagged mother meant that Rose was too cautious to believe in the simplicity of summer love. She had lived through youthful heartbreak when her father died and she knew that there was a difference this time around. Her feelings for Jack were not like a babbling brook that could dry up just as quickly as it began to flow after a rainstorm.

"Summer is thirsty work," Jack said suddenly, as if reading her mind. His voice was low and thoughtful. His eyes were fixed on the water. "Best take a drink before the river runs dry."

Rose turned to him, surprised. He hadn't spoken much all day, and his words echoed her own thoughts so closely that it made her heart skip a beat. "You're in heaven now," he added with a quiet smile, glancing at her. "Aren't you?"

She nodded, unable to find the right words. She was in heaven, sitting beside him on this dock, the rising moonlight wrapping them in a cocoon of silver thread. The world outside of their cocoon seemed so far away, like a distant memory. Here, in this moment, everything felt right.

"Do you think it will last?" she asked, her voice barely above a whisper. The question hung in the air between them, delicate and fragile.

Jack looked at her, really looked at her, his gaze deep and searching. "As the tides draw and close, and the seasons turn again," he said, quoting a line from a poem they had both read long ago, "Will the moon still wax and wane?"

Rose smiled, knowing what he meant. Time would keep moving. The tides would come and go, the seasons would change, and the moon would rise and fall in its eternal cycle, but right now, in this moment, they were in heaven, and that was enough.

"Jack, will you always colour my days?" she asked softly, echoing another line from that same poem, her voice filled with hope.

Jack didn't answer right away. Instead, he leaned closer, his hand finding hers. Their fingers intertwined, warm and solid, and in that touch was everything they hadn't said yet. "Yes. We'll always be in heaven," he whispered, his lips brushing against her ear. "This is heaven now."

And for a moment, it truly was. Time slowed, holding them in the fragile balance between day and night, light and shadow. They sat there, hand in hand, their fingers locked together, like two pieces of a puzzle finally finding their place. The air had that stillness that only comes at the end of a long day, when the world exhales and everything seems to quieten. It was as though the earth itself had paused just for them, granting this fleeting moment of peace.

The water shimmered with hues of white and yellow, like liquid fire, flowing silently onwards as if it too was part of the magic they were caught in. Rose watched the current move, steady and unhurried, carrying the remnants of the day away with it. She wished she could let her thoughts drift along with the river, to be carried away from the uncertainty that clung to her like a thin mist.

Beside her, Jack shifted slightly, his thumb gently brushing over the back of her hand in a motion so subtle, so tender, it sent a shiver through her. It was a small gesture, but it spoke volumes. It felt like a silent admission, a wordless understanding of all the things they weren't saying. She glanced at him, and the fading light caught the soft curve of his face, the way his lips were slightly parted as if he, too, was on the verge of saying something he couldn't quite form into words, but he didn't speak, and neither did she. They didn't need to. The silence between them felt full of unspoken promises, of shared memories, of things that were still too delicate to touch.

Above them, the first stars began to appear, tiny pinpricks of light that dotted the deepening sky. The stars blinked into existence, one by one, as if the heavens were stitching together a blanket to cover the earth. She tilted her head back to watch them, feeling a strange sense of wonder, as if she hadn't seen stars before. Each one felt like a distant promise, a reminder that there was more to the world than the small space they occupied now. Yet, in this moment, nothing felt as important as the quiet warmth of his hand on hers and the steady rhythm of his breath beside her.

It was almost too much, this closeness. The simplicity of it was alarming. The world around them seemed to fade into the background, leaving only the two of them sitting there, the soundtrack to their feelings being the river's gentle murmur. She wondered if he felt that their connection was hanging in the air like the stars, so far away and yet so near. She could sense the possibility of it, of something more, of something real, but like the stars, it was just out of reach, distant and glittering.

Rose wanted to speak, to break the spell. She wanted to tell him that this moment in time felt like the beginning of something beautiful, something they'd both been waiting for.

She wanted to say that the way he held her hand made her feel safe, and seen, and more alive than she had felt in years, but the words caught in her throat, tangled in the fear that saying them might break the delicate spell that held them in this perfect stillness.

So instead, she stayed quiet. She let the moment stretch out and settle over them like that heavenly blanket, soft and comforting. Her heart ached with the quiet hope that this feeling, this connection, wouldn't fade like the light of the setting sun. Maybe, just maybe, when the day broke again, they would still be here, hand in hand, facing the dawn together. For now, though, she would hold onto the warmth of his hand in hers. She would listen to the quiet hum of the river beneath their feet, and she would revel in the starshine above them, a silent witnesses to whatever this was.

They stayed like that for a long time, watching the night fall, knowing that tomorrow might bring something different. There would be new challenges, new uncertainties, but for now, they were here, together, in their own little slice of heaven, and that was all that mattered.

Rose glanced back at the river, the water now dark and shimmering under the moonlight. She smiled to herself, knowing that no matter what the future held, she would always remember this, the summer when she found heaven by Jack's side. Beside her Jack fished a joint out of a small canvas bag that lay on the deck by his left leg. He lit up, took a deep drag and held his breath for a long moment, before exhaling a stream of blue smoke into the night. He passed the joint to Rose. She took a hit and leaned back on her elbows. She never wanted to leave this perfect evening behind. "You're in

11

heaven," she whispered, feeling the warmth of his hand in hers, "and so am I."

The song behind the story: *"Colour Me" by Dot Allison is a song from her 1999 debut album Afterglow. The track, like much of her work, blends elements of dream pop, trip-hop, and electronica, creating an ethereal and moody atmosphere. I love Dot Allison's breathy and haunting vocals, which are a key feature, giving the song a delicate, introspective feel.*

The song's mood is one of yearning, where the speaker seems to desire connection, or perhaps even salvation, through love or intimacy. For me, "Colour Me" is a highlight of Afterglow, capturing the ambient, atmospheric quality that defines much of Dot Allison's work.

This one of those songs, like Horizon, that just moves me, and makes me want to find the story.

Album: *Afterglow*

Artist: *Dot Allison*

Year: *1999*

Composer(s): *Dot Allison*

Record Label: *Heavenly Recordings*

Mikey

Mikey sat on the edge of the playground bench, his fingers clenched tightly around his purple lunchbox. He wasn't just holding onto it, he was gripping it like an anchor in a world that often moved too fast and too loud. The laughter and shouts of his classmates swirled around him, a storm of sound that he kept at bay with the fortress of his mind. To them, Mikey was just the weird kid on the sidelines, but in his head, he was something much more powerful.

He was a superhero.

His parents' voices echoed in his mind, the words of their argument this morning ricocheting off the walls of his imagination. Mikey was not sure why they fought so much, and they always seemed to assume that he was not listening, or that he did not understand. One of Mikey's great talents was his ability to remember spoken conversations verbatim, having an eidetic aural facility. He replayed this morning's argument as he sat on the bench.

"He's different," his mother said, her voice tight with frustration but softened by an undertone of worry. "We need to think about alternatives."

"He's not broken," his father snapped back, but his voice lacked conviction, as if he, too, was still trying to convince himself.

"Don't you see how hard it is for him?" she pressed, gesturing toward the open door of Mikey's room. "He's struggling in school. The teachers don't understand him, the other kids don't invite him to birthday parties. And what happens when we're not there to explain things for him?"

"I know it's hard," his father admitted, running a hand through his hair. "But throwing him into a special school, pulling him away from everything familiar, I mean, how does that help?"

"He cries every morning before school. He hides under his bed when it's time to leave. Is that 'familiar' really helping him?" his mother countered. "Maybe he needs a place where he's understood. Where people know how to help him, instead of trying to make him fit into a world that doesn't make sense to him."

Her words landed heavily between them, a truth neither of them wanted to face.

"I just don't want him to feel like he's anything less than Sam or any other kid," his father muttered, his voice quieter now. "Like there's something wrong with him."

Mikey's mother sighed, her eyes glistening. "It's not about what we want, it's about what he needs."

Silence fell between them. From the bedroom, a quiet humming sound could be heard. Mikey was deliberately losing himself in his own world, repeating the same tune over and over. It was a simple rhythm that made sense to him, even as his parents struggled to make sense of everything else.

Different. Difficult. Special. The words cascaded through Mikey's thoughts like fat raindrops in a summer storm. Mikey knew that they were talking about him. He was the problem they were trying to solve. He could feel it in their silences, and in the way their eyes skittered away when he entered the room. His mother had a way of looking at him that made him feel small and vulnerable. He believed his brother when Sam said that their mother was scared and was trying to look sympathetic, but Mikey felt a sense of alienation anyway.

In Mikey's universe, he wasn't a problem. He was a legend. A guardian of the quiet spaces. He soared over rooftops, his cape rippling in the wind, his keen eyes scanning the city for danger. When the world turned against him, he didn't crumble. He stood taller, invincible and unshakable. His brother's words rang clear in his mind. "You're different, and that's what makes you amazing". That was his special phrase.

In his mind, he battled shadowy figures made of whispers and worried glances. He dodged the piercing lasers of their words, deflecting them with his unbreakable will. The more they tried to fit him into their box, the more he transformed, evolving into something greater. He was a protector of the unseen, a silent watchman in a world that never stopped talking.

And just when it felt like the villains were closing in, there was always Sam. His older brother didn't just see him as damaged little Mikey. Sam understood him. When Mikey felt like he was fading into the background, Sam was there, a steady beacon in the chaos.

"You're special, Mikey," Sam would say, ruffling his hair. "Not in the way they think. You're different, yeah, but that's what makes you amazing. You're like a hidden superpower. No one sees it until you show them."

Those words were his armour. Sam's belief in him was a force field, shielding him from the world's doubts. Whenever the weight of being different felt too heavy, Mikey clung to those words, wrapping them around himself like a cloak of invisibility, protecting him from the storm. He sat on the bench, gripping his purple lunchbox, and let his imagination run riot. Today a new villain had emerged: The Lobster.

Clad in an armoured exoskeleton, The Lobster had claws that clamped down on dreams, squeezing the life out of them with relentless force. Her words were sharp, snipping at Mikey's confidence. "You must be like the others," she hissed, her voice echoing through the streets. "You must fit into the mould."

Mikey stood firm, his purple lunchbox glowing in his hands. Inside it, his special powers pulsed. Mikey was infused with a force born from his imagination, his truth, and his uniqueness. He dodged The Lobster's crushing claws, leaping into the air with the grace of a summer swallow.

"You can't define me," he declared, his voice cutting through the fog of doubt The Lobster was trying to cast over him. "I am more than what you see. I don't need to fit into your world. I make my own!"

The Lobster lashed out, her claws snapping, her voice rising in desperation. But Mikey was ready. With a burst of light, he opened his lunchbox, unleashing a tidal wave of his own brilliance. Worlds unfurled, colours exploded, and suddenly, The Lobster was caught in a whirlwind of everything Mikey was, everything that she had tried to suppress.

"You fear what you don't understand," Mikey shouted, stepping forward as The Lobster shrank before his radiant smile. "But I won't be afraid of who I am."

With a final pulse of energy, The Lobster's armour cracked, and she tumbled backward, retreating into the darkness. Just before she disappeared from sight, Mikey caught sight of his mother's face returning to normal now that her alter ego, The Lobster, was bested. Mikey looked up and he was sure that he could feel every child in the playground sigh in relief, their hero victorious once more.

Mikey's fingers relaxed on the edges of his lunchbox. He let out a slow breath and looked up at the dull October sky. In his mind, the clouds weren't grey, they were star clusters, infinite and shining. Somewhere out there, in the vastness of space, heroes like him existed. They didn't always fit in, but they didn't need to. They were brilliant in ways the world couldn't always see.

Mikey knew he wasn't alone. He had Sam. He had his worlds. And one day, he'd show them all the power of being different. With a quiet smile, he stood up, his purple lunchbox swinging at his side. The world saw an awkward boy on the edges of the playground, but in his mind, he was already soaring, a hero in his own right, ready to take on whatever came next.

The song behind the story: *"Weird Friendless Kid" is a song by EG, featured on the album Adventure Man (2009). The song explores the themes of loneliness and social isolation through the perspective of a child who feels like an outsider. I picked up on this song via an article in a newspaper about Francis Anthony "EG" White, who has written some pretty amazing songs for major artists like Adele, Pink and many others. I love the compassion and the story-telling in this song and have wanted to do something with it for quite a while.*

In 2009, White released Adventure Man, his first solo album. This album allowed him to express a more personal, introspective side of his music, showcasing his skills in both lyrical storytelling and varied musical styles.

Album: *Adventure Man*

Artist: *Francis Anthony "EG" White*

Year: *2009*

Composer(s): *Francis Anthony "EG" White*

Record Label: *Parlaphone*

The Door

The house didn't need words to speak. It communicated through the creaking floorboards and through the cold drafts that whistled down the halls. The house's intent was revealed in the way the walls seemed to lean inward, pressing close, trapping me. And then there was the door... The door slamming echoed in my skull, and in that echo I thought I heard the heartbeat of something alive within the house, something relentless and hungry.

*

I remember as a child being told to lock the door, to keep the outside at bay. As I walked the hallways of the house that I grew up in I wondered at that. Locks work both ways. They keep bad things out, and they keep good things in, or was it the other way around? Halfway along the upstairs landing I heard the door slam shut behind me with a violent finality that rattled the bones of the house. It wasn't just the sound of it that unnerved me. The chalkboard scratch that crawled through the walls felt like it was shaking loose something ancient and unspeakable. I stood paralyzed on the landing, my breath shallow, my shadow clinging to the wall as if it, too, was afraid of the door. A fleeting thought flashed through my mind, a dark murmur with just enough menace to make me pause. *Don't move.*

I started to walk down the hallway, drawn by some unseen force, my feet moving almost of their own accord. Each step dragged me deeper into the heart of the house, where the air was viscose and sour, like old breath trapped in the lungs of a decaying beast. My vision blurred and I thought I saw he walls warp and bulge ever inward, twisting the space before me. The floor beneath me groaned, not just with age but with resentment. Each creak was a complaint, a growl of agony, as though the house itself loathed my presence. The door knew that I was here. A voice screamed in my head, shrill and desperate. *Lock the door! Lock the door!*

The walls trembled again, like a great, shaggy bear waking up with spring's first thaw. This house reeked of corruption. The air clung to me like damp layers of old skin, suffused with the memories of those who once walked these rooms and hallways. I could handle the memories, mostly, but it was the door that unsettled me the most. The door didn't belong here. The door moved like a predator, shifting through the rooms as if it were a lion hunting antelope on the savannah. One day it was in the kitchen, another day in the attic, and sometimes, just where you'd expect it, lurking at the end of a hallway. Tonight, it stood at the far end of this first floor landing, waiting for me, as it always did when I was about to try and leave. It was a door to nowhere, a door to everywhere, a door that I was terrified to touch.

The door at the end of the hallway swung open and then immediately slammed shut. The slam echoed like a gunshot, reverberating through the house's rotting bones. I felt it in my chest, a hollow thud, as if the house itself was exploding. The following silence was worse, as if the door was waiting expectantly. Then came the hiss, sharp and menacing, followed by a low growl that twisted my gut. I spun around, my eyes darting through the shadows, and there it was, the cat, its back arched in a grotesque silhouette, hackles raised like tiny spears. Its eyes glowed, reflecting the flickering lights, and for a moment, the cat seemed almost human. It too knew everything. It always did.

With shaking hands, I fumbled for the brass key that I always carried in my trouser pocket. The key was heavy and cold, a familiar and reassuring token of control. Today, though the key suddenly felt alien in my grasp. My breathing became heavier as panic seeped out of me through every pore.

"Lock the bloody door!" I hissed through clenched teeth. My voice trembled, barely audible over the pounding of my heart. My fingers scraped against the doorframe as I desperately tried to steady myself, the key now slick with my sweat. I jammed the key toward the lock, but the door, oh God, the door, flickered. It rippled, shivering between here and there like a dying creature that couldn't decide where it belonged. One moment, the door felt solid and heavy beneath my fingertips; the next, it was slipping away, as if it was teasing me, and toying with me.

It won't let me out.

The thought slammed into my mind like a wrecking ball, and for a moment, I was frozen in place again. I could feel the years of pain and sorrow seeping through the walls. My parents' endless warnings to stay safe came flooding back to me in whispers that must have been trapped between the cracks in the plaster, and as the house flexed and those whispers escaped, they seeped into my bones. My hands shook. I was losing time. I was losing myself.

"Lock it! Lock it!" My voice was cracked and raw with desperation as I shouted at the door. Finally, the key found the lock, and I twisted it. The grinding noise was deafening, as if the rust of a thousand years had fused the moving parts, the pins and the tumbler screaming their reluctance to move again. The moaning metalwork echoed inside my head, a sound of endings, of things that would never be undone. Then the key turned, the door shuddered, and everything stilled. For a moment, the door and I were one. We were connected in some awful, primal way. My hand, still gripping the brass key, felt the pulse of the wood beneath it. The walls seemed to shiver, and the cat's growl deepened.

The walls seemed to close in again, shrinking, as if they were breathing, as if they were alive. I could feel them tightening around me, pressing into my skin like invisible hands, warm and damp with the sweat of old memories. Every inch of the house whispered and moaned in a voice that slithered through the cracks, worming its way into my thoughts.

That was when I heard a voice on the other side of the door saying softly, "*Let me in*".

Oh, that voice. It was yours, papa. Or at least, it sounded like you, but muffled and distorted, as if you were trying to speak through layers of time and rot, through the decay of everything we once were. There was something cold in your voice, a chill that curled around each word, every memory laced with a bite of winter air. I clenched my teeth, forcing the sound away, pushing your ghost back into the darkness where it belonged.

"No," I whispered. Then louder, stronger. "No!"

Your voice echoed faintly in my mind, and I shook my head, trying to drown it out in a sea of silence. I wouldn't let you in. Not again. Not ever again, papa.

"Get out of my house!" I screamed, my voice ricocheting off the walls and bouncing back at me like a threat.

No one could enter. The door must remain locked. Too many had already crossed that threshold, bringing with them the totality of their sins and their horrors. Good or bad, I was the holder of the key and the door must stay locked. This house that had once been our joy, was nothing but a prison, a place soaked in torment, its doors barred and bolted against the world.

I heard it then, the scratching at the door. A slow, deliberate scrape of nails on wood, growing louder and more insistent. The door groaned under the pressure, as if something malign was clawing against it, trying to force its way in. My heart raced, panic rising in my throat like bile. I ran to the windows, desperate, my fingers shaking as I scrubbed at the glass, wiping away the grime that clung to it like old bloodstains. I could see the faint outlines of your face, papa, smudged and blurred. Your white hands pressed against the glass from the other side.

"Get out of my house!" I screamed again, my voice cracking.

I filled this place. There was no room left for anyone else. Not even for you, papa. The door swung abruptly open, nearly knocking me off my feet, and then it slammed shut again. The reverberation shook the walls, the echoes bouncing back, a cruel reminder that you were never truly gone. I made you leave, yes, but in my head, you never stopped knocking, you never stopped trying to come back.

Fists pounded against the door, sending vibrations through the floor. I stopped breathing, my chest tight with fear. "Daughter, let me in," you said, your voice a low hum, threading through the air like smoke. "Let me bring in the memories," you whispered, "The knife, my darling, remember the knife…"

No. I shook my head, refusing to allow the door to open again. The memories? *No.* Those had to stay out. They were dangerous. They were sharp and evil and too much to bear. I couldn't carry them again. I wouldn't. Not after what they had done to me. Not after what they had done to us, papa.

All the same, those memories twisted in the air, coiling through the silence like a snake curling around my thoughts. I could feel the snake's muscular body constricting around me, dragging at the corners of my mind. My knees buckled, and my hand reaching out to steady myself against the wall, but even the walls felt wrong. They were so cold. It felt as though the walls were waiting for me to break.

I heard the dream behind your voice, the dream that had slithered under the door on so many nights, looking for comfort. The dream suffocated me. It wrapped itself around my throat until I couldn't breathe, until I woke gasping for air, drenched in sweat, choking on the shadows that lingered even in the daylight. You were the bad thing, papa, You cannot come in.

No. Not again.

"Let me in," you whispered, and this time the words crawled under my skin, settling in my bones. I could feel you. I could feel the dreams. I backed away from the door, but it didn't matter. Your voice followed me, working its way through the house, through my mind.

"Get out," I tried to say, but the words came out as a whimper. The door rattled on its hinges, as if it was ready to break, as if it wanted to break. I wouldn't let you in. I couldn't let you in, but you were already here. You'd always been here. No matter how many times I screamed, no matter how hard I tried to bolt the doors and shut the windows, I could never escape you, could I papa. I was trapped here with you. And the worst part? I wasn't sure if I even wanted to leave anymore.

The change was subtle at first. My skin prickled, as if touched by static, the air around me growing sticky and heavy again. I tried to shake the feeling off, but the worm burrowed deeper, shifting under my flesh, an invading parasite. The door creaked in sympathy with the recollection of the years, the memories, and the madness that had nested here for so long.

Then it began. My bones and muscles twisted and contorted, bending in ways that defied nature. The familiar weight of my body grew foreign and lighter. I could feel the shape of me stretching, warping into something else. There was a mirror set into the door now, and it reflected a figure I no longer recognised, but I didn't need to look to know what was happening. I could feel it.

I felt a tearing in my back and something unfurled from inside me. Wings. My arms stretched, feathered and light, and for the first time in what felt like centuries, I wasn't bound to the earth or to you, papa. I had wings now, beating against the sour air, battering the walls that had once closed in around me. I was no longer trapped in the decay of this place, no longer drowning in the echoes of your voice, no longer caged by the curse of the memories you left behind. I soared higher than I ever thought possible, higher than your words and your whispers.

And then, from below, I heard you. "Daughter… Elizabeth… let me in."

Your voice was fainter now, distorted by the wind, a mere echo of the commanding sound it had once been. It no longer struck fear into my heart. It didn't root me to the spot or shackle me to my bed. I was something else now, free and beyond your grasp, but I wasn't just wind. I was more than the gusts that howled through the empty rooms. As I once was, so I was again. I was the storm. I blew past your voice, sweeping through the house, scattering the echoes and memories like dust. I slammed through the doors, rattling the windows, strong enough to silence the whispers that had once held me captive. In my right hand I carried the knife.

"Lizzie," you called again, but your voice was fading, weaker than before, drowned out by the roar of my wings and by the gust of wind that now carried me. You were losing your grip on me. I could feel it. I felt you try to reach for me one last time. I felt your presence swirl around the door like the ghost you had become, but you couldn't find your way in, not anymore. Neither I nor the door would let you in, because I was no longer your daughter. I was no longer the terrified, trembling thing you had left behind in this rotting house.

And you were gone, papa. I dropped the knife onto the landing floor, and watched the blood drip from the blade, staining the carpet a muddy brown. I stood firm, wings folded, braced against the wind that howled through the night. I was solid again. You would never pound at the door or whisper through the cracks again. You would never come back inside. Not ever again.

I locked the door.

The song behind the story: *"Get Out of My House" is the final track on Kate Bush's 1982 album The Dreaming, which is known for its experimental and dark tones. The song stands out as one of the most intense and emotionally raw pieces on the album, and has been a favourite of mine since its release.*

"Get Out of My House" is inspired by Stephen King's The Shining, with the theme revolving around isolation, paranoia, and self-defence. The track features wild, almost primal vocal performances from Kate Bush, including a powerful back-and-forth between angry, aggressive shouts and eerie, whispered lines.

For me, "Get Out of My House" reflects Kate Bush's fearless exploration of themes like personal boundaries, inner turmoil, and psychological survival. I think it highlights her ability to blend art rock, theatrical storytelling, and emotional depth.

Album: *The Dreaming*

Artist: *Kate Bush*

Year: *1982*

Composer(s): *Kate Bush*

Record Label: *EMI*

Beast

My machine let out a rhythmic hiss as the hydraulic press came down, moulding another lightweight metal housing into shape. There was a brief pause, and then a sharp release of air. The cycle repeated. Over and over. An endless loop of precision and routine.

I adjusted my gloves, the synthetic material already slick with sweat. I reached for another blank, the smooth, cold metal barely registering against my fingers anymore. I slid the blank into place, pressed the worn green button, and watched as the machine did its work. Hiss. Press. Release.

I pulled the newly formed housing out and inspected it under the fluorescent glare of overhead lights. No defects. No warps. Perfectly identical to the last hundred I'd handled that morning. I placed it onto the growing stack beside me, where dozens of others waited, each indistinguishable from the next, destined to disappear into the guts of a drone's CPU, components in a system I'd never see, never use, never think about again once my shift was over.

I rolled my shoulders, the ache settling in with quiet insistence. The workstation smelled faintly of oil and metal dust, a scent that had wormed its way into my clothes, my skin, my life. A clock hung on the far wall, but I had stopped looking at it hours ago. Time here was measured in cycles, not minutes. Hiss. Press. Release.

Occasionally, the supervisor walked by, clipboard in hand, nodding if the numbers were good, frowning if they weren't. But mostly, I was alone in the noise, an operator in a vast, automated system that needed only hands and patience. The world outside the factory floor felt distant, unreal. In here, there was only the next piece of metal. The next press. The next housing. I exhaled and reached for another blank.

The announcement was delivered by a tinny, superannuated Tannoy, the message crackling through the dimly lit factory. We heard the same reverberant voice that greeted us every morning. It was sharp, mechanical, and devoid of any warmth. The words echoed across the rows of worn-out bodies, each hunched over their workstations, hands trembling from the endless repetition of our work.

"Pack up your things. Your work here is done."

I took my gloves off and glanced down at my hands, blistered and calloused, branded with the mark of the beast, a small, charred emblem burned into the flesh of my wrist. It still ached sometimes, a reminder of the day when I was pushed into this life, stripped of choice and thrown into the grinding gears of this city. Time had long ceased to mean anything here. There came no mercy with the passing of days. Weeks, months and years moved forward relentlessly, without care or compassion, swallowing us bit by bit, one shift at a time.

The factory was a sprawling, metallic wasteland, its walls lined with rusting machines that hissed and clanked, producing the endless stream of things that fed the city above our bowed heads. They told us that we were the backbone of progress, the driving force behind the great society beyond these walls, but none of us had ever seen the fruits of our labours. We only knew the machines, their cold inefficiency, and their inhumanity. The day they branded us was the day they marked us as less than human.

Every so often, they would push someone into the sun, a cruel punishment reserved for those who could no longer keep up with the relentless demands of the machine. The sun was not the warm, life-giving star that once graced our world. In the aftermath of the global warming catastrophe, our star was now a punishing, scorching force, a blazing inferno that consumed everything it touched. Those who were sent to the sun never came back. It was a reminder, a warning to keep working, or be consumed just like the things that we made.

We had no names anymore. We were the number etched into the back of our necks. I was #79217, just another cog in the machine. There were whispers, of course, among the workers. Some hopeful souls murmured of a time before, when the land was free, and when people had choices, but those were just stories. This world didn't have space for personal freedom anymore. The free land had long since expired, choked out by the factories and by the endless sprawl of industry that ate away at the earth until there was nothing left. Open fields were a myth, a burnt out fairy tale under our withering sun.

The powers, those unseen faces who commanded our lives, wanted everyone to be numb. They wanted to stop us feeling, to stop us thinking. Our place, our role, was just to work, and in teaching us to embrace that numbness, they had succeeded in forging this mechanistic society. Most of us moved like ghosts, our faces blank, our minds dulled by the monotony.

I stood up from my station, my legs stiff from sitting in the same position for hours. The other workers didn't acknowledge me as I moved toward the exit. They rarely did. We were all too lost in our own exhaustion to notice anyone else. As I passed through the narrow corridor leading out of the factory, I could hear the distant echoes of the Glorious Leader's speeches on a loop. His words blared through the speakers at every corner, but no one listened anymore. His voice was a constant, droning reminder of our servitude.

I reached the checkpoint and handed over my slip to the guard. He barely glanced at it before motioning me through. I was on time, just like every other day. You couldn't afford to be late here. Not even once. The penalty was swift and final.

Outside of the factories, we lived in a series of interlinked workers' domes, each one the size of a small town. The air in the dome was thick with smog, the plas-glass roof panels now a sickly yellow from the pollution that poured from the factory chimneys day and night. I pulled my mask tighter over my face, trying to block out the acrid stench of burning metal and oil.

As I walked through the desolate streets, I watched our children with a careful eye. I passed a group of kids huddled together in a filthy alley, their eyes febrile, track marks visible on their arms beneath the tattered sleeves of their shirts. In the days before they were called to the production lines as young adults, drugs were pretty well the only escape left for them. I used to wonder how we ever let it come to this, but the truth was all too simple. This world had no place for love, or for innocence. By their fifteenth year, these children, our children, would be rounded up, branded, and turned into automata. Until then they would remain feral, and we would watch them carefully to avoid their malice.

I didn't stop walking. There was no point. I needed to get back to my sector, back to the small, cramped room that I called home, but home wasn't the right word for it. It was just a place, a space where I could lay my head for a few hours before it was time to return to the factory.

When I reached my building, I fumbled with the key, my fingers numb from the cold. In this sector, a worker's sector, the heating systems only ever worked intermittently. The door to my room creaked open, and I stepped inside, locking it behind me. The room was bare, with a single cot in the corner and a cracked mirror hanging on the wall. I had found a poster a few months ago on a pavement, a torn advertisement for a book festival in one of the better off districts. That was the only decoration that I had – a torn and foxed promotion for an event that I could never attend.

I stood in front of the mirror for a moment, staring at my reflection. The person looking back at me was a stranger who was gaunt and pale, with eyes sunken from too many sleepless nights. The brand on my wrist seemed to glow in the dim light, a constant reminder of what I was, of what we all were. I couldn't stay here much longer. The new machines were replacing us, one by one. Retrenchments were happening every day, and I knew my time was coming. Soon, I would be discarded and thrown away like the rest of them.

The thought filled me with a strange and bitter relief. Maybe it would be better to be retrenched, to be pushed into the sun and let it all end. This endless cycle, this suffocating numbness, was draining all hope from our lives. I felt it viscerally, but as I stood there, something stirred inside me. I felt a flicker of resistance, of defiance. I didn't know where it came from, but it was there, burning in my chest. Maybe it was the memory of something my mother used to sing, a song from before the factories took everything:

Last night, my love, as I lay dreaming,

I felt you safe within my arms,

But when I woke, love, shadows streaming,

I whispered soft to calm my heart.

You are my starlight, my only starlight,

You make me smile through the dark of night.

You'll never know, love, how much you mean to me,

Please stay close, my guiding light.

"Mama won't you sing?" I whispered to my reflection. I shook my head, trying to banish the thought. There was no place for songs here, no place for hope, but as I lay down on the cot, staring up at the ceiling, the song lingered in the back of my mind, a quiet reminder that once, long ago, there had been something more. I closed my eyes and waited for the day to come again, for the factory's call, for the machines, for the sun, and somewhere, deep inside, a small part of me refused to die. It was an idle daydream, but one that I indulged frequently. My escape wouldn't be a grand rebellion. It would be a quiet and subtle act of resistance, something that would grow from the tiny seed of defiance in my soul.

Day after day, the machines hummed with their clanking rhythm, the workers moving in synchronised patterns like shoals of herring. The dome overhead was a constant reminder of our prison, a protective cage against the wasteland outside, but a cage nonetheless. My small act of defiance was clear to me. I would try to retrain my mind to find beauty and hope. I would dig out fragments of humanity in a world where everything was designed to strip you of such things. This was how I would begin to escape.

That spark of rebellion first took root in the memory of my mother's song, that soft tune that cut through the fog of mental exhaustion. That song was a lifeline, a tether that tied me back to a world that existed before the factories swallowed our lives whole. It was an anchor, something to hold onto in the midst of the endless drudgery. Each night, as the machines fell silent, I would lie on my cot and hum that same song under my breath, a whisper of defiance that no one else could hear.

That quiet rebellion, though small, became my refuge, and from there, an idea began to take shape. I knew that I could never storm the gates or overthrow the system, for that was impossible. The dome was too well fortified, the factories too vast, the rulers too distant, but there was another way to escape. I began to observe the world around me, to pay attention to the smaller details. Day after day, I studied the factory, its routines, and its vulnerabilities. There were moments, brief but real, where the machine faltered, and where the system stuttered. There were moments of quiet chaos, when the automated guards lost track of time and place, when the surveillance grid would glitch, just for a few seconds. Everything was old and patched and rust dry. The systems and the machines that bound us were, themselves, failing with age. These glitches were small. They were brief moments in time, and barely noticeable, but if one was paying attention, if one was patient, they could offer a resourceful man a chance.

Weeks passed, and the song stayed with me, a silent chant of defiance that made my mind sharper and my senses keener. I began to collect small items, tools, scraps of metal, anything I could find that might help in my escape. I worked slowly and carefully, hiding my plan behind the dead-eyed expression of a loyal worker.

Then, during one of my night shifts, the glitch happened again. The spinning of wheels in that moment of systemic confusion was just long enough. While other workers briefly halted their repetitions at the factory, I slipped into the shadows behind my workstation, close by one of the outer factory walls. With trembling hands, using the tools that I had fabricated over time, I unscrewed the cover to an air-conditioning vent. During some routine maintenance I had discovered that the vents in the factory connected with the dome-wide air circulation system. The vent was barely large enough to squeeze through, but it led to the underbelly of the factory, an area rarely accessed by human hands. The machines and the workers around my night-shift workstation toiled tirelessly through their night rotation, unaware of the human being slipping beneath them like a ghost.

The dome had an edge, a place where it met the barren world beyond. As I wriggled through the narrow vent, my heart pounded with fear and anticipation. Years of indoctrination had burned a vivid image into my mind, one of a scorched wasteland, where the air would sear my lungs and the sun would blister my skin. I had accepted that this was what awaited me, that stepping outside of the dome was almost certainly leading to my death. Every worker knew the story. The dome was our only refuge, the last sanctuary in a world long destroyed. I was ready to face that death, to see the blackened earth, the charred ruins, and the endless horizon of ash, because I had hope. It was a forlorn sense of optimism, perhaps, but it was enough.

I unscrewed the outer wall mesh vent cover using my stolen and makeshift tools, I crawled out from beneath the dome's outer wall and the first thing that hit me was the air. It wasn't searing or toxic. It was fresh and clean. I froze, half in, half out of the vent, blinking against the bright moonlight in a cloudlessly black sky. I lay there in the scrubby dirt marvelling at the stars above me, a myriad sea of light. I half-remembered things from the worker's apprenticeship classroom. A galaxy called The Milky Way. My mind couldn't process what my eyes were seeing, and I lay there in a fugue as dawn's early purple hues heralded the rising of that killer sun.

As the light grew, and the early morning warmed me, so my confusion grew. Where were the barren deserts and smoking craters that I'd been warned about? Instead, I saw rolling hills of lush green stretching out before me, bathed in the soft dawn light. I saw tall and majestic trees, ancient trees that stood like sentinels, their leaves whispering in the breeze. I could hear birds, actual birds, their songs crisp and sharp, and a far cry from the endless hum of machinery I had known my entire life.

I stood up with my legs shaking and my head spinning. The ground beneath my feet was soft and alive with the scent of grass and damp earth. I crouched down, scooping up a handful of soil, letting it crumble between my fingers. The air I breathed was sweet and pure. I took a deep breath, and another, feeling fresh air fill my lungs in a way that made me dizzy. The warmth of the sun didn't burn me. It caressed my skin. I cried as I stumbled away from the dome. How could this be? How could everything they told me have been so wrong?

I took a shaky step forward, then another. The world outside was not just survivable; it was thriving. The sky stretched endlessly above me, clear and blue, dotted with white clouds. As I stood there on a slight slope, heading down and away from the dome I could see in the distance a river winding its way through a valley, sparkling under the morning light. My mind was reeling, spinning faster than my feet could move. Everything they told us inside the dome was a lie. The scorched wasteland they used to keep us imprisoned didn't exist. This world wasn't dead. It was alive, lush and vibrant. I had been trapped inside, toiling away in the factory, believing that the dome was my only protection from the horrors outside, but the truth was so much worse.

I dropped to my knees, overwhelmed by the sheer beauty of this natural, unchained vista. I ran my hands through the grass, needing to feel it, to know that it was real. The air was cool against my face, the wind was soft and gentle as it rustled through the trees. The ground beneath me pulsed with life. Behind me, the dome still loomed, its metallic frame and plas-glass panels catching sparkling fragments of sunlight. I turned to look at it, the rage rising inside me. That place, my prison, their prison, had no power over me anymore. It had never truly protected us. It had only trapped us, feeding us lies, keeping us bound by fear.

I stood up, my legs steadier now and with my heart racing. My previously vague sense of doomed hope was replaced by a vital, life-affirming joy. The factory, the dome, the lies, they were behind me now. I turned away from it all, toward the endless horizon ahead. I began walking, my steps growing stronger with each stride. This world, clean and vibrant, wasn't just a place to survive. It was a place to live, and I was finally free.

As I walked on, breathing in the crisp, unfamiliar air and marvelling at the vibrant world around me, something in this idyll shifted. A low hum, almost imperceptible at first, began to creep into my consciousness. It was a sound I knew too well, an electric whirr, steady and growing louder. My blood froze. I turned around quickly, scanning the sky, my heart hammering in my chest, and there it was, hovering just above the tree line a few hundred metres behind me. A drone, sleek, black, and menacing, sliced through the air with chilling precision. The moment I saw it for what it was, the sense of freedom I had felt just seconds ago shattered like glass. They were watching. They knew I that I was on the run.

Panic surged through me like a wildfire. I turned and bolted, my legs moving before my mind could fully comprehend what was happening. The lush grass I had been so mesmerised by moments ago now whipped at my ankles as I sprinted. The drone's hum intensified, a relentless shadow beast overhead, tracking my every move. How could I have been so stupid? How could I have thought I was truly free? The world blurred as I tore through the underbrush, branches clawing at my arms and legs. The sun, which had seemed so gentle and warm, now felt like a harsh spotlight, exposing me to their gaze. I heard the drone dip lower, the sound of its electric motors as menacing as a wolf's panting breath as it tracks a lame deer.

Run. Just run.

I veered toward the wooded hills on the opposite side of the valley into which I had so recently escaped. The terrain grew rougher, the ground beneath me uneven and treacherous, and then, as I pushed through a patch of dense foliage, I stumbled. My foot caught on something hard. I crashed to the ground, palms digging into the dirt, the breath knocked from my lungs. I turned to see what had tripped me, and my stomach twisted in horror. A skull, bleached white and half-buried in the earth, stared back at me with hollow eye sockets. My heart lurched. Bones. There were bones everywhere. Skeletal remains were scattered across the hillside, the forgotten relics of those who tried to escape before me.

The realization hit me like a punch to the gut. I knew that people had fled the dome before me, but we had all assumed that it was only to fry in the excoriating outside world. We believed it to be a sort of suicide, a final defiant act. The truth of it all lay around me now. Those poor people who had fled the dome before me, they had tasted clean air only to meet their end out here, hunted like animals. My throat tightened with fear and rage, but I couldn't stop, not now, not with the drone still hovering, still watching.

I scrambled to my feet, kicking the bones aside as I broke into a run again. My muscles burned and my chest heaved, but I kept moving, adrenaline the only thing keeping me upright. The thickly wooded hills were closer now, their jagged rocks and deep thickets offering a sliver of hope, a place to hide, a place to disappear in. I could hear the drone behind me, its whine growing louder and ever closer.

I reached a clump of thick bushes and dove behind them, seeking a brief respite from the chase, a chance to catch my breath. My heart pounded as the drone swept overhead. I glanced up and saw a sleek and efficient manufactured predator. More than that I recognised the dull metal gleam on the drone's underside. The main housing was familiar in a way that made my stomach twist. My hands had shaped that metal. My gloves had held it, turned it, checked it for defects before placing it into the finished pile beside my workstation. The very thing hunting me bore the mark of my labour.

A sick, bitter laugh almost escaped my lips, but I bit it down, my lungs heaving. I wanted to scream, to curse, to rip that piece of metal off with my bare hands. The factory had never just taken my time, it had taken me, piece by piece, pressing me into a shape just like the housings I'd made. And now, it had come to retrieve or exterminate what it still considered its own.

My mind screamed with desperation. I couldn't let them take me. I wouldn't let them drag me back to that life, to the endless factory shifts, to the soul-crushing existence under the dome. I wouldn't die out here, not today. If I stopped, if I faltered, I knew what awaited me. My bones would join with those whose remains littered the wilderness. With one last burst of energy, I flung myself toward the nearest patch of woodland, scrabbling up the rocky slope in desperate lunges. The drone's hum reached a fever pitch above me, and I dared not look back. All I could do was run, run for the hills, run for my life, knowing full well that I would be nothing more than another forgotten skeleton in the grass if I didn't make it.

I wouldn't be next. I couldn't be...

The song behind the story: *"The Beast" by Angus and Julia Stone is a haunting, introspective song from their debut album A Book Like This (2007). The track showcases the duo's signature folk and indie sound, blending soft, melancholic vocals with delicate guitar work. Angus Stone's gentle voice leads the song, and its lyrics centre on internal struggles, personal demons, and the complexities of relationships.*

For me, "The Beast" is a poetic exploration of inner battles and the challenge of navigating love and fear. The melancholic tone and reflective lyrics make it one of Angus and Julia Stone's most memorable tracks.

Album: *A Book Like This*

Artist: *Angus And Julia Stone*

Year: *2007*

Composer(s): *Angus Stone*

Record Label: *EMI Music Australia, while in the UK and the U.S., it was released under Flock Music and Nettwerk Records*

Rushed

The first moments of a child's life are a time of pure innocence, unburdened by the complexities and divisions of the world. Ellie knew this, abstractly, as she walked along the cobbled magnificence of Victoria Street in Edinburgh, her thoughts as muddled as the winter mist rolling away while rain began to fall.

The sandstone buildings took on a moody aspect, turning from their usual blend of greys, creams, and muted yellows to rich, charcoal tones. Those old stone buildings towered above her, making her feel small and insignificant, an apt metaphor for her current state. Someone had once told her in the Union bar that Victoria Street was the original inspiration for Diagon Alley in the Harry Potter books. That trivial fact seemed so distant now, belonging to a carefree version of herself that no longer existed.

In her belly, there was a gentle flutter of life, a constant reminder of how much her world had changed in the last few weeks. She was a third-year undergraduate, for God's sake, and here she was, engaged in one of the great mysteries of life. She was carrying a child. It made no sense, not logically. Not in today's world.

Ellie was painfully aware of her circumstances. The job market for graduates was abysmal, everyone knew that. Even her friends who had graduated last year were struggling, taking unpaid internships or jobs completely unrelated to their degrees, just to keep afloat. The cost of living was skyrocketing, and childcare? The figures she'd looked up online had made her so depressed. How could anyone afford it?

She hadn't planned for this. A drink at a friend's house party. A fumble with Akin. And here she was.

Why am I keeping this baby? The question plagued her, circling in the blue skies of her mind like a persistent vulture. Her friends hadn't directly asked, but she saw it in their eyes and in their carefully neutral expressions when she told them. "You know you have options," one had said gently. And Ellie did know. She was well-informed, pragmatic in most areas of her life. Termination would be the logical choice. The sensible choice. The choice that would allow her to finish her degree, find her footing in this unstable economy, perhaps travel a bit before settling down when she was actually ready for motherhood.

Ellie always thought she would have plenty of time to figure things out. She imagined that there would be a time to fall in love for real, just as there would be time to map out her future, but now, everything felt rushed. There was a life inside her that didn't care about her schedule, her insecurities, or the fact that she barely knew the man who helped her create this new little person.

She was terrified and curious all at the same time. What would it mean to be a mother? Could she do it? Could she really raise a child with Akin, a man who was still a near-stranger to her? The world felt like it was moving at double speed, while her brain struggled to keep up.

Every time she thought of Akin, a mix of emotions bubbled up. They were trying, though she wasn't entirely sure what they were trying to achieve. So much of what she felt was uncertain, but there was warmth between them as well as the tensions caused by fear and immaturity. They hadn't been looking for anything serious when they first met, just a few nights of fun, an escape from the pressure of exams and the hail-fellow-well-met loneliness of university life. She liked him, that much was true, but liking someone was different from building a life with them, wasn't it?

She worried about Akin, too. He seemed so calm, so sure of himself on the surface, but she wondered if he was as scared as she was. Their conversations to date had been somewhat circular. What would they do? How would they manage? Were they even a couple? Could they be? Or were they just two people thrown together by circumstance, now bound by something far more permanent than either of them had ever wanted?

Ellie rested her hands absentmindedly on her growing belly as she walked. The rational side of her brain kept presenting the facts. She was young, and financially dependent on student loans, with no job prospects secured. Akin was unreliable at best. The statistics for single mothers were grim. The cost of living was crushing even established families. It was madness to willingly walk into this.

Yet beneath all these practical considerations was something else, something that defied logic. She was both awed and overwhelmed by the idea that there was a little person inside her, someone who would rely on her for everything. The thought of tiny hands, a button nose, dimples and nappies, made her heart ache in a way she couldn't explain even to herself.

She wanted to be a good mother, but the thought of actually becoming a mother in such short order was so daunting. How could she raise a child when she didn't even know what her own life would look like in a few months?

Ellie felt torn between two lives, one where she was still a student, free to explore, to make mistakes, and to dream of a future that was hers alone, and another where she was suddenly responsible for another human being. As if that was not alarming enough, she would also now be tied to Akin way beyond the parameters of a kiss and a cuddle after party drinks. Could she have both? Could they, together, find a way to make this work?

The sensible choice was clear. Terminate. Wait. Build a career. Find stability. Find a partner who was committed, reliable, and ready for parenthood. Then have children if she still wanted them. That's what her mother would advise, or what her academic advisor might suggest if Ellie found the courage to tell her. It's what most of her generation seemed to believe was the right path. And maybe they were right.

Ellie felt emotional as she walked on along Victoria Street, veering from tears to laughter by the moment. The wind picked up as she neared the café where she was due to meet Akin. She pulled the collar of her coat up tighter around her neck. Whatever happened, she knew one thing for sure. Whichever way this thing fell out, there was no going back.

As Ellie pushed open the café door, she pressed a hand against her belly again. There was a small yet undeniable bump beneath her sweater. It was strange to think that in a few months, she could be holding her child. Or not. The café was warm, its familiar scent of coffee and pastries offering a little homely comfort. Ellie smiled. She slid into their favourite booth, the one that butted up against the window onto the street, her mind full of questions and conflicting advice from her friends at the university hall where she lived.

More pertinent was the obvious question based on recent experience. When would Akin really show up this time? He was always reliably late and could be quite unpredictable, as though he didn't understand clocks and watches, or had little regard for them if he did. It was a worry, she admitted to herself. Would she be relying on an unreliable man? Could she actually trust him with something as monumentally important as parenthood when he couldn't even make it to a coffee date on time?

Ellie absentmindedly traced the rim of her cup with her forefinger, her thoughts clouded by the uncertainty of their situation. The future felt as foggy as the dull, grey morning rain falling outside the café windows. She couldn't ignore her growing bond with the baby, a connection that was already so real and tangible to her, even if Akin hadn't quite grasped it yet. Did he feel the same responsibility?

The statistics flashed through her mind again. Student mothers were more likely to drop out. Single mothers often lived in poverty. The childcare system was broken. Housing was increasingly unaffordable. Climate change threatened everyone's future. The world was unstable and unpredictable. It was madness to bring a child into all this, especially when she wasn't ready.

It always came back to this single question; was she destined to face this journey alone, just her and the baby, figuring it out one step at a time? As she waited for Akin, Ellie's thoughts alternated between hope and fear. Maybe today would be different. Maybe Akin would walk through that door, take her hand, and tell her that they would face this together, no matter how uncertain the road ahead seemed. Or maybe, he would remain the enigma he had always been, present, yet distant and just out of reach. Maybe, she thought, she would tell him to sling his hook, and that she would go it alone.

When Akin finally appeared, his leather jacket draped carelessly over one shoulder, there was a palpable silence between them. He avoided her eyes at first, sliding into the seat across from Ellie with a strange feeling of awkwardness. Ellie studied him, trying to see some sign that he could be the partner she needed. His discomfort was obvious, and it only amplified her doubts.

"So," Ellie started, her voice small and hesitant. "Did you order a coffee?"

Akin mumbled that no he hadn't. Ellie sat by the window, her hands wrapped around a half-empty cup of tea that had gone cold. She turned her head to watch as the rain outside tapped softly against the glass, its rhythm calming and relentless. She almost willed herself to disappear into the quiet storm outside. Akin fidgeted for a moment before speaking again. The tension between them was thick. He raised a hand to signal for a waitress, ordered an espresso without glancing at the menu, and then finally met Ellie's gaze. Her eyes were filled with uncertainty. Neither of them spoke for another awkward moment.

"Well," Ellie began, her voice tentative, "what are we going to do?"

Akin exhaled sharply. He had been dreading this conversation. They ran over the same old ground every time that they met, and he still didn't have an adequate answer for her. He didn't know what to say. He wasn't even sure what he wanted to say.

"I don't know," he admitted. "I don't know what we're supposed to do."

Ellie looked down at her hands. "I've been thinking," she said quietly, a tremor in her voice that hadn't been there before. "About everything. All of it." She paused, her heart hammering so hard in her chest she thought it might break through her ribs. "I don't think I can do this, Akin."

The words hung between them, heavy and final. Inside, Ellie felt herself fracturing into a thousand pieces. Part of her wanted to take back the words immediately, to tell him she'd changed her mind, that they could figure it out together. But another part, the rational, practical part, knew this was the right choice. The only choice that made sense.

Even as she said it, a wave of grief crashed over her. She had already begun to imagine a future with this child, daydreams of teaching them to read, watching them take their first steps, their first day of school. Dreams that now felt like ghosts, haunting the edges of her mind.

Akin's expression shifted, a mix of relief and confusion crossing his face. "You mean..."

"I can't have this baby," Ellie said, her voice breaking. "I've made an appointment. Next week."

The words tasted like ash in her mouth. She'd spent nights researching, calculating, planning, trying to find a way to make it work. But every path led to the same conclusion. Bringing a child into the world now would mean sacrifice beyond what she could bear, not just for her, but for the child too. A life of instability, of struggle, of wondering if there would be enough money for rent, for food, for anything beyond the bare necessities.

"Are you sure?" Akin asked, his voice soft. There was no judgment in his tone, just a cautious concern that made Ellie's eyes sting with unshed tears.

"No," she admitted, a bitter laugh escaping her. "I'm not sure of anything. But I know we can't give this child what it deserves. Not now."

The waitress arrived with Akin's espresso. The waitress placed the cup in front of him with a sharp clink, and her eyes flicked between the two of them. She must have overheard part of their conversation because her expression softened into something like sympathy before she walked away without another word.

"I'll go with you," Akin said after a moment. "To the appointment."

Ellie nodded, grateful for the offer even as she knew it changed nothing. The chasm between them had been growing for weeks, and this decision, though they both seemed to accept it was necessary, would only widen it further.

"And after?" she asked, the question hanging in the air between them.

Akin didn't answer immediately. They both knew what she was asking. After the appointment, after the procedure, after they walked out of the clinic, what then? Would they try to build something from the ashes of what might have been? Or would they go their separate ways, each carrying a piece of this shared grief?

"I don't know," he said finally. "I don't think either of us knows what we want, Ellie."

The truth of his words cut through her. He was right. They were still practically strangers, thrown together by circumstance, by a few moments of connection that had spiralled into something neither of them was ready for.

"Seven seconds," she whispered, almost to herself.

Akin raised an eyebrow, puzzled. "What's that?"

"Seven seconds," Ellie repeated, her voice softer now, almost wistful. "That's all it takes for everything to change. For a new life to begin." She placed her hand absentmindedly on her stomach. "And this baby... it doesn't know yet. It's not burdened by anything. It has no idea about the struggles, about what's waiting outside."

The real world outside was harsh, a broken housing market, a fractured job market, a world rife with uncertainty. Ellie knew all of this. She'd grown up watching her own parents struggle through the 2008 recession, and she had seen friends' families torn apart by financial stress. She'd read the reports, seen the statistics. Having a baby now was objectively a poor decision by any practical measure. And that's what crushed her the most, that she was making the right choice, the responsible choice, and yet it felt like carving out her own heart with a blunt knife.

"I think," she said slowly, her voice steadier now though her hands trembled, "that we should end this. Whatever 'this' is."

Akin looked up sharply. "End us, you mean?"

"Was there ever really an 'us', Akin?" Ellie asked, not unkindly. "We barely know each other. We've been pretending we could make something work because of the baby, but without that..."

She left the thought unfinished. Without the baby, there was nothing binding them together. No reason to force a relationship that had begun as nothing more than a brief connection, a moment of escape from the pressures of university life.

Akin sat back in his chair, his expression unreadable. "If that's what you want."

"It's not about what I want," Ellie said, a sob catching in her throat. "If I could have what I want, none of this would be happening. I wouldn't be pregnant. I wouldn't be sitting here making the hardest decision of my life. I wouldn't be choosing between my future and... and this life inside me."

The tears came then, hot and fast, spilling down her cheeks. She didn't bother to wipe them away. Let them fall. Let the whole café see her grief. She was tired of pretending she was strong enough to bear this alone.

"I'm sorry," Akin said, reaching across the table to take her hand. "I'm so sorry, Ellie."

And she believed him. Sorry that they found themselves here, sorry that there was no easy answer, sorry that sometimes life presented choices that felt impossible to make.

"Me too," she whispered.

They sat in silence for a long time, the rain outside growing heavier, drumming against the window like a heartbeat. Ellie felt a hollowness spreading through her chest, an emptiness where hope had once resided. She knew this feeling would not leave her quickly, this grief for a future that would never come to pass, for a child she would never hold.

"I'll still go with you," Akin said eventually. "If you want me there."

Ellie nodded, unable to speak. It was a small mercy, not having to face this alone. But after? After the procedure, she would walk her own path. They both would.

As they finished their coffee, paid the bill, and stood to leave, Akin squeezed her hand one last time before letting go, his gaze lingering for a second longer than usual. They walked out into the Edinburgh streets, the skies still draped in the soft light of early morning. It was an ordinary day, yet everything had changed.

Walking in separate directions, Ellie carried with her a weight that felt too heavy to bear. That she had made the rational choice, the sensible choice, the right choice, was no comfort.

None of those words could ease the ache in her heart, the feeling that she was losing something precious before she'd even had the chance to hold it.

Seven seconds had changed everything. Seven seconds to create a life. And now, a lifetime to wonder what might have been. The path ahead was clearer now, unburdened by the responsibilities of parenthood, free to unfold as she had once planned. She would finish her degree. She would travel. She would build a career. She would do all the things she'd dreamed of before those seven fateful seconds.

But as she walked alone through the rain-slicked streets of Edinburgh, Ellie knew that some part of her would always wonder about the road not taken, about the tiny hands and button nose that she would never see, about the life that, for a brief moment, had been entwined with hers.

It was the right choice. The only choice that made sense.

But that didn't make it hurt any less

.

The song behind the story: "7 Seconds" by Youssou N'Dour and Neneh Cherry is a powerful song, and is one that I play regularly. It has always touched a nerve. The song blends themes of unity, resilience, and understanding, transcending cultural and linguistic boundaries. Released in 1994, the song became an international hit, praised for its unique fusion of world music, pop, and socially conscious lyrics.

The song is about the first moments of a child's life, highlighting innocence and the idea that they are not yet aware of the struggles and divisions in the world. "7 Seconds" is not just a song but a social statement, using music as a means of advocating for understanding and empathy across cultures, which is something I actively promote in my work on the "Tales From The World's Firesides" project.

Album: *Youssou N'Dour's 1994 album The Guide (Wommat) and later on some versions of Neneh Cherry's album Man (1996)*

Artist: *Youssou N'Dour & Neneh Cherry*

Year: *1994 as a single*

Composer(s): *Youssou N'Dour, Neneh Cherry, Cameron McVey (Cherry's partner and frequent collaborator), and Jonne Jarvis.*

Record Label: *The single was released by Columbia Records in most markets and Chaos Recordings in the United States.*

To The Woods...

The forest canopy loomed over Yevgeni. The trees' gnarled branches twisted into grotesque shapes that blotted out the sky. The air was concentrated with an unnatural twilight that clung to everything like a sticky residue from a hot summer day. The light cast long and distorted shadows on the pine needle litter by Yevgeni's feet. It wasn't day, but it wasn't night yet either. This was the pause in-between, the kind of time that could, if you closed your eyes, stretch on relentlessly. The path vanished beneath his feet, swallowed by the creeping undergrowth, but Yevgeni kept moving. He had to. The voice was everywhere now, weaving through the trees, a sound that echoed from all directions, impossible to place.

Come closer...

At first, it had been a faint whisper on the wind, easy to ignore, but now it was louder and more insistent, threading itself into his thoughts, urging him forward. His pulse quickened, not from fear, at least, not at first, but from a rising certainty that he must see this thing that called to him. He had to find the girl. Her voice was so clear now, as if she was just ahead, hiding behind the next tree or waiting in the shadows just beyond his eye line.

As Yevgeni pressed on, the forest seemed to close in, the tall pines leaning toward him, their twisted forms reaching out with skeletal limbs. Each step was slower than the last, as though the earth itself was turning to thick, viscose mud. His breath came in shallow bursts, his heartbeat loud in his ears, matching the rhythm of the voice that echoed in his mind.

Come closer...

The words were a spell cast upon his mortal soul. The certainty that had once driven him was unravelling, replaced by a creeping dread. Something was wrong. This wasn't a search anymore. It was a hunt, and he felt as though he was the prey, and still, the voice called out to him, sweeter now, more tempting, pulling him deeper into the labyrinth of trees.

Yevgeni had been here many times before. He knew this place. He knew every twist of the path and every darkened hollow, but today nothing seemed to stay still or fixed. The Holosiiv Park was a protected remnant of forest surrounded by urban Kyiv. It was a favourite weekend haunt, easy for Yevgeni to reach from his home in Demiivka district. Today, though, the usually clear details were flowing around, as if the forest itself were alive and watching him. The trees were the worst. Their ancient, gnarled trunks loomed over him, their bark splitting open like raw wounds, appearing to Yevgeni like mouths caught in eternal, silent screams. The trees seemed to breathe and the air felt as though it was clogged with damp earth. All around Yevgeni there was the rotten aroma of things long dead, yet underneath the decay there was a tantalising and seductive a sweetness that didn't belong here. That sickly-sweet scent curled around him like the perfume on a recently embalmed cadaver, luring him deeper into the woods.

Come closer… see…

The girl, the lace-white nymph at the heart of Yevgeni's troubled mind, called again and again. He was as convinced as ever that finding her, that touching her alabaster skin, would quieten the voices that made his waking hours so confusing and threatening. Her voice slipped through the trees, soft as a whisper, but with a gravity that brooked no deviation. The voice tugged at him relentlessly, continually changing his orientation, so that now Yevgeni was quite lost. His pace quickened and his feet crunched on the brittle twigs that littered the forest floor. Dead leaves from ancient oaks crumbled underfoot. The ground felt wrong to Yevgeni, as though it might give way at any moment.

In his mind Yevgeni could still hear that cacophony of inner voices as they buzzed and rasped out their warnings. Her voice filled the spaces between those thoughts as if her words were the glue that bound his deliberations together in an incoherent whole. Every time Yevgeni blinked, he thought he saw her. Those glimpses were brief and fragmentary, just an image of a pale figure slipping between the shadows. He caught only the briefest glimpses, but he was certain that he could see the sway of a white dress teasing him at the edge of his vision. Each time he turned to look directly in her direction she was gone again, always just out of reach. Yevgeni swore out loud and pressed on. He was certain that she was waiting for him. He could feel her… watching.

Yevgeni had been running for what felt like hours. He was out of breath and tired. His eyes flicked wildly through the oppressive gloom, searching, always searching, for the girl. She had to be there. Just one glimpse, he thought, just one full glimpse. "Find the girl…" The words tumbled from his lips in a low, sibilant whisper, like a desperate prayer to the lowering darkness.

And then, everything stopped. Yevgeni froze. He felt as though invisible hands had gripped him tight, holding him in place. The air solidified around him. The once-rustling leaves now hung limp and still. The wind had hushed, leaving behind a silence so absolute that it hurt his ears. Yevgeni's heart pounded like a bass drum. It was the only sound that Yevgeni could hear in the suffocating quiet. The forest, once alive with its eerie whispers, now seemed to be silently stalking him. The voice that called to him, the girl's voice, had vanished. All sense of her seemed to have been swallowed by the unmoving air. Yevgeni's throat tightened. Panic began to gnaw at the edges of his mind. Yevgeni was utterly alone.

"Hello?" Yevgeni called out tentatively. His voice broke. He cried out again, shattering the silence, but only emptiness answered him. The oppressive quiet swallowed his call, as if the forest had devoured his words. She was gone. That sweet and elusive voice was a mirage. Yevgeni suddenly wondered if she had ever been there at all. Was the forest playing tricks on him, twisting his mind and warping his senses until reality itself was a shifting, unreliable thing? Yevgeni's hands trembled. No… no, she's real, he thought, she has to be real.

Yevgeni felt that the forest was mocking him. He couldn't help but think that the trees' branches were curling closer, their shadows lengthening like grasping claws. His mind, once filled with the girl's voice, was now a maze of doubt and terror, as the forest's silence wrapped around him like an iron band, squeezing the breath from his chest. The voices in his head mumbled words of warning, but even they were reluctant to break the forest's silent embrace.

Yevgeni forced his feet to move again, but each step felt heavier. The forest seemed malevolent, the shadows deepening all around him. The shadows warped into grotesque shapes that scratched and cut into his bare arms. Twisted roots became gnarled hands, reaching for him from beneath the earth, and the hollows of the trees seemed to pulse with ember eyes, watching and waiting.

The deeper he plunged into the forest, the more the world seemed to twist and turn in on itself. The ground beneath his feet softened once again, giving way as though the earth was trying to devour him. With every step, he felt as if he was sinking into something far darker than dirt. The trees loomed like sentinels, their crooked branches forever curling inwards to trap him. The early evening chill bit at his skin, seeping into his bones

Come closer...

The girl's voice returned, faint as yet but unmistakably hers. Yevgeni's inner turmoil was making his thoughts disorderly, and he wasn't sure if the voice was real or just a memory, or maybe a hallucination. Whatever it was, the voice beckoned him on, pulling him deeper into the suffocating woods. He stumbled forward, desperate and blind to reason until he pushed through a tangle of nettles and trailing brambles into a clearing, where the oppressive canopy above his head parted just enough to let in a sickly sliver of twilight.

And there she was.

Just ahead of Yevgeni, she was standing as still as death itself with her back to him. She was draped in white, the fabric swaying gently as though caught on a breeze that wasn't blowing. Her long, tangled hair cascaded down her back, and for a fleeting second, Yevgeni felt a sense of relief, but that feeling degenerated almost immediately into the deepest sense of foreboding. He was deeply afraid, afraid that she would disappear again like a whisp of smoke on a windy evening.

"Wait!" he rasped, his voice cracking with desperation. "Don't go!"

She didn't move. Not even a flicker. Her form wavered at the edges, blurry and insubstantial, like a ghost suspended between two worlds. The knot of terror tightened in Yevgeni's gut. His legs felt heavier than ever, but he staggered forward, each step more laboured than the last.

Come closer...

His fingers trembled as he reached out, the tips just inches from her shoulder. The air around her felt cold and dense, and the dread that he had been holding back surged through him. Something was terribly, impossibly wrong, but he was too far committed now to stop.

Close enough ...

The voice whispered from nowhere and everywhere. Her words were a disembodied murmur that curled around his mind, slipping through his thoughts like an icy thread. Yevgeni's hand froze in mid-air, suspended in an awkward gesture toward the space where she had just stood, but there was no one there. Yevgeni visibly trembled. A thought came to him, a borrowed thought. The girl in white… she had never been real.

Adrenaline surged through Yevgeni's body as his mind recoiled from the truth. The realisation slammed into him with the force of a physical blow. His knees buckled, and he stumbled back, a scream catching in his throat, only to die there, strangled by the sea of silence flooding in on him. The trees were watching. Their crooked branches stretched toward him, their limbs yearning to drag him down amongst their roots where they could bind and hold him forever. The cold earth beneath him seemed to pulse, as though the ground had become sentient and alive with dark intent. Yevgeni could hear the earth, he could feel it beating a drum tattoo through his skin. Yevgeni knew then that he was no longer alone.

"It's always the same…" he mumbled to himself. How many times had he chased her? How many times had he wandered into these cursed woods to run and run toward nothing? His breathing was ragged now, coming out in short, tattered bursts. He wasn't just lost. He was trapped, trapped in the loop, the endless repetition of his own madness.

The whispers in the trees grew louder and more insistent. They were speaking now with overlapping voices, a return to that cacophony of murmured warnings and malevolent promises. He clutched his head, trying to block them out, but the sound was inside him, crawling beneath his skin. Yevgeni's was exhausted. He felt as though his sanity was being carved away from his soul. He had been here before, so many times before, always chasing her. The girl. The phantom. His tormentor. Yevgeni's vision blurred as the cycle began again.

Come closer… come closer…

The words sounded soft and melodic, but they were tinged with malice. The cold seeped into his bones as he sank to the ground, too weak to fight anymore, too broken to resist. The forest claimed him, as it always had, as it always would, and as his eyes fluttered shut, the last thing he felt was her presence. The girl in white hovered at the edge of his consciousness, just beyond reach, always just beyond reach.

And then there was nothing but the endless quiet of the forest, the unyielding grip of the dark, and the faint, mocking echo of her voice.

Come closer…

The song behind the story: *"A Forest" by The Cure is one of the band's most iconic songs, originally released in 1980 on their second album, Seventeen Seconds. I first saw The Cure around this time and this song has stayed with me ever since. It became one of their signature tracks, marking a pivotal moment in their transition towards a darker, moodier post-punk and gothic rock sound.*

"A Forest" is characterised by its driving bassline, atmospheric guitar riffs, and haunting synthesizers. Robert Smith's vocals are distant and ethereal, complementing the song's eerie, almost dreamlike quality. "A Forest" evokes feelings of alienation and existential anxiety, themes that would become central to The Cure's later work.

Album: *Seventeen Seconds*

Artist: *The Cure*

Year: *1980*

Composer(s): *Robert Smith, along with other members of The Cure at the time: Simon Gallup, Matthieu Hartley, and Lol Tolhurst*

Record Label: *Fiction Records*

The Jakey And The Nae Chancer

Elliott had built his life around solitude, but it wasn't any kind of isolation that felt peaceful or chosen. It was a necessity, a form of survival that he had learned long before he'd even realised that he was acquiring such a skill. The small, windswept coastal town in the Scottish Highlands was remote enough that people minded their own business, and that suited him fine. The wind howled off the sea, rattling against the thin walls of his cottage, and on some nights, when the storms rolled in, he could almost imagine that he was somewhere else, back in a world where he knew the rules, where there was an objective, a mission, something to structure the chaos in his head.

Elliott hadn't always been like this. Once, he had been a man of action. In the military, emotions were a luxury few could afford or admit to. He spent years perfecting the art of detachment, keeping his feelings in check because that was the only way to do the job right. Fear, grief, doubt, none of it had a place when you were clearing a building, when you were waiting in the back of a transport plane about to drop into unknown territory, when you were holding the hand of a mate whose life was slipping away beneath the brutal sun in Iraq.

But war left its mark, and not just in the obvious ways. The transition back to civilian life had been a slow, grinding process of disconnection. He had walked through supermarkets feeling overwhelmed by the choice, by the bright lights, by the chatter of people who had never heard a gunshot fired in anger. Conversations at dinner parties, when he still bothered to go through those social motions, felt like they were happening in another language. There was an invisible thread between him and the rest of the world, but it was stretched so thin it barely held.

The worst of it wasn't the flashbacks or the nightmares, though they came often enough. It was the hypervigilance, the sense that even here, on the edge of the world, something could go wrong at any moment. He scanned every room he entered, his back never to the door, his ears tuned for sounds that didn't belong. The habit was burned into his nervous system, a relic of a life that he was trying to get away from. He knew it was irrational, but knowing didn't make it easier to stop these default actions.

And there was the loneliness. He would never admit it, not to anyone, not even to himself most days, but it gnawed at him in quiet moments. He missed the camaraderie, the feeling of knowing that someone had his back no matter what. That kind of trust wasn't something you found in a pub with strangers, or even in the polite small talk of the phlegmatic Highland locals who had long accepted him as an odd and distant presence. The reliance on others had been forged in the field, in the exhaustion of long marches, in the unspoken bond of men who had seen too much and didn't need to talk about it.

He missed his dog. A rescue mutt, scrappy and full of fight, just like him. She had been with him through the worst of it, her quiet companionship the only thing tethering him to the earth when the gravity of his former life threatened to smother him. When the divorce came, bitter and inevitable, there had been no question of who the dog would stay with. But now she was gone, old age finally taking its toll, and the house that he rented felt emptier than ever. He didn't miss his ex-wife. He did miss the idea of what their marriage could have been if he had been someone different, someone who hadn't come home carrying ghosts.

He knew people thought he was cold, maybe even unfriendly. He spoke with caution, his words deliberate, his engagement with the wider world sparse and fitful. He didn't see the point in small talk, nor did he have the energy to pretend to care about things that felt trivial. For Elliott, survival depended on silence and blunt strength. It always had.

But there were days when he felt the weight of it all pressing down on him. There were days when the isolation didn't feel like a choice but a sentence. He had lost so much, brothers-in-arms, a sense of purpose, the ability to close his eyes at night without seeing things he wanted to forget. And so, he built walls, thick, unyielding walls of guilt and anger, and of painful memories. He told himself he was better off alone.

And maybe he was. But it didn't mean he wasn't lonely.

Elliott told himself it was better this way, better to be the man on the outskirts, the one people nodded to in passing but never tried to know. It was easier this way. No expectations, no need to explain himself. No one to disappoint. He lived simply, his days marked by quiet rituals, early mornings spent watching the mist roll in from the sea, afternoons doing odd labouring jobs that kept his hands busy and his mind just distracted enough. His service pension was enough to get by, and when he needed extra cash, he found work where he could. The locals knew him as reliable. Strong. A man who didn't talk much but got the job done.

That was the way he liked it. Or at least, that was what he told himself.

In the evenings, when the work was done and there was nothing left to keep the past at bay, he'd sit in his small cottage, watching the walls, a large malt in hand. He drank for the warmth, for the quiet hum that dulled the sharp edges of his thoughts. He tried not to drink too much, not anymore. He'd seen too many men drown in their own sorrow, and he had no intention of following them. Elliott drank enough to smooth the jagged edges of his memory, and to make the silence a little less hollow.

Some nights, he fished at the loch, the water still and dark, mirroring the sky. The rhythmic cast of the line, the slow tug of the reel, it was one of the few things that gave him peace. He liked the solitude of it, the way the world seemed to shrink down to just him, the water, and the whisper of the wind. But even there, alone in the wild, the ache was ever-present.

He felt it most in the quiet moments, in the way the empty chair across from him was never filled, in the way his bed stayed cold on one side. He could have gotten a dog again, he supposed, something to keep him company, something to fill the space with its presence. But he wasn't sure he deserved that kind of comfort, not anymore.

Elliott ached for connection in his more thoughtful moments, though he rarely let himself dwell on it. He had tried once, tried to be a husband, to build something that resembled a life. But war had left its scars. Since then, he had convinced himself that love was something for other people, people who hadn't seen the things he had, who didn't wake up some nights gasping for breath, or reaching for a weapon that wasn't there.

The idea of meeting someone who could understand all that, who could see the scars criss-crossing his hidden heart and not turn away, seemed impossible. So he stayed alone. It was safer that way. It was easier. And yet, some nights, when the wind howled outside and the fire burned low, when the whisky did little to warm the hollowness inside him, he found himself wondering, if only for a moment, what it would be like to let someone in.

*

Fiona lived just a few houses away from Elliott's rented cottage, though they had never crossed paths. If they had, she might have recognised something in him, a familiar wariness, an unspoken reluctance to let the world in. She had learned not to dwell too much on strangers, nor to let curiosity draw her in. Once upon a time, she had been drawn to people like a moth to flame, seeking connection, laughter, an escape from herself. Now, she was careful. She too kept herself to herself these days.

Once, she had been the kind of woman who lived loudly, who laughed with abandon and danced like no one was watching. She had been reckless with her love, throwing it at people who weren't equipped to catch it, drinking too much, saying too much, trusting too much. And for a time, it had felt thrilling and intoxicating. The parties, the wild nights, the fleeting affection of people who disappeared with the sunrise, it had been fun until it wasn't. The hangovers lasted longer than the good times. Mornings were filled with shame and confusion. Eventually Fiona looked in the mirror and didn't recognise the woman staring back.

She had told herself she was the life and soul of the party, but somewhere along the way, her soul had retreated. It had curled up in the corner of some shabby and forgotten room inside her head, battered and bruised by the damage she had done with the bottle.

Fiona had not been a happy drunk towards the end. The laughter had soured, the charm giving way to bitterness. She had burned bridges, hurt people who had only ever tried to help, and driven away those who had seen the worst of her and had no more kindness left to give.

Getting sober had been like clawing her way out of a deep pit, one handful of dirt at a time. The programme had helped, though at first, she had resisted, convinced she could do it alone. But she wasn't alone, not really. She found others like her, people who spoke a language she understood, who knew what it was to feel utterly lost. It saved her. Even now, years later, she still went to meetings, still carried the small token in her pocket, smooth from the nervous way her fingers ran over it when the cravings whispered at the edges of her mind.

But sobriety was only part of the battle. The real war was fought every day in the quiet moments, in the loneliness she had to keep at bay, in the fear that if she let someone in, if she risked her heart again, she would break, and this time, she might not be able to put herself back together. She was much more careful now. Careful with who she let into her enclosed world, careful with her love, treating it as something fragile and precious. Fiona was almost certain that her heart was too delicate to risk breaking again.

And yet, she still had hope. It was a small, flickering flame, buried deep inside her, but it was there.

Fiona treated her emotions like intimate secrets, things to be guarded, locked away until the right person came along. Someone who wouldn't push too hard, who wouldn't try to fix her, who would understand that some wounds never fully heal, but only fade into scars.

Fiona still liked to sing. It was the one part of her old self she had kept, the one thing that had never turned sour. The melodies she hummed to herself while she cooked, the quiet songs she sang in the solitude of her cottage, they were her solace. They were proof that despite everything, despite the loneliness and the fear, her heart was still very much alive. She was waiting for the day when it would be safe to share again.

But waiting was hard. In her many moments of solitude, Fiona dreamed of love, of finding someone who would understand her, and care for her without her needing to explain how the drink had shattered her dreams. She longed for a connection that would make her feel as if the world might take notice of her as a worthwhile person once again. Outwardly, though,

Fiona kept herself hidden away behind a scowl and a frown, and a reputation as that Jakey lass from number sixty-two.

*

Elliott and Fiona passed each other on occasion, usually walking along the strand to the little Co-op store that served as the town's convenience shop and post office. On the odd occasion they might have reached for the same packet of garibaldi biscuits, their hands brushing ever so briefly, or perhaps, they might have stood one behind the other at the till. If either was aware of the other it was only ever contrived through a polite smile, both of them totally unaware of any opportunity to develop a deeper connection.

Fiona sometimes passed Elliott as he sat in the little café just opposite the self-service petrol station at the top of the High Street, as she walked to her work as a cleaner at the doctor's surgery. Fiona was originally offered the job as part of her rehabilitation by a sympathetic GP, and she had stayed on now for two years. Fiona always walked quickly and with purpose, that purpose being chiefly to avoid the Highland rains. On more than one occasion she had glanced in through the window at the brightly lit café interior just as Elliott glanced up from a book or newspaper. For a fleeting second, their eyes met through the condensation on the window, his brow furrowed in thought, she clutching her umbrella. Neither of them held the gaze long enough to consider that it had any meaning at all. The Jakey looked through the "nae chancer", who looked through the Jakey. It was as simple as that.

*

Fiona tugged the hood of her jacket tighter around her head as the rain came down harder, soaking into the fabric. She cursed under her breath, more annoyed at herself than the weather. She should have known better, this was the Highlands after all, where rain was as much a part of life as breathing. It was a mistake she made too often, always assuming she could outrun the downpour.

The late afternoon winter darkness had settled in, the kind that came early this far north, stretching the nights into long, dark vigils. The streetlights cast an eerie glow, their sodium oranges reflecting off the wet pavement, giving everything a hazy, dreamlike quality. Fiona stepped sideways to avoid a puddle, her shoes already ruined, and that was when she collided with someone unseen. Elliott.

He had not seen her either, being too preoccupied with his take-out coffee and a folded-up newspaper tucked under his arm. He had been frowning down at the coffee cup, lost in thought, his focus on a crossword clue when they danced their awkward, clumsy misstep.

"Och! I'm pure sorry, I... I wisnae lookin' where I wis goin'," Fiona said, fumbling with the strap of her bag.

Elliott had stepped back instantly, instinct taking over as his left hand shot out to steady her, only for him to withdraw it just as quickly, as if second-guessing whether contact was welcome. His voice was low and steady, but tinged with hesitation. "No, no, my fault. I... I didnae see you. Are you okay?"

Normally, Fiona would have nodded, muttered a quick "Aye, fine," and hurried on her way. That was how she handled interactions these days, short, polite, distant. But something about the way he spoke, about the way he had stepped back in his own uncertainty, made her pause. She laughed, though it was a nervous, slightly self-deprecating sound. "Aye, just my pride that's hurtin'. An' these shoes o' mine. This dreich weather's not done them any favours."

Elliott caught her smile, and for a moment, he found himself looking into hazel eyes that seemed so full of life. He hesitated, then surprised himself by smiling back. It wasn't something he did often, not with strangers. He lifted his coffee cup slightly, as if that explained everything. "Aye, tell me about it. I'm fair drenched, and I just came fae the bloody café. Should've brought a brolly... again."

Fiona glanced up at the sky, rain splattering against her face. "Aye, but where's the craic in that, eh? Bide here long enough and you either take tae the dreichness or you pack your bags for someplace more clement."

Elliott made a soft sound, part scoff, part quiet amusement. "Clearly, I've embraced the misery."

For a moment, the rain filled the silence between them, the quiet patter of it hitting the pavement, the gentle dripping from shop awnings. People hurried past, heads bowed against the cold, hurrying home to warm houses and waiting dinners.

Fiona shifted on her feet, unsure whether to keep talking or to make her excuses and go. But there was something oddly comforting about the moment, about this stranger who wasn't quite a stranger anymore. She had seen him before, of course. Small towns didn't allow for complete anonymity. But seeing someone and meeting them were entirely different things.

"You live round here, then?" she asked, her voice careful, not wanting to pry too much.

Elliott nodded. "Aye, not far. Just renting a place further up the road." He hesitated before adding, "You?"

"Same. Few houses away, I think."

Another beat of silence. This was where she should say, Right, nice meeting you, and walk away. But she didn't. Instead, she glanced at his coffee cup. "So, what's good in there, then? I always get masel' the tea.

Elliott lifted a brow, mildly surprised at the continuation of conversation. "The coffee's decent. No life-changing, but it does the job." He lifted the paper under his arm. "I mainly go for the quiet. And the crossword."

Fiona smirked. "Och, a crossword? Is that why you near walked right into me?"

Elliott gave a small huff, somewhere between a laugh and an exhale. "Something like that."

Fiona hesitated. It had been a long time since she'd entertained the idea of chatting with someone like this, even in such a casual way. She had built her life on careful avoidance, on keeping things measured. But now, here she was, standing in the rain, talking to a man who looked just as lost as she sometimes felt.

And so, before she could overthink it, she took a breath and said, "Well… I'm frozen. I was just heading home, but I suppose there's worse ways to dry off than a coffee."

Elliott's expression wavered. He too could have said no. He could have mumbled an excuse and retreated to his rented cottage where the silent walls waited for him Instead, he glanced at the rain, then back at Fiona.

"Aye. Could be worse."

And together, two guarded and lonely souls stepped out of the rain and into the dim glow of the café, neither of them entirely sure what they were doing, but neither of them quite willing to walk away.

The song behind the story: *"I've Got This Friend" is a song by The Civil Wars (Joy Williams and John Paul White) from their debut album Barton Hollow, released in 2011. The track reflects the band's signature blend of folk, indie, and country influences, characterised by their harmonies and emotionally rich storytelling.*

I think I came across this watching Jools Holland one Friday night, and was blown away by the song. This piece absolutely had to offer something positive and join this collection of tales.

For me, the song's simplicity, both musically and lyrically, makes it a tender, hopeful reflection on love and the idea that the right person might be just around the corner, waiting to be found.

Album: *Barton Hollow*

Artist: *The Civil Wars*

Year: *2011*

Composer(s): *Joy Williams and John Paul White*

Record Label: *Columbia Records*

Aphrodite

The bass line thumped through the floorboards of Club Elysium, a mechanical heartbeat that seemed to mock the organic rhythms of its patrons. Under the dusty crystal chandeliers, the light fractured and dim like broken memories, the dancers moved with an eerie precision. Their steps were too perfect, too rehearsed, as if they were clockwork figures performing on command. The air shimmered with sequins and silk, punctuated by the sharp glint of military medals that adorned shoulders and chests like fantastic constellations.

A superannuated colonel, or at least that's what his epaulettes made him out to be, spun past in a blur of midnight blue and tarnished brass. His medals clinked together with each turn, a discordant melody that spoke of battles no one cared to remember anymore. The wars had taken everything, even the meaning of valour, leaving behind only these trinkets that people now wore as fashion statements rather than battle honours. In the hazy light, his face was a mask of calculated revelry, painted with the same desperate joy that seemed endemic to the club's patrons.

The air was thick enough to chew on, a potent cocktail of cigarette smoke, cheap perfume, and expensive regret. It clung to the velvet walls and settled on the lungs of the dancers like a second skin, a shroud they wore willingly in their nightly ritual of forgetting.

Aphrodite observed it all from her position against the wall, one hand holding a half-empty glass of wine, the other bringing a cigarette to her lips in a gesture as old as vice itself. The wine was mediocre, but that hardly mattered anymore. Nothing here was quite what it pretended to be, herself included.

Her eyes, ancient and knowing, cut through the elaborate masquerade before her. These weren't party-goers, they were survivors, each one carrying on their own personal war beneath layers of makeup and manufactured glamour. They moved faster and faster, as if they could somehow outrun the ghosts that chased them across the dance floor. The music aided their flight, its relentless rhythm demanding movement, insisting on distraction from the ruins that waited outside the club's heavily draped windows.

She'd been watching long enough to see the patterns. Seven out of every ten faces were unremarkable, blending into the backdrop like particularly well-dressed pieces of furniture. Four out of five moved through the space in a daze, their eyes glazed and distant, their bodies operating on automatic as they performed the expected motifs of enjoyment. They were sleepwalkers in their own lives, barely conscious enough to maintain the illusion of living.

The cigarette burned down between her fingers as she observed them with the detached curiosity that came from millennia of watching civilizations rise and fall. This wasn't her first death dance, nor would it be her last. Pride had become their last refuge, their final fortress against despair. They wore their carefully constructed identities like costumes in this designer world, changing personalities as easily as they changed their clothes.

The wars had stripped everything else of meaning, leaving only this desperate dance in a crumbling temple to a god that no one remembered how to worship anymore. Even she, Aphrodite, once revered as the goddess of love and beauty, now walked among them unknown and unrecognised. Her former divinity had become just another accessory in a world too broken to believe in gods.

She could taste the misery, bitter and sharp beneath the veneer of shallow laughter and cynical conversation. It was her misery too. Some sought solace in each other's arms, in darkened corners and on plush divans, but even their passion was hollow. These were mechanical pleasures that never quite reached the hearts of the revellers in the club. Real love had become as rare as the stars, now hidden behind the perpetual haze that shrouded the city. No one loved anymore, and so her divinity had faded, until she too was now mortal and resigned to her fate.

Tonight felt different, though. She could feel it in the air, in the subtle shift of cosmic weights and measures. Something was coming, a comet, a revelation, a moment of truth that would tear through their carefully constructed reality like tissue paper in a soaking storm. The balance was beginning to tilt, though the dancers were too lost in their revels to notice.

But they danced on, clinging to their illusions, too proud to stop and too broken to stand still. Aphrodite watched as a young woman in a tattered ball gown twirled past, her face a perfect mask of ecstasy that didn't quite hide the trembling of her lower lip. They were all like that, beautiful, desperate, doomed.

With a deliberate motion, Aphrodite stubbed out her cigarette on the marble floor, adding one more scar to a surface already pitted with similar marks. The truth would fall upon them all soon enough, burning away their fabricated world like morning mist. But tonight, for this one last night, she would let them have their moment of false grace. Let them dance and drink and pretend that tomorrow would never come.

After all, even moribund gods could be merciful sometimes.

The song behind the story: *"States of Grace" by Loveswing was released on April 12, 2021, as part of an EP on Bandcamp. The EP includes several other tracks such as "The Brave," "Gravity," "Nightingale," "Rollercoaster," and "Rue De La Promenade."*

Loveswing began back in 1993 when 3 old hippies did a fundraiser for their local school. Originally billed as The Tantric Loveswing, Sting fans kicked off, so they dropped the Tantric part. Songwriter Rob Swan kept the name and alongside a merry band of minstrels , he has now released a couple of singles / EPs and the album, "Archetypes" on Bandcamp.

I should come clean on this one. I've known Rob for a few years through some shared activities that our wives indulged in and through some of the editorial work on my books.

Album: *States Of Grace EP*

Artist: *Loveswing*

Year: *2011 & 2021*

Composer(s): *Rob Swan & Justin Welch*

Record Label: *Cr8sound / Bandcamp*

Mara Ness

Gazing out at a star field, Mara Ness couldn't help but think that those far distant suns were revealing fragments of their ancient past, fragments that held the memories of countless lives lived, loves lost, and of a betrayal too deep to be forgotten. Mara had spent years chasing one of those memories, roaming the vast expanses of the void, searching for the physical embodiment of own, personnel demons. She was searching for one man, a man who once meant everything to her, but who left her with nothing but a criminal record and a deeply rooted sense of injustice. Mara was a balanced woman, the chips on each shoulder carrying equal weight, and these stars had borne witness to her agony, her resolve, and her transformation. They blinked in the distance, indifferent to the rage that drove her on, but their cold light guided her forward, illuminating the path to vengeance. She had danced on the edge of survival for so long and now the thought of finally seeing him again, of finally reaching him, made her pulse race.

"Dex…" Saying his name out loud stoked the embers of her hatred. Her fingers trembled slightly on the controls as her ship's scanners locked on to the final coordinates, the last-known location of the man who betrayed her. He had once been her closest ally, her most trusted confidant, and her lover.

Together, they shared their dreams. They planned a future in partnership, an immortal future, but Dex turned those dreams to ash, leaving Mara broken and abandoned on a forsaken outpost, while he disappeared into the stars.

Their lab existed in the shadows, buried beneath layers of secrecy and deception. On paper, it didn't exist. The authorities had scoured every registry, every database, every research grant for any sign of it, and they had found nothing. That was because Mara and Dex had built it in the places where no one thought to look, deep beneath the derelict industrial zones of an outpost moon, in repurposed biotech facilities whose official records had, they believed, long been lost to bureaucracy.

Here, away from the eyes of regulators and ethics committees, they worked relentlessly, their hands stained with the ghosts of the laws that they had shattered.

Immortality. The word was almost mythological, but for them, it was a problem waiting to be solved. Aging was a disease, one written into the fragile coils of human DNA, a series of biological failures stacked one upon another, leading to cellular collapse. But Mara and Dex had spent years untangling those failures, treating time itself like a pathogen that could be eradicated. Their project was compromised. Word got out and the authorities got in. Dex got a tip-off and he disappeared without a word a few hours before the raid, leaving Mara to face the music.

But the time that she spent in the penitentiary wasn't wasted. She spent those years rebuilding herself, forging her body and mind into tools of precision and vengeance. She was no longer the woman he had left behind, and that thought brought her a twisted sense of satisfaction. When she finally faced him, he probably wouldn't recognise her, but she would remember every scar carved on her skin by his hand. She could recall every teardrop that had fallen.

"Approaching target," her ship's AI announced in a monotone voice. For this specific task Mara travelled alone, her usual crew enjoying furlough on a mining station just out of reach of the sector authorities. She preferred the company of machines because they were indifferent to the storm raging inside her. The small research station that she tracked was drifting in the dark void ahead, its engines and systems largely powered down, its faint digital silhouette barely visible against the backdrop of the great expanse.

Mara's heartbeat quickened. Was this it? After all these years of chasing rumours and following trails that evaporated into nothing, could it really be him? A thousand scenarios flashed through her mind. Would he beg her for forgiveness? Would he try to explain away his betrayal and tell her it was all a mistake? Would he even remember her? Now, in her seventies, Mara felt that time had betrayed her too, but that feeling only fuelled her anger. She held herself taller, defying the stoop her body wished to give in to. She could feel the span of her hard-earned years as if they were carved into her skin like the rings of an ancient tree. Her once-black hair was now a silver-grey halo, her fingers gnarled and stiffened with arthritis, and her eyes had lost their brightness, but no, none of that mattered anymore. She took her meds and carried on, fuelled by cold, hard vengeance. It was all she had. The rest of her life was mechanistic and hollow. To some degree that emotional dislocation was what made her a good privateer captain.

Mara's attention was suddenly drawn to her tactical displays. There was an abrupt spike in energy readings. Alarms rang their metallic warnings on the bridge of her ship., and through the forward viewport, she saw the glint of movement. Tactical screens showed a horde of drones activating from the hull of Dex's apparently abandoned station. They swarmed like mechanical hornets, buzzing with lethal intent, and Mara's stomach churned. This wasn't just a chase anymore, where two humans would face each other in a final denouement. It was a battle.

Without thinking, Mara engaged manoeuvring thrusters, her ship jerking violently as she veered away from the oncoming swarm. Her stiff fingers flexed and then danced over the controls, engaging tactical patterns designed to dodge the bulk of the drone swarm as the machines closed in. The skeletons of derelict ships littered the area, a graveyard of broken hulks and superannuated craft that Dex had used as cover for this, his final hiding place. Although her ship was shielded, there was only ever a finite amount of energy that she could deploy, so Mara dodged in and out of those rotting wrecks, using them as cover herself.

Her mind raced, fuelled by a mix of fear and that ever-present rage. He was close, and she wouldn't let him escape, not again, but as the drones closed in, she realised with a sickening dread that she might not survive this initial encounter, and that was too much for her to bear. With a roar, she engaged her ship's weapons, firing at the nearest drones, but there were too many. They surrounded her, cutting off every obvious escape route.

Her ship jolted under the impact of their blasts, the hull groaning under the strain. Readouts flashed numbers at her. Shield strength at seventy percent and falling. Weapons buffers emptying rapidly.

"No!" she screamed, her voice a mix of fury and despair. Mara gritted her teeth, her breath ragged, refusing to give in. She wasn't done yet. She would survive this. She had to. Mara needed a better plan. She looked again at the field of battle. The starship graveyard stretched out before Mara's eyes, a desolate expanse of broken vessels and shattered hulks. Massive wrecks, the twisted remnants of long-forgotten wars, drifted lazily in the cold expanse of space, their metal bones silhouetted against the backdrop of distant stars. This was a graveyard where dead ships rested, but Mara's fast picket ship, although equally ancient and scarred, still functioned in all of the right places. She threaded her way between the wrecks with purpose.

Her ship, formerly a patrol vessel with the Apparat Alliance, had been retrofitted for moments like this. Mara had converted and adapted the ship over the years. She was renegade, an outsider, living on her wits. Her vessel now had strengthened energy shields, reinforced hull plating salvaged from forgotten cruisers, and a plethora of awkwardly mounted weapons turrets that hummed to life, anticipating what was coming. The small bridge was dark except for the cold glow of the tactical screens, and Mara's hands gripped the controls tightly, her fingers reaching out with certainty across the flickering panels as she navigated through the debris field.

Dozens of drones were converging on her position She could see them buzzing through the tangled remains of derelict ships, their small, sleek frames glinting like daggers in the dim light of distant stars. If she stayed out in the open they would overwhelm her defences. She needed cover, and there it was. She pinpointed the hulk of an old ice hauler, swinging round and backing her ship into its vacant interior so that she could force the drone swarm into a direct frontal assault. Mara's pulse quickened, but she was ready. She had fought these types of automated sentinels before. They were the remnants of some long-dead warlord's final defence, co-opted to guard the station at the heart of this junkyard, the station where she would find her quarry. The drones weren't intelligent, but they were fast, relentless, and dangerous in numbers.

Her ship's weapons roared to life as the first of the drones darted toward her, its red eyes flashing as it fired a stream of plasma bursts. Mara steadied her own ship, shifting to the left, letting the shot graze the side of her ship, the metal hull plates shrieking as the ordnance scraped across her shields. A few more seconds of delay, and her shield system would overload.

Mara brought all of her weapons turrets to bear. With a flick of her wrist, she targeted the closest drone and fired. A volley of searing light erupted from the cannons, slicing through the drone's thin frame. It exploded in a burst of flame and debris, fragments spinning off into the void, but there were more. They swarmed in front of her, dozens of them, weaving through the wreckage with unnatural agility, marshalling their formation to gain maximum advantage for their frontal assault. The drones' ability to manoeuvre was compromised by the close confines of the old ice hauler's interior. Mara's pulse pounded in her ears, but she remained focused and calm.

Another burst of laser fire erupted from her ship's cannons, tearing through a cluster of drones. Explosions lit up the graveyard like fireworks, reflecting off the crumbling hulls of long disabled ships. As the drone swarm thinned out, she pushed the throttle forward, diving back out into the graveyard, skimming the surface of a derelict battleship, its massive guns rusted and useless. The drones followed, relentless in their pursuit.

Suddenly, one of the drones broke formation, accelerating toward her with suicidal intent. It slammed into her ship's rear thrusters, sending a shockwave through the superstructure. Alarms blared as warning screens switched back and forth between damage reports. Mara cursed, wrestling with the controls as the ship spiralled. She pulled it back, just barely, righting the ship and sending it barrelling toward a massive hulk, half-buried in the debris field. With a swift manoeuvre, she brought her ship into the shadow of the hulk, using its wreckage as cover. For a brief moment, the drones lost her in the cluttered mess of broken ships.

But Mara wasn't done. She fired up the auxiliary thrusters, pushing the freighter through a narrow gap in the debris. The drones surged back into view, but this time she was ready. Her ship emerged from behind the wreckage with all cannons blazing. The drones didn't stand a chance as they flew straight into her trap. One by one, they erupted in flames, their lifeless frames scattering across the junkyard, adding to the sum total of decay. Breathing heavily, Mara surveyed the destruction on her radar screen. The swarm was reduced to a few stragglers, and those quickly vanished into the debris, retreating into the darkness. Warning lights flashed, but she had survived, and now she could resume her mission. Somewhere in this vast field of death, her ex-lover was hiding, and she would find him.

Mara moved the ship cautiously back towards the derelict station that was orbiting a dead moonlet at the heart of the junkyard. Mara's heart pulsed in sync with the hum of the ship's engines, her hands steady on the controls despite the storm of emotion swirling inside her. Dex was on that station. Dex, who had once been a beacon of humanity's ambition. His was the brightest of minds, and he sought to transcend human limits, reaching for the stars and immortality, but the dream did not become reality. When Dex fled and left Mara to take the blame, their work was incomplete. Mara wondered who she would find. Would Dex be in his eighties now, or did he actually find a way to stay young?

Mara felt nervous. She would come face to face with Dex in minutes. The encrypted signals that she had followed across the void and through the last forty standard years, had finally led her here. A man who had once meant everything to her, the man who betrayed her, had hidden himself away in this forgotten place. Every step she took now felt like walking back into a nightmare. An inner voice begged her to turn back, to give up this foolish pursuit. That voice told her she was chasing ghosts, that she was throwing away the last remnants of her future on a past that was already written in the stones, but forgetting was no longer an option. She had tried. For years, she let herself believe that time would dull the sharpness of his betrayal, and that she could rebuild what he had shattered, but every message, every trace she uncovered, burned away her hope and reignited her fury. The betrayal was alive inside her, festering, a wound that refused to heal.

As her ship neared the station's main air lock, she watched the screens as the automated docking sequence kicked into life. The derelict station loomed larger, its massive structure casting shadows on the dead moonlet below. The place was a ruin, a monument to lost ambition, but she knew he was here, hiding like the coward she believed him to be. Mara Ness was about to finish what he had started.

The readouts were in the green. There was atmosphere and gravity on board the station, which she took as a positive sign. With a sharp hiss, the docking procedure completed, and the airlock creaked and groaned as it opened, releasing a rush of stale, cold air that made her shiver. Mara hesitated, standing on the threshold of the station's dark corridors. She felt the density of the station's silence as if it were a wall, a silence that mirrored the void inside her where once upon a time her love for Dex had burned so brightly.

She stepped into the darkness, her boots echoing in the empty hallways. Every shadow seemed to whisper his name, and every creak of the station's aging metal felt like a reminder of the time they had lost. The deeper she ventured, the stronger her resolve grew. She would find him, and this time, there would be no escape, no more lies. In the distance, she heard the faint hum of an active power source, which meant that something here was online. He was definitely here. Mara could feel him. Somewhere in these darkened halls, he was waiting, thinking he could hide from her fury, but she had tracked him through a galaxy, wading through the ashes of their shared past. She would not stop now.

Mara tightened her grip on the plasma blade at her side. She lifted it from its sheath and felt the comforting weight of it in her hand. She would make him answer for what he had done. There would be no forgiveness. Only justice.

Mara's breath was shallow and her heartbeat was steady, even though she felt tense as she stepped forward. This place had once been alive, humming with the excitement of progress and innovation, but now it too was a graveyard of twisted metal and faded echoes. She had expected nothing less. Time destroys all things.

"Fool," she muttered under her breath as she descended deeper into the station. "Why couldn't I just forget you."

The corridor stretched ahead, its end shrouded in darkness. Every step brought her closer to him, to the answers she dreaded and longed for in equal measure. She paused, her hand grazing the cold metal wall. Through these walls and conduits Mara could feel the faint hum of energy that still suffused the wreckage. That would be his signature, his handiwork. She was more certain than ever that he was here.

Mara approached the lab at the heart of the station. This was the place where his last transmission had reportedly come from. A surge of adrenaline mixed with bitter rage coursed through her veins as she stared at the towering servers. Their faint hum was the only sound in the cold, desolate room, a testament to the thin filament of energy that kept this station's basic systems running. Mara's focus wasn't on the machines, though. She stared intently at the stasis pod in the centre of the room.

The pod's soft glow illuminated the dark corners of the lab, casting eerie shadows across the walls. Slowly, she approached it, her breath catching as she saw the silhouette inside. The glass was fogged, but the shape was unmistakable. She knew that figure. She had once known every inch of him. Her hands trembled as she wiped away the frost from the glass, revealing his face beneath. Mara swore then and turned her gaze away. How dare he, she thought. How dare he!

Dex had beaten time, true enough, but only by entering stasis He had barely aged, while she had lived every agonizing year that had passed since their last meeting. He still looked like the man she had fallen for, the man who sold her a dream of immortality, of a life beyond the stars, a promise that was crumbling to dust as surely as the hours ticked down day by day.

The pod's control panel was just within reach, waiting for her to make a decision. She hesitated. What would she say when he woke up? The fury that had fuelled her for so long faltered for a moment as the memories of their past crept back in. Mara swooned as she remembered the way that he had held her, and the way he had whispered his dreams of eternity in her ear. As she looked at his familiar face she could almost hear him speak those words, and part of her wanted to believe that he really had meant them, and that this was all one huge and lousy fuck-up.

But then the lies flooded her mind again. The betrayal. The truth he had hidden from her until it was too late. He left her behind. When things got hot, he left her to carry the can. He hadn't cared what it cost her, as long as he achieved his goal. With a deep breath, she activated the pod's reanimation mechanism. The soft hiss of air filled the room as the stasis field dissipated, and slowly, after a few minutes, his eyes fluttered open. He blinked, disoriented, and then he saw her.

"You came for me," he whispered, his voice cracked and dry, barely more than a whisper.

Mara clenched her fists, her nails digging into her palms. She had come, but not for him, not for the man she once loved. She had come for closure, for justice, for vengeance.

He was still groggy. He searched her face, asking, "Who... who are you?"

"Don't," she interrupted, her voice cold and steady. "Don't say another word. Look at what you've done to me!" she replied, her voice low, each word manufactured from her iron will.

Her words struck Dex like sharpened stones. He searched his memory for a name. Dex tried to rise, but his body was weak from stasis, his movements slow. "He wiped at his eyes, trying to see her clearly. He stared at her for long seconds before saying hesitantly, "Mara? Is that...is that you, Mara?"

A flicker of recognition passed over his face. Dex looked confused and uncertain, and Mara felt a sense of satisfaction, in that and she tasted a hint of the revenge that she had sought for so long. Her anger was no longer just for him. It was for herself, for the years he had robbed, for the dreams abandoned, and the other lives that she might have had that would always remain unlived. She wouldn't be satisfied with mere words; she wanted to leave him stripped and laid bare.

Mara stared at him, her thoughts a riot of confusing impulses and memories. "You don't need to explain," she spat, her anger rising to the surface.

His expression shifted, confusion replaced by desperation. "It wasn't like that. You have to understand..."

"I don't need to understand," Mara said, her hand hovering over the pod's controls. "I just need to decide what to do with you."

Mara stood next to the stasis pod and stared down at Dex. She was frozen, her heart a battleground of conflicting emotions. Part of her yearned to close the gap between them, to hold him and pretend that the years hadn't passed, and that betrayal hadn't scarred her beyond recognition. The girl within who had once loved him whispered of forgiveness, of picking up the shattered pieces of their past and mending them, but the other part, the part that had crawled through the wreckage and lived with the consequences of his deception, was much louder.

"I never forgot," she said at last, her voice a cold blade cutting through the silence. "But I wish I had."

He blinked, as if trying to grasp the full meaning of her words. His muscles twitched in feeble attempts to sit up, but years of stasis had weakened him. His body moved sluggishly, still adjusting to the shock of life after so long in the cryogenic hold.

"Mara," he croaked, his voice barely more than a rasp.

"Don't," she snapped, stepping back. "Don't say anything. You lost that right a long time ago."

His gaze wavered in his desperation. Mara looked into the same eyes that once captivated her and were now pleading for understanding, for forgiveness.

She barked out a bitter laugh, the sound harsh in the sterile lab. "You wanted power, and you didn't care what it cost. You left me to pick up the pieces when you got scared, when you ran away. You don't know what I had to sacrifice."

He reached out a trembling hand toward her, but she stepped back, her eyes narrowing. The room felt smaller, the air full of the years of her unspoken pain.

Silence stretched between them. His hand hovered in the air for a moment longer as his eyes, wide and pleading, searched hers for a glimmer of hope, for the woman who had once adored him, but Mara made her choice. She stepped away from the pod, moving behind it to where the power lines lay tangled on the floor. She bent down and her blade flashed through the air in a trail of sparks. Then Mara turned on her heel, the fading glow of the pod casting long shadows as she started to walk away.

How ironic, she thought, that he would die without aging a day, while she, old and decaying, would continue for a while longer at least. The lights flickered ominously as Mara walked away from the impotent Dex still lying in the stasis pod, her steps echoing loudly in the cavernous station. The hum of the remaining power systems stuttered. The once-vibrant energy of the lab was dying slowly. She didn't look back. She couldn't. Not now. Not after anything.

"Don't leave me, not like this," his voice rasped, barely audible, swallowed by the fading sounds of the lab. She paused at the lab door, her fingers trembling on the control panel. For a brief moment, she almost faltered, but then she spoke, her voice cold, the sharp edge of her words cutting through the dimly lit silence.

"You'll never fade, will you?" she whispered, the words barely louder than the dying hum of the machines. "But that doesn't mean you need to be alive." Her finger pressed down, and with a soft hiss, the lab door sealed shut. She thrust her blade into the control panel on her side of the door and shorted the control.

As Mara stepped onto her ship, the familiar hiss of the airlock closing felt like the closing of a chapter. It was a story that she had been bound to for far too long. Mara wanted the weight of the past, of the betrayal by the man she had once loved, to lift from her shoulders. The door behind her, now sealed, was not just a barrier between her and him, Mara wanted it cut off the years of pain that he had caused. Mara reached the bridge of her small ship and went to the forward viewport. As much as she wanted closure, that inner rage still burned. For a moment she stood there looking at the station superstructure, feeling confused. Her retribution was imminent, but her anger was only partly focused on Dex. She was, she realised, angry with herself too for letting the man dominate her life for so many years.

She settled into her ship's pilot's seat, her hands moving across the controls with the ease of routine. The ship hummed to life, and she gazed out at the stars beyond the viewport. They shimmered, cold and distant, just as they always had. As she undocked she sent one final coded command to the old station's core CPU. It was an old protocol but a good one nonetheless. She was a privateer. These were things that she knew about, and these were the things that she did. The station's systems powered down, plunging the entire complex into a suffocating darkness. The last vestiges of light flickered out, leaving only silence in their wake. Life support faded. He was gone now. Truly gone. Dex would be frozen in time. He would never fade. His lies, his deceit, they would remain entombed in that dark and lifeless station, just as they were in her own broken heart..

Mara looked down at her hands, seeing the wrinkles and the stiffened, arthritic joints. She grimaced as she gripped the controls, her lips curling into a determined smile. The ship surged forward, its engines roaring to life, as she flew toward an appointment with her crew. Although her time might be growing shorter, she was going to make the most of what she had left.

The song behind the story: *"Never Fade" by Alice In Chains, from their Rainier Fog album, is a great track that delves into themes of grief, memory, and resilience. Written by William DuVall and Jerry Cantrell, the song addresses the emotional weight of loss and the attempt to keep someone's memory alive. DuVall was inspired by both his grandmother's passing and the memory of Layne Staley, Alice In Chains' original lead vocalist.*

For me, the song's lyrics suggest a struggle between the suffocating nature of grief and the determination to hold on to the presence of those who have passed, with the repeated line "Never fade" emphasizing that their memory will never disappear. The song captures this duality with a sense of raw emotion, balancing the pain of the past with the hope of carrying forward what has been lost.

Album: *Rainier Fog*

Artist: *Alice In Chains*

Year: *2018*

Composer(s): *William DuVall and Jerry Cantrell*

Record Label: *BMG*

Be Well

Rain pattered softly against the window, a constant, muted rhythm that matched the ebb and flow of life in this place of healing. It was the only sound in the room, save for the faint and shallow breaths that Karen took and the rhythmic stirrings of the syringe driver strapped to her left thigh. I sat beside her, one hand resting gently on the edge of the bed, the other tracing absent minded patterns on the blue weave of the hospital blanket. The room we were in was a godsend. It was our small and private corner of the world, usually an oasis for us in these troubled times, but today the space felt oppressive. We had spoken so many times about these days, but any preparation that we thought we had made was laid low by the true fragility of life.

Karen's form was almost motionless under the thin sheets, her slight frame dwarfed by the hospital bed. She had turned her face away from me, muttering under her breath, as though she was having a secret conversation with the far wall. Her eyes, once so lively and filled with light, now just stared past everything. The intravenous morphine was taking her far away from me, beyond the haze of its numbing relief and into a space where I couldn't reach her anymore. I tried to stay with her, but nothing could bridge the drug induced chasm between us.

"Karen," I whispered, my voice barely audible in the stillness. Her name, once a source of comfort, now felt foreign, as if the woman who carried it with grace and strength had already slipped away.

The syringe driver clicked softly, releasing another dose of morphine into Karen's thigh. I watched her face, waiting for some reaction, some glimpse of recognition, but there was nothing. Her hands, so familiar and yet so alien now, twitched faintly on the bed. Her skin was thin and almost translucent, and the veins carrying blood and morphine around her body stood out. I wondered what dreams the morphine spun for her, and what landscapes her mind wandered through. Did she even remember me? Was she really still in this room, or had she already gone somewhere I couldn't follow?

The silence between us was unbearable, like a thick fog that blurred everything including our memories. I could still see the curve of her shoulder beneath the blanket. I looked at the cascade of her regrown hair spilling onto the pillow. "Where do you go?" I asked, my voice barely breaking the stillness, knowing I would get no answer. She didn't stir or blink. The bright and vibrant Karen that I once knew seemed trapped in some unreachable place, staring beyond the walls, beyond me, into something only she could see.

I leaned closer, feeling a sense of helplessness settle deeply into my bones. "Is it darkness?" I murmured. My chest felt tight as the bitter truth was sinking in. Her silence was a presence in its own right, one I could neither challenge nor understand. She had crossed a threshold, and I, still tethered to this world, was powerless to follow.

Her breath remained steady and her body lay still. Karen's absence hung above the bed like a stale pocket of air. It was as if she had taken the first steps into the unknown without saying goodbye, and I was left to sit in the wake of her quiet departure, wondering what lay on the other side of the wall that her eyes were now fixed upon. I closed my own eyes for a moment, pressing my fingers harder against the blanket, trying to ground myself in the here and now. The ache in my chest was unbearable, a constant reminder of everything I was losing.

I stared at the back of her head, willing her to turn, to give me a glance, a word, some sign that she was still here with me, but Karen remained motionless, her body sinking deeper into the hospital bed, cradled by the soft sheets and the relentless obfuscations of the morphine. She seemed miles away, not just in body but in spirit.

There was a time when the warmth of our love filled every moment. As I looked at her emaciated figure I remembered that wonderful New Year. It was just the two of us. We sat across a candle-lit table. I remember scallops and venison and red wine. We made love in the living room at the farmhouse, and then, as we sat back in each other's arms, tasting a red Corbières, Karen sighed. I asked her if she was OK and she started to cry. She wanted the night to be perfect because, she said, she had found a lump in her breast, and she was frightened.

Even in this room, before the drugs took effect, when Karen's hallucinations had been mild and she drifted in and out of our world, laughter echoed off these sterile walls. On one occasion, just days previously, she held a conversation with drip stand, believing it to be a nurse in need of fattening up. There had been moments where our connection was so strong that words weren't needed. A look or a brush of hands was enough, but now, the cancer had stolen all of that. It wasn't just eating away at her; it was hollowing out our shared moments, and then filling those voids with this unbearable silence.

I felt the dull ache of it as I stood up, every movement heavy with a kind of grief that words can't describe. Moving to ease the stiffness in my legs, I sat in the chair beside her, lowering myself slowly, my knees groaning with the effort, but the pain in my body was nothing compared to the sadness that was settled in my soul.

"Karen," I whispered, my voice barely holding together, "where will you go when you leave me?" I trembled as I spoke, the words coated with the tears I refused to let fall from my eyes. "When you go silent... I feel your soul slipping away."

Her breathing was slow, too slow, and the stillness of the room threatened the world with paralysis. I thought of all the things we had never said to each other, the things I had kept buried because I didn't want to weigh her down with my own fears. I wanted to tell her how afraid I was, and how lost I felt with the thought of her absolute absence, but it seemed selfish now, amidst all that she was enduring, so the words stayed trapped in my throat, choking me.

"Does it seem lonely?" I asked, my voice soft, almost lost in the sterile hum. I watched her closely, desperate for any flicker of recognition. Then, just as I was ready to give up, I thought I saw something. There was a slight relaxation of her shoulders, a shift so small it could just have been my imagination. Was it a response, or was it simply the morphine pulling her deeper into oblivion? I couldn't tell, but I clung to the idea of it anyway. In this endless and oppressive quiet, I pinned my hopes on the idea that maybe, even in the haze of her pain and sedative induced catatonia, she had heard me. Maybe, just for a second, she knew I was still here, and that I hadn't given up on her.

My fingers brushed against hers where they lay cool and limp on the white sheets. "I'm still here," I whispered, but even as I said it, I knew that someday soon, she wouldn't be. When that day came, the silence that had fallen between us would be permanent. I reached out, hesitant, and took her hand in mine. Her fingers were cold, their once strong grip now limp, but at least she didn't pull away. That was something, wasn't it? Even in this fog of morphine, where her mind drifted somewhere between pain and peace, Karen hadn't yet let go completely.

"Be well," I whispered, my voice trembling. It was like a ritual now, those same two words, a mantra that I repeated in the darkness. I said these words for her, and I said them for myself, hoping each time that they would carry some hidden power, some magic that could somehow undo what had already been written into her genes.

She didn't stir. The rhythm of her breathing remained the same; slow and deliberate, as though she was fighting a battle with each breath. I knew the morphine was stealing her pain, and dulling the edges of her decline, but it also stole the woman I had known. I was speaking to the shell of someone who was already slipping away, leaving me alone in a sterile room that smelled of antiseptic.

"Please, Karen," I said again, more to fill the silence than to call her back from wherever she was. "Be well."

The rain tapped lightly on the window, a gentle and natural counterpoint to the hospital's mechanical beeps and the soft sigh of the saline drip feeding into her veins. I watched that drip with an obsessive fascination, feeling like the world was being measured out in droplets. I wanted to scream at the universe. I wanted to break the silence with all the things I had left unsaid, but I couldn't. Not now. What words would change anything? What good would my confessions, my fears, or my desperate love do for her now?

"What will my arms do," I murmured, my voice cracking, "when you're not here for me to hold?"

That question had become a nightmare that haunted me. What would I do when she was truly gone? The emptiness was already there, looming like a shadow, waiting to consume me once she no longer occupied this space. Would I learn to live with the void? Or would I drift into it myself, just as she was fading now?

Her chest rose and fell with an agonizing slowness. I squeezed her hand gently, though I knew she wouldn't feel it. Maybe, in some faraway place, she was listening, maybe she heard me, but maybe not. All I knew was that I was here, anchored to her, unable to imagine a world where she wasn't, a world where I didn't have this hand to hold.

And then, for a brief, fleeting moment, her fingers twitched in mine, as if in recognition. I held my breath, wondering if it was real or just my mind playing cruel tricks, but then it was gone.

She was gone, still breathing, still here, but not here. I stayed with her, counting her breaths, waiting for the rain to stop.

"Be well," I whispered again, my voice barely audible, as though speaking too loudly might break the fragile cord that held her here with me. I leaned back in my chair, the cold stiffness of it matching the numbness settling deep into my bones. I was losing count of the days that we, the extended family, had been keeping vigil. I was exhausted. We all were. I was tired of watching her drift further from me. I was so tired of continually sweeping up the hope that had long since turned to dust. I was tired of the fight that had worn us both down to mere shadows of who we once were. Her face, pale and almost translucent, seemed more a memory than reality, but as I sat there, lost in the overwhelming silence of my thoughts, her hand tightened around mine. It was faint, but it was there. A small, almost imperceptible squeeze. She was still with me. Somewhere in the fog of morphine and pain, Karen was still holding on.

That was all I needed. I choked down a sob, pressing my free hand to my lips as I leaned closer to her, my forehead resting on the pillow's edge. "May your heart be open," I whispered, my words breaking in the air between us. My words were fragile, like the life we were clinging to. "Whatever changes come, whatever darkness surrounds you now… find peace, Karen. Please, please find peace."

My heart burned, and it felt as if it was being pulled apart vessel by vessel. I didn't know what lay ahead. A world without her seemed too cruel and too impossible to accept, but I knew it was coming. Her body, once strong, was losing its battle, and soon the light in her eyes would fade to nothing. I blinked against the stinging in my eyes, refusing to let the tears fall, not yet, not while she was still here, still fighting, but for now, for these final moments, I would be with her. I would sit in this sterile room, my hand clasped in hers, a fraying lifeline that tethered her to the world for just a little while longer. I would love her, even as the pain of it hollowed me out.

"Be well," I whispered, my voice cracking. The rain continued to patter against the window, a steady rhythm that was indifferent to the lives of people in a room set aside for the dying. Outside, the world turned on, unknowing, uncaring. Life moved forward, even as ours stood still. I squeezed Karen's hand one last time, and waited.

The song behind the story: *"May You Be Well" by The Lone Bellow is a heartfelt and introspective track from their album Walk Into a Storm (2017). It reflects the band's signature blend of Americana and soulful harmonies, bringing warmth and emotional depth to the listener. The lyrics express sentiments of care, longing, and a deep wish for well-being, even as the protagonist seems to navigate through hardship and distance.*

This story is inspired by those sentiments and is one of the very few fictional stories that I've written based on my late wife's fortitude in her ultimately unsuccessful battle with cancer. It has taken me fourteen years to find the words, so I have a lot to thank this song for.

"May You Be Well" centres on resilience and the desire for peace despite life's challenges. Its repetitive refrain of "may you be well" feels like a blessing, wishing strength and love for those going through personal struggles, and these sentiments are something that I think we can all empathise with.

Album: *Walk Into A Storm*

Artist: *The Lone Bellow*

Year: *2017*

Composer(s): *Zach Williams*

Record Label: *Descendant Records*

Horizon

It was the glow of neon lights and the buzz of a dangerously exciting world hovering in the shadows that first lured Rose and her lover to this place. The streets hummed with life, the noise of this alien landscape utterly compelling, and yet within this tangled mess of sound and touch and smell, Rose managed to find space for her own silence. Back then, when this was all fresh and addictive, it was as though she walked in a bubble, while all around her a human maelstrom swirled and eddied. That was the story that she told herself. The bubble was a fragile thing and soon pricked. Now, with her lovers long gone and the maelstrom firmly pulling her down beneath the surface of the city's waters, these city alleyways were as much a prison as they were a refuge, and this particular street, with its fractured windows and cheap motels, was the limit of her horizon, forming the boundaries within which she survived each day.

The people who came here didn't ask too many questions. They took what they needed and left what they didn't want any more. Rose lived in a world of transactions. This was a place of constant withdrawal, a bank without tellers, where overdrafts had no limits. This was a place from which the frayed threads of a life were picked at in random sequence.

Rose wasn't sure what she had left to give, but every night, she had to give something. Tonight would be no different. A John was due to knock at her door any minute now. Rose was resigned to the fact, almost stoic in her anger and frustration at her addict's impotence.

Rose hadn't always been this person. Once, she'd danced under a star filled sky, her feet twirling, her arms flung wide to catch the wind by a slowly drifting, moonlit river, but those were different days, a time when there was still sugar in her veins, and when hope wasn't some distant, unreachable thing. She sometimes felt as though she had broken her neck. When the bubble burst, she fell to the dusty pavement, a limp and paralysed creature bathed in a flood of neon yellows. She recovered, but she couldn't dance now, not in the way that she once had. Her assimilation into this narrow and grimy little space suffocated her spirit. She danced, but only to the edge of the world, where she inevitably hung back and waited for someone to join her, but that special individual never came for her. The men who did pay her a call now never cared enough to pull her back from the edge. This next customer was a regular. He liked to talk. Rose shuddered at the thought as she refreshed her lipstick.

"Let me put the water in the bowl for your wounds, babe," she whispered to herself sometimes. Such words of tenderness, once whispered by others, her mother, perhaps, were now her one small comfort. Rose's inner world had shrunk, so that now she crouched in a small, painful corner where she sought comfort in whispers, not from others, but from herself. The words she imagined that she once heard from her mother, gentle reassurances that soothed her wounds, were her last refuge. Her mother was a cold, self-centred gadfly, who had rarely ever paid her daughter much attention. As Rose whispered the word that she longed to hear from her far-distant mother, each syllable felt like an echo of ta childhood nightmare, now distant, leaving her clinging to fragile imaginings. As Rose's world narrowed with her dependence on the needle, so too did her ability to express her emotions. Her language became sparse, filled only with terms like "wounds" and "scars" and "hurts", symbols of the violence that surrounded her.

All the men who came to her wanted something, always something. Mostly, they wanted the warmth of her skin, the hollow comfort of a body pressed against theirs in the night. Sometimes they craved the thrill of a fantasy, asking her to play a role in their fractured dreams so that they could pretend for just a while that they were someone else. At other times, they came seeking a fleeting confession of love, whispered between the sheets, something temporary enough to fill the emptiness in their existence, but without the permanence that weighed on their hearts in their other lives.

Every instance was the same, a repetitive ritual of superficial connections. They came, took what they needed, and left, and she, like a well-rehearsed actress, smiled through it all. "You can't lose, babe," she'd say, her voice playful, like it didn't matter, and it didn't, not for them. In this game, they always won, their desires fulfilled, their egos soothed. They left feeling lighter, victorious in their quest for momentary distraction, never realizing that the cost was paid by another. Sat at a worn out dressing table, Rose applied a little blusher, thinning about the men who came, and the disaster of her love life before the addiction took hold.

With every anonymous touch, she lost a piece of herself. With every smile she forced, a little more of her soul slipped away like sand falling through her fingers. She would sit in the silence after they were gone, feeling smaller, her edges blurred, her identity dissolving like smoke on a summer breeze. She couldn't remember when it began, when her heart had started to wither, or when the smile had first become just a mask. The game never seemed to stop, never giving her the room to breathe or to reclaim what was hers.

She tried to feel nothing, to wall herself off from the emptiness, but it always seeped in, filling the cracks in her spirit, until there was almost nothing left of the girl that she had been. "You can't lose, babe," she whispered again as her reflection in the mirror looked back at her with vacant eyes, as if asking the same silent question; when would she finally let herself win?

When she played their game, did it really feel so bad, she wondered? When they chose her and then left her, did it hurt them like it hurt her? She doubted it. It was not the hurt of loss, though, that mattered. For Rose the hurting came as another slice of her was carved away, to sink into the grubby waters in the gutter. She was their dark, forbidden princess for a few fleeting moments. Afterwards, they'd walk away, back into their world of light and comfort, while she stayed behind, here, in this place. Rose caught sight of the reflected fire in her eyes. Time to smile. It never stopped the anger, but there was a time and a place for that, and dealing with her imminent John was more urgent. She needed the action to score.

Rose stared out of the cracked window of the dingy room that she rented from her pimp. The room smelled of sweat and cigarettes and semen. Outside, the sky hunkered down, setting limits to hopes and dreams. "Here is your princess," she said softly to no one in particular, her eyes tracing the skyline. "And there is the horizon." Beyond the crumbling buildings and flickering neon signs, the city seemed to stretch on endlessly, but for Rose, the thought of distant places made her feel giddy, as though she was standing on the edge of a cliff, the drop below bottomless. The skyline was mostly made of squat brownstones, with the towers and the glass of the financial district rising in the distance. The street below her window was littered and grubby, with a smattering of the homeless and the hopeless milling about. A yellow cab crawled to a halt outside her building. She watched as a middle aged man paid his fare and turned. He looked up at Rose's window, saw her, and waved.

Rose wasn't sure why the thoughts of her former lovers' many betrayals kept creeping into her mind like shadows crawling into the light from the corners of her consciousness. It wasn't something she wanted to think about, but it was there now, lingering, a persistent whisper that refused to leave her alone. It wasn't that those thoughts reminded her about her own sordid outcomes. No, she wasn't afraid of that. It was their repetitive desertions of her when things got tough that rankled. Those men pulled the thread that unravelled her entire life. All except one. Rose hated those men who, with cruel precision, used their needles to prick her bubble of innocence, setting her adrift in a world that felt cold and dark.

Sometimes, when she was alone with her thoughts, one man's face would drift back into her mind like a ghost, uninvited, unwanted, yet always present. She could still see the sharp lines of his jaw and the way his eyes never quite softened, even when he pretended to be kind. His voice echoed in her head. She could still hear the words that he used like weapons, carving his way into her heart, and every time his image appeared, she would find herself wondering, how, how did everything turn so sour?

Rose wondered if she would ever be free of him, free of the hope that she still held in his memory. There were days when wondered if she might drop everything and go off to find him, but she suffered from a disease that rotted out her core every day. She imagined hearing the news, a simple phrase to the effect that his place in her memory was gone, and she would try to picture how it might feel to be free of those thoughts and images. Would it be a rush of relief, like air finally filling her lungs after too long spent holding her breath? Or would it be something else, something heavier, a new wound slicing open in a heart already too scarred to heal?

There was a flood in her mind, and the waters never stopped flowing. The memories surged and crashed like waves in a storm, relentless and unforgiving. She tried to fight them, tried to push them back, but they were too strong. They always had been. Every word he'd ever spoken to her, each one soaked in promises, in love, became an anchor that dragged her deeper beneath the surface. His lies, his promises, his casual cruelty, all tangled together like chains around her ankles. She couldn't swim. She couldn't breathe.

Rose wanted to scream, to cry out against the injustice of it all, but even her voice felt distant and muffled by the flood in her head. All she could do was sit with the weight of it, feeling the pull of the anchor as it dragged her under, again and again, until all that was left was quiet suffocation in the dark. "I don't belong in these waters," she whispered, her hands trembling as she ran them over her own bare skin. This place, this life, it wasn't meant for her, and yet, here she was. This was a moment of clarity amid the black waters of the maelstrom. "Yes, I can see it, take me home, babe," she said, her voice barely audible over the background hum of the city, but there was no one to take her home. Home was a distant memory, a place that existed only in her dreams.

Rose was tired, the kind of tired that sleep couldn't fix. She'd scratched it down, every promise she'd made to herself that things would get better, that she'd amount to something, but now, the sugar in her veins had run out. She didn't know what to say anymore. At heart, Rose no longer knew how to convince herself that she still mattered.

There were nights when she stood at the window, watching the people pass by below, wondering if anyone else felt as lost as she did. Did anyone else feel like they were dancing on the edge of the world, just waiting to fall? She could hear their voices sometimes, muffled through the thin walls of the motel; laughter, arguments, and the murmurs of paid for lovers. In those moments, she felt the deep well of her loneliness sucking the life from her chest, so powerfully that she could barely breathe, but then, she'd remind herself, "I am a princess, and there is the horizon." She wasn't sure what that meant anymore. Maybe she was trying to tell herself that she still had some kind of power, some kind of control over her own fate. Or maybe it was just a lie she told herself to make it through another night.

The men who came and went, they didn't really see the princess, and they definitely didn't see her horizon. All they saw was a body, a place to leave their pain for a little while. They never noticed the quiet desperation in her eyes, or the way she clung to those last fragments of herself, and when they left, they never looked back. But every now and then, in the quiet hours before dawn, Rose would think about leaving. She would try to imagine what it would be like to step out of this place and never come back. She tried to visualise a new horizon, one that wasn't tainted by so many ghosts, but then, the sun would rise, and the city would wake up, and she'd realise that she didn't have the energy or the will to go anywhere else. This was her life now. She had to stay here because this city gave her the means to fulfil an endless and never assuaged hunger.

One day, she knew, it would end. Maybe she'd just disappear and fade into the background like the other forgotten souls who wandered these sordid streets. Or maybe, one day, someone would finally see her. Not the rented body, not the mask she wore for them, but her, the girl who used to dance under the starry sky with the boy in her dreams. Rose heard a cough and then a knock at her door. The John. She smiled at her reflection in the dressing table mirror. She sighed, knowing that the girl who dreamed of something more was here, in this place, and there was only this horizon, under which the needle pricked the balloon.

The song behind the story: *"Horizon" by Aldous Harding is a hauntingly beautiful track from her 2017 album Party. Aldous Harding, a New Zealand singer-songwriter known for her atmospheric and genre-blurring style, weaves a complex narrative in "Horizon" that showcases her ability to create both eerie and emotional music. The song blends elements of folk, gothic, and avant-garde pop, with Harding's ethereal vocals taking centre stage.*

"Horizon" is often interpreted as a meditation on emotional distance, vulnerability, and unspoken tension in relationships. The lyrics are minimal but packed with meaning. I think that the song explores themes of self-realization, the tension between freedom and confinement, and the challenge of communication in relationships. There is a feeling of longing and loss throughout, but also a sense of empowerment.

Ever since I first heard it, I've found "Horizon" to be a captivating track that showcases Aldous Harding's talent for creating emotionally charged, enigmatic music, inviting listeners to delve into the complex layers of meaning beneath its minimalist surface.

Album: *Party*

Artist: *Aldous Harding*

Year: *2017*

Composer(s): *Aldous Harding*

Record Label: *4AD Records*

Ulfhednar...

The wind sounded like a banshee's wail and it was relentless as it tore across the fields, pulling at the warriors' furs and whipping bare skin with the sharp bite of winter. The sky bled with the first light of day, casting everything in a crimson hue that foretold of the coming violence. Ulfhednar stood like a solidly carved figure at the edge of the battlefield, his silhouette framed against the lowering sky, his every breath rolling out in clouds of mist. His spear, long and sharp, felt good in his hand, and he was eager to taste blood once more.

Beside him, Ulfric, his great wolf, stood as still as death itself. The beast was no mere creature; he was kin to the gods, a wolf of unnatural size, his fur as dark as the night, his amber eyes gleaming like molten gold. The air vibrated with tension as his low growl rumbled through the ground beneath Ulfhednar's feet. Ulfric had always been his shadow in battle. Ulfric was more than a companion. The wolf was as much a part of Ulfhednar as he was a part of the wolf. Together, they had carved their way through countless foes, but today the odds were different.

Across the field, a sea of Danish shields glinted in the rising light, their numbers seeming vast and overwhelming. The enemy forces stretched across the field, a serpent of warriors coiling and preparing to strike. Ulfhednar's band was smaller, no more than sixty men, each as scarred and weathered as the stones that lined the fjords. They stood behind him, axes and swords at the ready, knowing that victory was a distant hope, but they were willing to give their lives for the rights of their kin and for the blessing of the gods. To fall in battle was an honour they craved. If fate willed it they would meet their end and join the revelry in the halls of Valhalla.

But Ulfhednar wasn't ready to die. "Tyr, guide us," he muttered under his breath. He glanced skyward where the evening star still gleamed as a reminder of the god who watched over them, the god who had tamed this beast at his side. Tyr was the one-handed god, and the feeder of the wolf. The god Tyr had raised Ulfric from the beginning and had kept him close until the time of binding came. That binding was one of blood and loyalty, a binding that Tyr reserved for his greatest mortal warrior in each age. Of men. Ulfhednar was just such a warrior, and so Ulfric was Ulfhednar's companion, bound not by chains, but by true blood fealty. Together they fought, and together they survived, carving their path through long years of struggle and bloodshed. War was their life and now they stood on the brink of another battle.

"Hail Tyr," Ulfhednar whispered, echoing the ancient prayer. His voice was swallowed by the wind, but Ulfric's ears twitched, as if he too understood the gravity of the words. "Tyr is our guiding star, and we will not stray from his path."

The wolf gazed at his companion, unblinking, before he let out a low, guttural growl, a sound that sent a chill down Ulfhednar's spine. They had fought alongside each other for so long that words were no longer necessary. Ulfric's growl was a promise. Blood would flow today.

Behind them, the men shifted, readying their shields and making final adjustments to spears, axes and swords. Metal bosses and blades gleamed in the morning light. The army was small, a band of hardened warriors who had fought for seasons unending, but tonight, they faced a larger enemy, an army driven by greed and now seeking to conquer their lands. Ulfhednar could hear the murmurs of his comrades. He knew the odds and he could feel their fear, and yet none of them looked away. To a man they stared at Ulfric. The wolf was sacred. He was a creature of the gods, a beast bound to their fate. To question his presence or his purpose was to question Tyr himself.

A horn sounded in the distance, long and mournful, signalling the enemy's advance. Ulfhednar tightened his grip on his spear, his pulse quickening as the call to war echoed through the valley. The enemy's banners crested a low ridge at the bottom of the field, revealing a sea of armoured men, their shields locked, and their weapons gleaming like fangs in the rising light.

"We go to battle," Ulfhednar called out to his men, his voice steady despite the chaos swelling within him. He raised his spear, and Ulfric bared his teeth, a snarl rolling from his throat. The men echoed his cry, their voices rising in a crescendo of fury and determination. They were outnumbered, but this was their land and their people. They wouldn't yield.

"By the strength of the Gods, we are chosen men!!" Ulfhednar shouted, his voice rising above the din. The response from sixty voices standing firm and ready behind him came with raw courage, "We fight with fury! We fear no death!"

Ulfhednar slammed the butt of his spear into the earth, feeling the vibrations travel up his arm. His heart pounded in rhythm with the advancing footsteps of the enemy, but he didn't waver, not with Ulfric at his side. With a guttural cry, he lifted his spear, and Ulfric's howl rose in answer, a primal sound that echoed across the plains, chilling even the bravest of the enemy. The Danes hesitated, their formation faltering for just a heartbeat as the wolf's eerie wail filled the air. In that moment, Ulfhednar surged forward, his legs pumping with the strength of a prime stag, his spear gleaming like a lightning bolt in the bright sunlight. Ulfric bolted beside him, a streak of black fury, his powerful frame leaping effortlessly over the rocks and snowdrifts as he raced towards the enemy.

The clash of steel and the sickening crunch of bone filled the air as Ulfhednar slammed into the Danish line, his spear punching through the first shield with a splintering explosion of wood. The tip drove deep, impaling the man behind it, ripping through flesh, ribs, and lung, before Ulfhednar wrenched it free with a brutal twist, spraying blood in thick, dark ribbons across the mud.

A heartbeat later, he was already onto the next. His warriors surged behind him, howling like beasts, their battle-madness turning them into frothing demons. Axes bit into necks, split skulls, and cracked collarbones like dry tinder. The scent of iron, of freshly spilled guts, thickened the air. Men screamed, gurgled, and died in heaps as the Vikings carved through them like farmers through grain.

But it was Ulfric who turned the tide. The great wolf leapt into the fray, a hulking shadow of fangs and fury, his jaws snapping shut on the throat of a Danish captain. The man's eyes bulged as Ulfric's teeth crushed his windpipe, his hands clawing uselessly at the beast's fur while blood gushed from the gaping wound. A ragged death-rattle tore from his lips as Ulfric ripped his head back, flesh tearing, arteries snapping, the captain's lifeless body dropping in a heap as the wolf flung the ruined man aside.

Terror rippled through the enemy ranks. They had come to fight men, not this monster wolf with fire in its eyes and blood dripping from its fangs. Ulfric did not stop. He barrelled forward, tackling another warrior, teeth sinking deep into a shoulder, ripping muscle from bone, leaving the Dane howling in agony, his blood hot and steaming in the cold air.

All around Ulfhednar and Ulfric, the battlefield was a maelstrom of horror. Shields shattered as limbs were hacked away, guts spilling in slick, steaming coils onto the churned-up earth. The mud turned slick with blood, men slipping, falling, dying in droves. The air was thick with the stench of sweat, fear, and ruptured bowels.

And in the centre of it all stood Ulfhednar, grinning through a mask of crimson, his breath coming in ragged gasps, his body soaked in the ruin of men. He did not care for mercy. Only for the kill.

Still, the Danes were too many. For every warrior Ulfhednar split open, three more surged forward, their blades slick with the blood of his kin. He did not falter. His axe, wet with gore, shattered skulls and split ribcages as he carved his way through the horde. The air was thick with the iron stench of blood, the screams of the dying mingling with the howling wind. Flesh tore, bones cracked, and severed limbs thudded onto the frozen ground, steaming in the cold.

His muscles burned, his breath came in ragged snarls, but the battle had consumed him. He revelled in the agony, in the warmth of blood that coated his arms, and in the way his axe cleaved through muscle and marrow. He was not a man. Ulfhednar was more. He was a beast, a scourge, a harbinger of death clad in wolf's hide, his eyes alight with divine fury.

A spear rammed into his side, the tip grinding against his ribs, but he only laughed, an unholy, guttural sound as he wrenched it free, feeling the wet suction of flesh resisting the pull. He turned, hacking down the fool who dared wound him, his axe biting deep into the Dane's collarbone, splitting him open like a rotted log. Blood fountained, hot and dark, spraying Ulfhednar's face as he roared in triumph.

The gods watched from the heavens, their hunger for slaughter sated with every warrior that fell beneath Ulfhednar's blade. The earth drank deep of the dead, and still, he fought on because he was Ulfhednar. He was born in the womb of war, baptised in blood, and forged in the slaughter of men. He would not stop until the last of them lay cold at his feet.

Because of his flesh wound, Ulfhednar's breath came in short, ragged bursts, his lungs burning with the fire of battle. The air was thick with the stench of blood, sweat, and iron. Around him, the clash of steel rang like a violent symphony, punctuated by the guttural screams of the dying. The sky, choked now with dark clouds, loomed overhead as if the gods themselves revelled in the slaughter below.

His spear dripped crimson, slick with the lifeblood of those who had dared to stand against him. A severed hand still clung to the shaft, fingers twitching in the last throes of death before he wrenched it free with a grunt. No hesitation. No mercy. Only the raw instincts of a wolf-warrior, honed through years of carnage, would see him through this day.

Ulfric, his monstrous wolf companion, had already carved a path through the enemy ranks, a nightmare of bristling fur and snapping jaws. A Danish warrior howled in anguish as the beast's fangs locked onto his throat, his flesh splitting like overripe fruit. Blood gushed in a steaming torrent, painting the frozen earth in thick rivulets of red. Another man swung his axe, desperate to end the wolf's rampage, but Ulfric twisted mid-leap, his powerful jaws crushing the attacker's face in a splintering explosion of bone and cartilage.

A blade whistled toward Ulfhednar's neck, but he spun, his instincts sharper than thought. The sword skimmed past, grazing his shoulder, but he welcomed the pain, for it only sharpened his fury. With a guttural roar, he drove his spear deep into the attacker's gut, twisting as he yanked it free. Entrails spilled in a steaming heap, the dying man's shrieks turning to a gurgling whimper as he collapsed, hands feebly trying to shove his intestines back inside his torn belly.

Ulfhednar did not pause to watch him die. There were more foes to send screaming into the afterlife. The battlefield was a feast for wolves, and he would leave no meat unclaimed.

The enemy surged like a black tide, their shrieks a maddened chorus, their desperation reeking like a dying beast. Ulfhednar met them with steel and fury, his breath a ragged growl. A shield crashed into his arm, the force splitting skin and sending a violent throb through his bones, but he did not yield. With a snarl, he drove his spear forward, the iron tip punching through flesh and gristle. His foe's eyes bulged, a wet gurgle bubbling from his lips as blood frothed from his torn throat. Ulfhednar wrenched the weapon free, dragging sinew with it, and the man collapsed, clawing at the gaping ruin in his neck.

His face was warm with the splatter of crimson. He wiped it with a calloused hand, smearing the gore across his cheek. No time to linger. No time to breathe. The air was thick with the iron tang of blood, the stench of open bowels, the sickly perfume of death.

His war-band held the line, outnumbered but unbroken. They fought like wolves in a pit, teeth bared, their axes singing a dirge of splintered bone and sundered flesh. A Dane lunged at Ulfhednar, a wild, desperate strike, but he twisted away, his blade hacking into the man's side, parting mail and skin alike.

Ulfric, his great beast of a wolf, was a demon let loose. The hound's fangs clamped onto a warrior's face, tearing into the soft flesh of his cheek and yanking away a strip of meat, leaving the man screaming with his jaw half-torn from his skull. The wolf did not stop. He buried his maw into the Dane's throat, shaking wildly, until the head lolled back with nothing but shredded meat and vertebrae holding it in place.

Still, the enemy came. More of them. Staggering over the corpses of their kin, their faces twisted with horror and rage. A man, some chieftain by his gilded helm, charged Ulfhednar, a bearded axe raised high. Ulfhednar met him with his own blade, the impact jarring his arms, but he pressed forward. Their weapons locked, but he had the greater strength. He smashed his forehead into the Dane's nose, heard the wet crunch, and as the man reeled, he hacked downward. The blade carved into his collarbone, splitting ribs, slicing deep until it found the heart. Blood erupted in a hot spray over Ulfhednar's arms, and the man spasmed, coughing red mist, before slumping against him.

Ulfhednar shoved the body aside and turned to find another kill. The ground beneath him was a slick quagmire of blood, brains, and severed limbs, bodies twitching as the last of life drained from them. The wounded wailed, clutching at their ruined flesh, their prayers to their gods lost in the frenzied clamour of steel. But there was no mercy here. Only the will of the strong.

They would not fall today. Not while they could still fight. Not while their gods still hungered for slaughter.

The sun clawed its way to its zenith, glaring down upon the battlefield like an indifferent god, its heat mingling with the stench of blood, bile, and opened entrails. Ulfhednar sensed the shift, the moment when steel and sinew gave way to terror. The invaders, once so assured in their conquest, now flinched beneath the weight of the slaughter. Their shield walls, once unbreakable, splintered like rotted wood as his warriors tore through them with axe and fang. Flesh ripped. Bones cracked. The dying screamed, their voices drowned beneath the frenzied roars of the wolf-clad berserkers. The Danes staggered, their footing lost in the mire of gore, their swords slipping from trembling fingers slick with the blood of their kin. Panic curdled in their bellies, replacing their lust for war with the cold realization of death.

Ulfhednar stood amid the carnage, his breath ragged, his body slick with the blood of friend and foe alike. His spear, its tip clogged with meat and viscera, hung loosely in his grip. Around him, the dead lay in ruin, some gasping out their last breaths. Others were barely human anymore, their bodies hacked apart, their faces frozen in twisted grimaces. A dying Dane clutched at his leg, his mouth gurgling a plea, but Ulfhednar wrenched his blade free from its sheath and drove it through the man's throat, silencing him with a wet gurgle.

Ulfric slunk to his side, his thick fur matted with gore, his golden eyes burning with the unrelenting fire of the hunt. His maw dripped red, pieces of flesh clinging to his fangs as he panted, a beast made for war. Wounds marred his body, but he stood tall, defiant, alive.

The few Danes who remained turned and fled, their courage shattered, their dead left to be feasted upon by carrion and beasts. Ulfhednar watched them vanish into the trees, his lips curling. They would return. More would come, drawn by greed, by vengeance, by the ever-hungry maw of war. He dropped to one knee, his bloodied fingers tangling in Ulfric's thick coat. The wolf did not flinch. They had fought. They had bled. And they had lived. Tyr had guided them today. He would guide them again tomorrow. And when the next battle came, Ulfhednar would stand once more, wreathed in death, and garlanded in the glory of war.

The sky above was brighter now, with the sun breaking through the morning clouds, shining like a distant fire. With a glance at the bodies strewn across the blood-soaked earth, Ulfhednar took a deep breath, letting the pain and the stress of the day leave his bones to drift on the wind. He stood once more and raised his spear to the sky, a silent salute to the gods, and then turned to join his remaining men.

Together they stood on the blood-soaked ground, breathing in the icy air that clung to their lungs like iron. Their chain mail and their thick leðr brynja were marked by deep cuts and smeared with the blood of fallen Danes, but they had held fast, though the sharp edges of battle had taken their toll. Above Ulfhednar, the heavens stretched wide. The wind carried with it the scent of iron and death, but also a feeling of triumph. Ulfhednar lifted his gaze, the fire of battle still burning in his veins, and offered a silent prayer to Tyr, the god of war.

"Hail Tyr," Ulfhednar whispered, his voice carried away on the cold wind. "One-handed god, the feeder of the wolf, guide my hand in the wars to come."

Beside him, his great wolf Ulfric stood tall, muscles rippling beneath his shaggy coat. The beast's golden eyes glinted in the sunlight, and were fixed on the horizon, where the shadows of the fleeing Danes disappeared into the forest. A low growl rumbled in Ulfric's throat, a sound that seemed to echo across the battlefield, as if the wolf itself was acknowledging the god's power. Ulfhednar placed a bloodied hand on Ulfric's head, feeling the warmth of his companion's body beneath his fingers.

Now, with the battle behind them, Ulfhednar could feel exhaustion tugging at his limbs, but the adrenaline of the victor surged through him like a second wind. He knew this was not the end. The Danes were sure to return, stronger and in greater numbers, but Ulfhednar was ready. He had Ulfric, the wolf blessed by the gods, and together, they were unstoppable.

The sun shone steadily above them in silent acknowledgment as Ulfhednar and Ulfric stood amidst the fallen, the only sounds the distant cries of the wind and the last groans of the wounded who were left to rot on the field. Ulfhednar smiled, his hand still resting on Ulfric's fur. They would send these fallen men to the halls of the gods. It was a fitting end.

"We are not finished," he said to his men, his voice strong and rough. "Let them come again. We'll send more of them to their gods. Let's finish this by giving these brave men their final release."

… and Ulfric

The wind carries a thousand scents to my nostrils. I catch the sharp bite of winter, the musk of warriors, of their fear, of the battle-hunger in their blood, and the acrid tang of Danish steel. I stand beside my kin-brother Ulfhednar, as still as the death that I have dealt to our enemies so many times before. My fur, black as the deepest night, ripples in the relentless wind, but I remain unmoved, a shadow given form and purpose by the gods themselves.

I feel the vibrations of my own growl through the earth, a warning to the enemies that gather across the field like scavengers before a feast. They do not understand what they face today. They see only men, outnumbered men at that, but they do not see me for what I truly am. I am kin to the gods, a wolf of unnatural size, my eyes gleaming with the fire of divine purpose.

Ulfhednar is more than my companion. Our blood-bond transcends the meagre connections between most men and beasts. Where he ends, I begin. We are two halves of the same savage whole, forged in countless battles. Together we have sent legions to their final rest, but today the Danish shields that glint in the distance seem numberless, a great serpent coiling to strike.

My ears twitch as Ulfhednar whispers, "Tyr, guide us." The name sends a ripple through my mind. Tyr, the one-handed god, raised me from my first days. He is the one who has nurtured me until the time came to bind me to the greatest mortal warrior of the age. I am not bound by chains, but with blood fealty. I understand the gravity of Ulfhednar's prayer, for Tyr has chosen us both.

"Hail Tyr," he whispers again, and I answer with a low, guttural growl from the deepest part of my being. Words are unnecessary between us. My growl is my oath. Blood will flow today, and we will send many souls to the afterlife.

I can smell the fear rippling through the Danish ranks. Their scent carries uncertainty as they stare at me, for I am no ordinary wolf. I am sacred, beast-made-god, and to face me is to face Tyr himself. Their hesitation is palpable, a sour note in the air.

When the enemy's horn sounds, mournful and distant, I bare my teeth. The time for waiting has ended. Ulfhednar calls to his men, and their voices rise in answer, a battle-cry that stirs the blood. But it is my howl that truly shakes the enemy, a primal sound that echoes across the plains, a promise of violence that makes the bravest Dane falter.

I bolt forward alongside Ulfhednar, my powerful legs carrying me effortlessly over rocks and snowdrifts. The battlefield opens before me, a canvas of virgin snow soon to be painted crimson. The Danish line approaches, and I can pick out the fear in their eyes as they behold me, a monstrous wolf with jaws that can crush shields and tear through mail.

The first kill is swift. I leap into their formation, a hulking shadow of fangs and fury, and find the throat of a Danish captain. His flesh yields easily beneath my teeth, his windpipe crushing as I clamp down. His hands claw uselessly at my fur, his eyes bulging with terror and disbelief as I rip my head back. Arteries snap, hot blood gushes across my muzzle, and I fling his ruined corpse aside, already seeking my next prey.

Terror ripples through their ranks. They have come prepared to fight men, not a beast sent by the gods. I barrel forward, tackling another warrior, my teeth finding purchase in his shoulder. I can taste his fear as much as his blood when I rip muscle from bone, leaving him howling in agony.

All around me, the battlefield transforms into a maelstrom of destruction. The air grows thick with the iron tang of blood and the stench of opened bowels. Men slip in the gore-slicked mud, falling to the earth where my kin-brother and his warriors descend upon them with axes and swords.

I carve my own path through the enemy, a streak of midnight bringing daylight-death. For every warrior that falls beneath my fangs, more surge forward, but I do not tire. This is my purpose, this is the reason that Tyr has bound me to this world and to Ulfhednar. Death is my gift to deliver, and I give it freely.

A Dane lunges at me with his spear, the tip grazing my flank. The pain only fuels my fury. I twist mid-leap, my jaws finding his face, tearing into the soft flesh of his cheek. I can feel the resistance of skin and sinew before it gives way, taking with it a strip of meat. His screams are a symphony as I bury my maw into his throat, shaking wildly until his head lolls back, attached by nothing but shredded tissue and bone.

The battle continues without pause, the sun crawling across the sky as we fight. I never stray far from Ulfhednar, always aware of his position, always ready to defend him. When a chieftain in a gilded helm charges him, I am prepared to intervene, but my kin-brother meets the challenge with his own strength, splitting the man from collarbone to heart.

I sense the change in the air when the tide begins to turn. The Danes, once confident in their numbers, now flinch at my approach, their courage crumbling beneath the weight of our savagery. Their formation splinters, warriors breaking ranks to flee into the forest. The ground beneath my paws is a slick quagmire of blood and viscera, littered with the fallen, some still gasping their last breaths, others dismembered beyond recognition.

When the last of the enemy disappears into the trees, I slink to Ulfhednar's side. My fur is matted with gore, wounds stinging across my body, but I stand tall. We have survived another day together. My kin-brother drops to one knee, his bloodied fingers tangling in my thick coat, and I do not flinch. This is our bond, forged in battle, tempered by survival.

The sun breaks through the morning clouds, warming my blood-soaked fur. I fix my golden eyes on the horizon where the shadows of the fleeing Danes have disappeared. A growl rumbles in my throat, an acknowledgment of Tyr's power and a promise of more blood to come. Ulfhednar places his hand on my head, and I feel the connection between us strengthen.

I know, as he does, that this is not the end. The Danes will return, and we will meet them again with fang and steel. For now, we stand victorious among the fallen, and I am content. Until the next battle comes, I will remain at Ulfhednar's side, ready to deliver Tyr's judgment once more.

The song behind these two stories: The song "Týr" by Wardruna is from their album "Runaljod – Yggdrasil" released in 2013. Wardruna is a Norwegian music group known for their use of ancient Nordic instruments and themes based on Norse mythology, runes, and Viking culture.

In Norse mythology, Týr is the god of war, justice, and law. He is known for his courage, particularly for the myth in which he sacrifices his hand to the wolf Fenrir.

The song embodies the group's signature sound, blending traditional Scandinavian instruments such as the lyre, tagelharpa, and frame drum, along with ambient vocals and chants. The atmosphere created is one of reverence, power, and an ancient connection to Norse beliefs.

I find these sorts of songs and groups very compelling, often using them along with film scores as a backdrop when writing, as the vocals are not in English meaning that they don't influence my thoughts directly, although the music definitely sets a mood.

Album: *Runaljod – Yggdrasil*

Artist: *Wardruna*

Year: *2013*

Composer(s): *Einar Selvik*

Record Label: *Indie Recordings*

Reflections

In the Kingdom of Reflections, time was measured quite differently to the simple march of days or the steady cycles of the seasons. Time was measured by the mirror. Time was marked by the way one's reflection gradually faded from the surface of the looking glass. Each citizen was bound to the mirror, and mirrors didn't merely reflect their features, but offered glimpses into the deep currents that flowed through their souls. The mirror held everything; beauty and despair, ambition and fear, dreams and regrets, all of it captured in the polished surface like delicate threads spun in crystal.

For some, their reflection was a source of pride, a reminder of accomplishments and moments of happiness. For others, it was a haunting image, one that showed too much of their true natures. For such people, lines of grief would be etched on their faces as an indicator of the hidden scars that they couldn't bear to confront. No matter the life that anyone might lead, as the years passed, so the image in the mirror grew dimmer, fading like the detail of an old memory as it slips away. The mirror was both a gift and a curse.

There were rumours that whispered of how the mirrors didn't just fade but sometimes shattered, revealing truths too unbearable for the mind to comprehend. That was, they said, the root cause of madness. I had avoided looking into mirrors for as long as I could remember, terrified of what I might see. I knew that my life was full of dualities. My outward attempts at grace contrasted with the awkward shadow that I cast upon the world. As my reflection in mirrors darkened, so that image became less a likeness of my present self and more a glimpse into what I feared. I was vain and self-serving, and so despaired at things like crows' feet and wrinkles. As the years wore on, I wondered when I would be forced to see the undeniable truths of my life.

Eventually though, one has to look, to really look. My hands trembled as I stood before the glass that day in the bathroom of a shabby rented room, my breath shallow, my heart pounding in my chest. The dim outline of my face seemed to pulse, as though the reflection were alive. My mother warned me long ago about this moment. There comes a point in life, she told me, when a person could no longer look away from the things revealed by their reflection.

Perhaps I should explain this a little more clearly…

I was born into a world where mirrors were sacred and revered as portals to the truth. To truly see yourself, we were taught, was to unravel the threads of destiny and understand the role we played in the grand tapestry of existence. Early on in my life I came to fear the mirror. The reflection I saw was never what I expected, for it wasn't just my face staring back at me. I saw something darker, something layered beneath the surface, lurking in the space between the light and the shadows.

Every time I stood before a mirror, it transported me to a place that I didn't want to go. My past stretched out behind me like a tattered ribbon, each mistake fraying that ribbon a little more and casting a faint but grotesque shadow in the glass. It was as if I had become trapped in an infinite loop, forever replaying the worst moments of my life. Every heartbreak, every lie, every promise broken by my own hand was reflected back at me, mocking me and taunting me.

So it was that I stood there in that tattered bathroom, frozen before the mirror, my fingers clutching the bowl of a cracked porcelain sink. What began as the routine washing of my face, transformed into something else entirely. The face staring back at me wasn't mine. Not entirely.

In the glass, I saw myself, but the eyes... the eyes were Katarina's, my daughter's. She looked at me through my own reflection. Her eyes were the same emerald-green that she had gazed up at me with complete trust some sixteen years previously, before I walked away, claiming that I 'needed to find shadows.' The reflection's mouth twisted into a bitter smile, so like Paulo's had been when he'd handed me the divorce papers.

"You're running again," the reflection whispered, the voice shifting between my own and a chorus of others, Paulo, Katerina, my mother, everyone I'd ever disappointed.

The bathroom light flickered, and in that moment, the reflection showed not my face but a kaleidoscope of abandoned moments: the empty chair at Katarina's coming of age celebration, the unanswered birthday cards, the wedding invitations returned to the abandoned senders, the callously abandoned lovers. Each image flickered across the mirror's surface, indicting me with silent evidence.

I reached out, wanting to touch the glass, to explain, to justify, but my hand trembled. Anything that I might say would be a lie, just like my life.

"Stop," I whispered.

But the reflection only leaned closer, its features a horrifying blend of my own and of my abandoned responsibilities. "You can't outrun yourself," it said, wearing my face but speaking with my lost daughter's voice. "I'm still here. We're all still here."

I backed away, my shoulders bumping into the wall. The mirror held me captive with truths that I'd spent a lifetime fleeing. In its unforgiving surface, I finally saw myself clearly, not as I pretended to be, but as I am, a woman who has spent her life running from her own shadow.

Mirrors are not just glass. They are memories, tethered to your soul and to your innermost fears. In my mind's eye I remembered seeing myself in the calm of a midnight window or in the still surface of a rain puddle. The truth always found me, and the truth was that I couldn't escape who and what I was bound to this earth to be. I was tethered to the people in the mirror. They were the other half of me that I could never fully exorcise. They watched me, always waiting but just out of my reach. There was something terrible in their eyes, something I couldn't bear to confront. Was it regret? Was it hate?

The mirror shimmered before me, calling to me and drawing me in like a moth to a flame. I was tired of running. I was tired of fearing what lay behind the glass. This time, I decided, I would face my reflection and my terrible twins in the shadows. The truth of it was that I was no longer sure which side of the mirror I belonged to. Was I the woman standing in the light, or the one lost in the darkness? Taking a deep breath, I reached out, my fingers trembling as they brushed the surface of the glass. It was cool and smooth, and almost comforting, but then it rippled, and in that moment, I knew I wasn't just looking into a mirror. The mirror was looking into me.

My reflection suddenly wasn't clear. I was barely more than a shadow. The glass distorted my features and dimmed them, as if the mirror itself was erasing me, piece by piece. I could feel my history reaching out to smother me. Every mistake, every heartbreak, every betrayal and every joy was laid bare. The mirror didn't show beauty or youth. It showed the sum of my life.

I reached out, my fingers trembling as they touched the cold surface of the glass. For a moment, I hoped that the mirror would shatter beneath my touch, leaving me free from the truth it held, but the mirror remained whole and unbroken. As I stood there, I realised what that dark truth was that I had been running from all along. The mask that I wore for the world, the beauty, the confidence, and the laughter had only ever been a charade. The mirror forced me to face my duality. There was nowhere left to hide. I was both the light and the shadow, the beauty and the beast. I could no longer pretend otherwise.

The bathroom grew unnaturally cold as I stared, transfixed by my distorted reflection. Something shifted in the glass, a ripple, as if the surface had become liquid mercury. My own face fragmented, dissolving into the faces of those I'd wronged.

"You always said you'd come back," whispered the reflection, its voice a haunting blend of my daughter's childish plea and adult accusation.

My fingertips brushed the mirror's surface for a second time. It yielded like cool water, sending concentric ripples across the glass. It was a mistake. I tried to pull back, but invisible hands seized my wrist. The grip tightened, fingernails digging into my flesh as the mirror began to pull me in.

"No," I gasped, my free hand grasping for the towel rack, but missing it by inches. "Please, I can make it right…"

But the mirror knew the hollowness of my promises. The surface undulated, bubbling with faces. I saw my ex-husband as he was on our wedding day, young and hopeful, my daughter at five, at twelve, at sixteen, each face marked by progressive abandonment, my mother on her deathbed, calling me by name, but I never came.

Pale arms reached through the mirror, spectral yet solid, seizing my shoulders. I struggled, but every movement drew me closer to the glass. My reflection smiled with terrible understanding, not mocking, but knowing. This moment was always coming.

"You can't outrun your shadows forever," the reflection whispered, its breath cold against my face. "It's time to admit what you've become."

The mirror's surface stretched like a membrane. I felt the cool glass touch my cheek, enveloping my face like a shroud. My scream remained trapped in my throat as the looking glass consumed me, inch by terrible inch. The bathroom light flickered overhead, casting grotesque shadows across the walls as I was pulled deeper.

My fingernails scraped desperately against the porcelain sink, leaving ghostly trails as the mirror claimed me. The glass rippled one final time as it swallowed me whole, its surface smoothing back to perfect stillness. For a moment, my terrified face remained visible in its depths, a prisoner of my own reflection.

Then the bathroom went dark. The mirror hung innocently on the wall, reflecting nothing but an empty bathroom, as if I had never existed at all. But exist I do and now I have an eternity to… reflect on my past life.

The song behind the story: *I came across this song one evening randomly flicking through music vids on Apple Music, and fell in love with the song straight away. "All Mirrors" by Angel Olsen is the title track from her 2019 album All Mirrors. The song is characterised by its dark, cinematic atmosphere, blending indie rock with orchestral elements. Olsen's powerful vocals carry a sense of vulnerability and reflection, underscoring themes of introspection, change, and emotional transformation. The track builds slowly with haunting synths and swelling strings, reflecting the inner turmoil and complexity of dealing with one's identity and confronting harsh truths.*

Album: *All Mirrors*

Artist: *Angel Olsen*

Year: *2019*

Composer(s): *Angel Olsen*

Record Label: *Jagjaguwar*

Michel

The room was bathed in a soft, amber glow, the late afternoon sun filtering through the lace curtains, casting delicate shadows on the wooden floor. Helene sat by the open window, her head resting lightly against the cool glass, her eyes tracing the gentle sway of the trees outside. The rustling of the leaves in the breeze seemed to mirror the quiet rhythm of her breath. A stillness settled over her. It was a peace tinged with melancholy, a silence that carried questions and daydreams.

She closed her eyes, letting her thoughts drift back, and in that space between memory and longing, Michel's voice echoed in her mind. "And so it is, just like you said it would be," she whispered softly, repeating the words he had once spoken to her in that calm, measured way of his. She could hear him still. She could picture him sitting at the piano, his hands hovering just above the keys, his eyes meeting hers seeking permission to play.

Life did go easy on her, most of the time, anyway. That was the story she told herself. That was the narrative she lived by. On the surface, everything was as it should be. She had her quiet routines; her students, her music, her books, and the small circle of friends that she met with for tea on Sunday afternoons. Her apartment on the Rue de Caumartin in the ninth

Arrondisement, le neuvième, in Paris was modest but charming, typically Parisian and filled with tastefully affordable items, all of it comfortably worn by time. The piano, its varnish slightly faded from decades of use, sat at the heart of her living room like an old and faithful companion. Her days passed in measured cadence, one much like the other, marked by small pleasures and familiar comforts.

But beneath that surface another story ran its course It was a short story and incomplete, a story that lacked the sweeping romance that she had once imagined her life would hold. Helene was in her mid-thirties but as yet had found no grand love. There had been lovers of course, but nothing that really stuck. There was no one to whom she could surrender her heart without reservation. Instead, there was Michel, with his quiet intensity and steady gaze, who had briefly stood alongside her at the edge of love.

It was absurd, really. She knew it, even as she thought of him now. He was only eighteen, her student, barely a man, with the world still unfolding before him, and she, at thirty-five, had no place in his brave new world. Her role was simply to be his guide and his teacher, not his generational equal, and certainly not the object of his affection, but somewhere along the way, between the Chopin nocturnes and the long conversations after lessons, she allowed herself to feel something deeper, something that had settled quietly into her heart before she even realised it was there. The frustration came with his need to be home for dinner or to cancel piano lessons for commitments at school.

Helene sighed, tracing a finger along the window's edge, watching the sunlight flicker across her hand. The feeling she harboured for Michel was a quiet and reserved one. Helene's emotions played a delicate melody that somehow always remained unresolved. When she watched him play with such grace, his fingers moving across the keys with passion, she forgot that he was still at school, and in those moments, she felt something stir, but nothing was ever said. How could it be? Michel was young and so full of life and possibility. After a few lessons Helene watched aghast as Michel fell for a girl of his own age, a fleeting romance that made her smile in public even as it pierced her heart. She remained silent, letting the feelings stay buried. Her love for Michel was a song of obsession left unfinished, its final notes hanging in the air.

As Helene sat there, watching the world pass by her open apartment window, the golden light fading slowly into dusk, she realised that her life, with all its quiet moments and unspoken desires, would have to be enough. Yet the echo of that unfinished love for Michel lingered on stubbornly. Helene let his name drift through her thoughts, drawn-out like a delicate musical note suspended in the air. She was trying so hard to forget him, to erase the feelings that had swelled unbidden in her chest, but it was no use. His presence was woven into her memories like a melody that she couldn't stop humming, no matter how many times she told herself that she had to move on. His mother had been quite clear on that.

Michel had been in her life for such a fleeting season. Events transpired so quickly that there had barely been long enough to justify his continuing presence in her thoughts, and yet it was enough, more than enough. His absence now felt like a dull ache, a hollow space she carried within her, though it had been months since they last spoke. She hadn't seen him or heard from him in all that time, and yet it was as if he had never truly left. His name still hung in the corners of her mind, his presence lingering in the smallest details of her days.

She thought of him often, usually triggered on quiet afternoons when the sunlight filtered through the windows of her studio, casting soft shadows across the piano keys. That was when she could feel him most, as though he were just there, seated beside her, his fingers tentatively tracing the notes of a piece they had worked on together. She could almost hear the gentle and unsure way that he'd ask for her guidance. His voice was soft but deep at the same time.

Helene closed her eyes and allowed herself, just for a moment, to fall back into those memories. She revelled in the way that he would look at her with those brown eyes searching hers as if he was trying to see past her carefully crafted façade and touch the parts of her she kept hidden from the world. The intensity of his gaze unnerved her at first. That slightly confused boyish lust made her feel superior and in control, and there had been something intoxicating about it, something that stirred a longing inside her that she had been unprepared for. That look. How could she ever forget it? He was just a boy.

It wasn't love, not really. That was both the tragedy and the excitement of it. Helene stayed on the edge of it, dancing around Michel's infatuation. He was her student, and she was his teacher. They were bound by an unspoken promise that she dared not break, a promise that felt like safety and torture all at once. She never said the words. She never confessed the truth that she believed she could see in his eyes, and she kept herself at a distance, telling herself that she was in control and that what she felt was something that would fade with time.

But it hadn't. Even now, months later, she could feel the strength of her wanting as it distracted her in these quiet moments. She suffered a restless ache that settled in the pit of her stomach. They, the mother and the girl, took him away, but he had never left her thoughts. She could still see him so clearly, his dark hair falling into his eyes as he bent over the piano with his long fingers caressing the keys. He always hesitated before he played the first note. He was beautiful in that way. Michel possessed the kind of beauty that wasn't showy or loud but was understated and quiet. The way that she felt drawn towards him had caught her off guard at first. The way he moved through the world seemed to carry a depth of feeling that belied his years.

Nothing was ever said, and nothing was ever done. They remained in their roles, teacher and student, navigating a relationship that was, for Helene, filled with unspoken possibilities. Had they played their games in public an observant voyeur would have seen that they lingered just a little too long in their looks. That same observer would have seen how their fingers almost brushed but didn't. actually touch. It was a game, Helene told herself and nothing more, but the truth was far more complicated. She wanted to win the game, but she wasn't quite sure what winning looked like.

Now, in the quiet of her studio, with no one but the piano to witness her thoughts, she allowed herself to feel the full grandeur of the what-ifs and the moments that might have been, had she been braver and allowed herself the freedom to act without the normal societal constraints. Now Helene was left with nothing but fragments of conversations, fleeting glances, and the way his name still tasted bittersweet on her tongue. Michel was in the music she played and in the silence between the notes.

Ice cold water. That's what it had felt like when he left that last time having told her that the lessons were at an end. Her breath caught in her throat. She closed her eyes and tried to imagine that moment in soft colours, in gentle strokes of pastels and hushed tones. It was easier that way, easier than facing the raw, jagged edges of his absence. She pictured Michel walking away, not with cold indifference, but with the quiet grace of a drifting cloud, something light and inevitable. Not a rejection, she told herself, just a change of seasons. Just a leaf slipping free from its branch, carried by the wind.

She tried to frame it as something natural, something meant to be. People came and went like tides, didn't they? And wasn't it lovely, in a way, that he had been part of her world at all? She wanted to shape Michel, to nurture him, to guide him with careful hands. Helene still believed that he would have been willing had he not been driven away from her by the jealousy of his prudish mother.

Beneath the soft glow of this imagined version, a slow, aching bruise pulsed beneath a layer of silk. No matter how she painted it, Michel had left. He had turned away from the world she wanted to build for him. He stepped beyond her reach, his footsteps fading like watercolour in the rain. She told herself it was fine, that she wanted him to be happy, that love was about letting go. But love, her love, had never been so gentle. It had been fierce, consuming, absolute. And the thought of him moving on, of him smiling without her presence in his life, was a betrayal wrapped in pastel hues.

Helene inhaled deeply, willing herself to be still, to be composed. She would not chase. She would not beg. She would wrap herself in the softness of altered memories, and cushion the sharp edges to make it something beautiful. To see her time with Michel int any other way would be too much. Too painful. Too real.

Now, months later his voice still echoed in her mind. What was that thing he'd said a few days before he left? Helene scratched around in her memories. Yes, that was it; "We'll both forget the breeze, most of the time." It seemed like an offhanded comment at the time, but it stayed with her, refusing to leave her thoughts for days thereafter. Forgetting the breeze. Helene thought that he was saying that they should forget the little things, the fleeting moments they had shared. Even now Helene wondered how he could believe that was possible. How could he think that time would erase everything? She could still feel the gravitational pull of those moments. She could still see the way he glanced at her when he thought she wasn't paying attention She could still hear the way his laughter would fill the room with warmth, making her heart race.

Dusk was falling, and with it came a lessening of the fever in her heart. In the evenings, when the world slowed down, when the quiet settled upon her soul, there was a moment when she could almost relax.

"I can't take my mind off you," Helene whispered to world beyond the open window, the words barely audible in the stillness of her small apartment. Her voice trembled as she said it. No matter how much time passed, no matter how many new students she taught, Michel remained written into her soul, like a dark melody that lingered long after the piano fell silent. He was the unfinished sentence, the song that never reached its final note, a composition she had poured herself into but could never quite complete.

She stood up from the window where she had been watching the world drift by as the day closed, and she walked slowly to the small table where her phone rested. It had been weeks since she'd heard from him, but that didn't stop her from staring at his name in her contacts, her thumb hovering over the call button. The desire to hear his voice again and to feel that connection they once shared, was overwhelming. She wanted to ask him questions. She wanted to know if he ever thought of her the way that she thought of him. The words caught in her throat before she could even imagine tapping the call button.

Helene sighed and closed her eyes, allowing the bittersweet memories to wash over her. She could see him so clearly, sitting across from her, his long fingers absentmindedly tracing the rim of his coffee cup while he listened to her speak. She remembered the warmth in his eyes when he looked at her, the way he seemed to hang on her words, as if her thoughts mattered more than the rest of the world.

Now she was living her life in the quiet spaces between her students' lessons. She was settling into the solitude of evenings spent staring out at the world beyond her window. Helene waited for time to dull the sharp edges of these memories. She waited for the day that she would wake up and not think of him first thing in the morning, nor feel the echo of his presence in the room when she played the piano. She waited for someone new to come along and fill the space he had left behind. She tried to convince herself that it was for the best, that Michel was too young, and that their connection had been nothing more than a passing infatuation, but none of it stuck. The truth was, she didn't want to forget him. Not just yet.

So she waited. A day would come when she would be ready, when she would see a new boy walk into her life. Until that day came Helene would sit here in this quiet room, the sunlight dappling her inner sanctum, waiting for her next pupil. She stared out at the world as all of the creatures and all of the possibilities moved on without her. Helene fixed her thoughts on Michel, and waited impatiently until she might find another bright young thing to fantasise about.

The song behind the story: "The Blower's Daughter" is one of Damien Rice's most well-known songs, featured as the lead track on his 2002 debut album O. I defy anyone not to be moved by the song's haunting beauty and the melancholy driven by Rice's emotive vocals and sparse, acoustic instrumentation.

I was introduced to this song by friends (Doug & Emma) some twenty years ago and it has remained in my top tracks playlist ever since. I couldn't resist the opportunity to write something inspired by such brilliant original writing.

The title of the song, "The Blower's Daughter," is somewhat enigmatic. Damien Rice has mentioned in interviews that the "blower" refers to a clarinet teacher, and the "daughter" was someone he had feelings for. This backstory adds a personal layer to the song, but it is also left deliberately vague, allowing listeners to project their own interpretations onto the song.

Album: O

Artist: Damien Rice

Year: 2002

Composer(s): Damien Rice

Record Label: 14th Floor Records (UK) and Vector Records (US).

Down South

The Louisiana heat was relentless, a heavy, suffocating blanket of warmth that seemed to draw the breath out of your chest, but Jimmy barely noticed these things anymore. He had grown accustomed to the oppressive summer heat over the years. The air outside was thick and sticky with humidity. It was the kind of day that made you feel like you were constantly wading through a thick broth. Even the salty breeze that occasionally wafted in from the Gulf couldn't cut through the densely layered atmosphere. It only made the air heavier, and with it, Jimmy's chest got tighter. He sat alone in his old, battered GTO, the engine idling as the AC sputtered weakly in a half-hearted attempt to fend off the heat. It didn't stand a chance. Jimmy's eyes were fixed on his phone screen, scanning the messages again. For the third time in the last ten minutes.

Where you from? Way down south?

It was a simple message, harmless even, but the words gnawed at Jimmy's sanity. A casual text from a coworker he barely knew, yet it burrowed into his mind like a maggot latching on to a dirty wound. There were at least a dozen other unread texts beneath it from his friends, friends who hadn't seen him in days, all of them checking in, asking if he was okay. He hadn't responded to any of them. His mom had called six times that morning alone, leaving increasingly frantic voicemails, her concern crackling through the speaker in that oppressive way that only she could muster. It felt to Jimmy as though his mother was the human embodiment of this overbearing summer heat. Even the delivery guy, the one who dropped off his groceries on the porch of his run-down rented trailer, barely looking him in the eye, had asked, "You okay, man?" as if he could tell something was off just from the way that Jimmy opened the door.

"Nah, man, but thanks," Jimmy had muttered, his voice sounding disjointed and diffident to his own ears. No, he wasn't okay. Jimmy hadn't been okay for a long time, but admitting it was something else entirely, especially not to the delivery guy. Hell, not even to himself. He had moved out of home to give himself the space and time to think things through, but, like the heat haze rising off tarmac, Jimmy's mental state was in a constant shimmer.

The town of Jonesboro felt small and claustrophobic in a way that had nothing to do with its size. The long stretches of pine and cypress trees, the cracked pavements, and the familiar faces, none of these things brought comfort anymore. It was all a constant reminder of what was missing. Jimmy could barely picture the man who left without a word when he was twelve. No warning. No note. Just an empty seat at the dinner table and a mother who never quite let him forget it.

She tried to fill the space that Jimmy's father left behind with her loving presence, but it ended up feeling like suffocation. As Jimmy passed through puberty and into his teenage years, his mother's ever-present intrusion felt to him as though she was always hovering above him or watching him, her concern wrapping itself around him like the heat, impossible to escape. He tried to be enough for her, to make up for what they'd lost, but the more he tried, the tighter her grip became. Now, sitting here in his car, staring blankly at his phone, he felt that grip tightening again. Her voice echoed in his mind. It wasn't the canned voice from her voicemails that Jimmy heard. There was a version of his mother who lived in his head that constantly whispered, "Don't leave me like he did."

Jimmy let out a shaky breath, rubbing his palms against his jeans, trying to ground himself. He wasn't sure what was worse; the resentment simmering inside him or the guilt that followed it like a shadow. He knew she meant well. She was just scared, scared of losing him too, but that didn't make it any easier. Her insecurities didn't make the walls of this town any less stifling, and yet, now that he had bought himself a little space, he wanted to make things right. The problem was understanding how.

He looked at his phone again, at the unanswered messages and the missed calls. He could respond. He could call his mom back and tell her that he was fine. He could reassure his friends, but what would he say? "I'm good"? He'd said it so many times that he even started to believe it for a while, but it wasn't the truth. The truth was something he wasn't ready to face. Not yet.

So instead, he turned off the engine, letting the silence wash over him. The quiet hum of cicadas filled the air around him. He closed his eyes and let the heat sink in, swallowing him whole. Whatever it takes, he thought, he would figure it out on his own.

Jimmy stared at the quiet, narrow street ahead. His rented trailer in J-Ville, as he called Jonesboro, was supposed to be his fresh start, a place where he could bury the ghosts of his past and rebuild. He was nineteen years old and now, seven years after his father walked out just maybe he could carve out something that resembled a life, but it wasn't working. This town felt small and asphyxiating, and all he'd done since gaining his small freedoms was drift through the days like a shadow. He took labouring jobs when he could, but his life was largely aimless and haunted by memories he couldn't shake off.

He rubbed his temples, trying to ease the throbbing ache that had taken permanent residence there. Every day it was the same; the pressure building, his thoughts scattering like dry leaves in the wind. *Temple throb, dust lakes, black gold, tigers, and saints;* the words floated through his mind, fragments of a half-forgotten dream. The words were disjointed but persistent, hovering just beyond any rational explanation.

Jimmy's chest tightened, and a low buzzing filled his ears. He closed his eyes, but the pressure in his head only grew worse, like a vice slowly clamping down on his skull. For weeks now, the headaches had come and gone, but lately, they had grown sharper and more insistent. It felt like something inside him was clawing its way out. Jimmy was scared. Something was buried deep within him that he didn't think he could control. His hands trembled as he gripped the steering wheel, knuckles white against the worn leather. He needed to move. He had to get out of the car and breathe, but his body seemed immobile and without any sense of purpose. The depression that flowed through everything, the town, the past, his father, his mother, it all crowded in on him, holding him captive in the front seat of the GTO.

Jimmy's phone buzzed. He didn't even glance at it. He already knew what the messages said. They all blurred into the same worried, well-meaning static.

You okay?

Hey, man, let's catch up.

Your mom called me...she's worried.

She was always worried. She was always calling or texting to check up on him as if he were still the scared little boy his father left behind. A tight knot of anger twisted in his stomach. It wasn't her fault, not entirely. She just didn't know how to let go, but her concern choked him, with every call being a reminder that he wasn't free. No matter how far he ran, she'd always find him, tugging him back with those invisible strings that tied them together.

The phone buzzed again. Jimmy ignored it. His pulse quickened. He could feel his heart beating against his ribs as a wave of anxiety flooded through him. The walls of the car seemed to close in on him, the air still thick and heavy. His mind raced. Monroe, Jonesboro, Haynesville, Ruston. These were the small towns that had shaped his life. The South clung to him like a second skin that he couldn't peel away, no matter how far he drove. This wasn't what he wanted. This wasn't the life he had imagined.

He felt the appeal of the road beneath him, and the temptation to drive, to disappear across the horizon and never look back, but he couldn't outrun his past. The ghosts within were his family and they were a niggle inside him that just wouldn't let go. He blinked hard, his eyes grimy with exhaustion. The sun was setting, casting long shadows over the quiet street, but he felt no closer to finding any kind of peace. Jimmy felt trapped in this town, trapped in his own skin, with no clear way out. And the messages kept coming.

Memories crept in like a rising tide, seeping into the corners of his mind, unbidden and unstoppable. He could almost hear his father's voice again. He could feel the fleeting presence of the man who had once filled their house with the scent of cigarette smoke and sawdust. Jimmy alternately hated and loved the man who left them with nothing but a shallow excuse. He mumbled a mental afterthought, "He went away, real far away…"

That's what his mom always said when people asked, as if those words meant anything to a kid who didn't understand why his dad couldn't just come back. He'd walked out all those years ago, but it felt like yesterday and a lifetime ago all at once. Jimmy still remembered that last morning with vivid clarity. His father sat across from him at the kitchen table, his tired eyes fixed on the paper, sipping his coffee like any other day, but then, in a blink, he was gone. No goodbye. No explanation. Just the slam of the door and a stack of bills that seemed to grow taller by the week.

Jimmy spent months trying to understand and then fill the emptiness his father left behind. He tried to figure out what he could have said or done to make him stay, but it was useless. He never did understand why. Maybe that was the worst part, and it was this sense of not knowing that gnawed away at him.

Jimmy carried an invisible wound that never quite healed, no matter how hard he tried to pretend it didn't hurt.

The familiar throb of the headache pulsed behind his temples, more insistent now. He closed his eyes and took a slow breath. When he was younger, his dad made a promise to him with the kind of certainty that made Jimmy believe him. "We'll be alright," he'd said. "I'll always be here, kiddo. You can count on that."

But promises didn't mean a damn thing when you were sitting alone at the kitchen table, staring at the empty chair where your father used to sit. There was just silence in that house now, a silence that filled every room like a fog. Jimmy clenched his fists so hard his knuckles turned white. The anger started slow, creeping in around the edges of his sadness, but now it was simmering just beneath the surface, threatening to boil over.

His vision blurred as he stared at his phone, her latest text glowing on the screen; *You alright?* She'd sent it ten minutes ago, but he hadn't responded. He didn't want to. How could he explain what was happening? How could he tell her about the confusion that clouded his thoughts or the guilt that bedevilled him like a parasite? How could he expose her to the rage that simmered just beneath the surface, ready to explode. He didn't want to be like his father, vanishing without a word, leaving behind nothing but questions and heartache. He hated him for that. Jimmy hated the way his father's absence still controlled everything.

The phone buzzed again, a sharp, insistent vibration that rattled the GTO's centre console, snapping him out of his trance. He snatched the mobile up, his pulse quickening. Another message, this time from one of his friends.

Your mom keeps calling me.

His stomach twisted, the words burning into him like a brand. He wanted to fling the phone across the car, and make it shatter into pieces, but that wouldn't solve anything. His mother was always there, always standing at the periphery of his life, trying to pull his strings, reminding him that he couldn't escape her.

His fingers hovered over the screen. He wanted to respond, but what could he say? That he was sorry? That he didn't mean to drag his friends into it? That his mother didn't realise how controlling her hold on him had become? It would all be lies. He knew it, and deep down, so did they. Everyone could see the cracks because they were too wide to be hidden anymore. He felt sick, the kind of sickness that rooted itself deep inside, twisting into something black and heavy.

But it wasn't just about the grief. There was the responsibility too. Jimmy saw in his mind's eye how his mom started looking at him, her eyes filled with desperation, her voice clinging to him like she'd drown without him. She called him her "saint," over and over, as if the title itself was a lifeline, but the meaning of the word changed with every utterance.. Being her saint meant being the glue that held everything together. It meant being the man of the house when he was still way too young to know what being a man meant. His stomach churned with bitterness. She's a saint, he thought, a sharp edge to the words as they echoed in his mind. And I'm her shell of a man.

The thought reverberated inside him like a scream in an empty room. He was hollow and brittle, stretched so thin that one wrong step would break him. He closed his eyes, trying to push it all away, but the darkness was already creeping in. Then, out of nowhere he heard his father's voice whispering in his ear, saying, "Nah, you're a hell of a man, Jimmy. You're stronger than you think."

The words felt wrong. It had to be a lie. The man who left him couldn't be right. Jimmy knew that he wasn't strong. He was a muted creature, pretending to be okay, pretending for the sake of his mom, and for the sake of everyone around him who needed him to keep it together. If he didn't, if he cracked, if he let the flood of anger and sadness and grief that swirled inside him spill out, then everything would come crashing down.

His headache pounded at the base of his skull, sharp and relentless, pushing him to the brink. His vision blurred for a moment, the world fading to black. He clenched his jaw, gripping the steering wheel as if it were the only thing keeping him anchored to reality. His fingers dug into the worn leather. His mind repeated the same mantra, trying to drown out the chaos building inside him. Jimmy repeated the phrase again and again; "Gear up, stand up. Gear up, stand up."

But for what? The streets of Jonesboro stretched out ahead of him like a never-ending labyrinth, the familiar highways winding into places that didn't feel like home anymore. Each street sign, each corner of this small Louisiana town, felt like a reminder of everything he'd lost. *Black gold, tigers, saints.* He was spiralling, and he knew it. Something inside him was breaking, splintering like glass under pressure, and no amount of pretending could fix it. The messages kept coming, the phone buzzing again and again. His friends, his mom, even people who barely knew him, were all reaching out, all asking the same question. They could see the cracks and the fractures that he tried so hard to hide.

Are you okay?

He hated the question. He hated how easy it was for them to ask it. No. He wasn't okay. He hadn't been okay in a long time, maybe never. And what scared him most was that he wasn't sure he ever would be again. He had to find a way to accept the responsibilities that had been thrust upon him at such a young age. He had to…

"Fuck, no…" he muttered under his breath. Jimmy turned the ignition key with a rough twist, the engine roaring to life in the quiet stillness of the late afternoon. He hit the gas hard, the tires screeching as the car jolted forward, tearing through the streets of Jonesboro. He didn't have a destination in mind. All that Jimmy cared about was this sudden desperate need to escape, to outrun everything that had been lacerating his soul for years. The city blurred into a smear of concrete, tarmac, and a rainbow of neon shop signs. The familiar landscape was distorted by the speed and the pounding headache that throbbed at his temple, sharp and relentless. His hands shook on the wheel, his breath ragged and uneven. It felt like the world was slipping away from him, unravelling faster than he could hold it together.

"Cheer up, cheer up," he muttered under his breath, forcing the words through gritted teeth. "Gear up, stand up." It was a mantra, a shield that he had crafted, repeating it again and again to ward off the evil eye within, but the words felt hollow today, meaningless echoes bouncing around his mind. They couldn't stop what was coming.

The phone buzzed again on the centre console, vibrating like an accusation. The noise cut through the pounding in his head, sharper than before, and without thinking he snatched it up. His mother's name lit up the screen. He could imagine her on the other end, sitting in that bleak house that she called home, waiting for him like she always did, her need as dull as the Louisiana humidity.

You okay, Jimmy? her text read.

The question felt like a punch to the gut. He stared at the screen for a long moment, the words blurring. With a snarl of frustration, he threw the phone out of the driver side window, watching it disintegrate briefly in his door mirror. He pressed harder on the gas, the speedometer creeping higher as the car hurtled through the backroads, past old gas stations and empty lots. The heat of the day whipped through the open windows, but it did nothing to calm the storm raging inside the car.

Jimmy didn't have an answer, not for her, and certainly not for himself. All he knew was that he had to run. He had to keep driving, as far and as fast as the car would take him. There was no going back to the trailer or to that house and its empty promises of safety. He couldn't bear it anymore. His father had run, and now it was his turn. Maybe that was the only thing he'd ever learned from the man…how to leave.

He sped past the town limits, the narrow road winding into the thick stands of cypress trees that lined the outskirts of Jonesboro. The road ahead carved out a path through the dying day, but everything outside of the GTO was a blur. Jimmy gripped the wheel tighter, his heart racing faster than the engine, and for a moment, he felt like he was on the edge of flying, but he didn't slow down. He couldn't stop running. Not now. Not ever.

The song behind the story: *This was another one of those random but serendipitous finds while scrolling through music videos. I had heard odd tracks by Sleigh Bells before but this one is quite different, and It got me hooked. "And Saints" offers quite a shift from their typical high-energy noise-pop sound, being more stripped-down. Alexis Krauss' vocals are prominent, creating a haunting atmosphere, reminiscent of a hymn in an empty chapel.*

The track is part of their mini-LP Kid Kruschev, and it's a track that has stayed with me for a while now and, obviously, provides the backdrop for this story.

Album: *Kid Kruschev*

Artist: *Sleigh Bells*

Year: *2016*

Composer(s): *Derek E. Miller and Allison Krauss*

Record Label: *TBD Records*

Planet Hunter

The stars burned brightly through the viewport of *Quaoar Station*, a skeletal relic adrift in the frozen expanse of the Kuiper Belt. Once a beacon of humanity's eager hope to find new worlds, it now floated in silence, a monument to the follies of the past. The station had been named after Quaoar, a creation deity of the Tongva people. They said that Quaoar sang and danced the world into existence. How fitting, Pyotr thought, for the place where he once believed that he could find new life by dancing through the folds in space and time, but that was before everything went wrong.

Now Pyotr stood alone, his breath faint against the thick quartz-glass viewport. He pressed his hands against the ice cold surface as if he could reach out and touch the stars themselves. The familiar hum of the station was the only sound left now apart from the soft notes as he inhaled and exhaled. The sound of voices, of the laughter and the chatter that he once found annoying was long gone. The crew that he once commanded were entirely absent. The stars outside felt different now as well. Everything around Pyotr seemed distant and unknowable, as though the universe had turned its back on him. The stars used to guide him, as if he were joining the dots of understanding using those pinpricks of light. Now, he saw them as ghosts in the void, haunting his every step.

He could hardly remember Earth's constellations anymore. That felt like another lifetime. 2215, he thought. How many years have passed since then? Every time that Pyotr folded space, time got twisted out here in the Kuiper Belt, and after so many jumps, it had become impossible to track exactly when he was. For all that Pyotr knew, he could have been out here for decades, or centuries, or millennia. To ease the madness Pyotr had stopped counting some time ago.

Pyotr wasn't a planet hunter anymore. He wasn't even sure if there was anyone left on Earth who remembered them. The planet hunters, his crew out here on the station, had been legends once. They were bold explorers venturing past the known reaches of the solar system, looking for habitable worlds where humanity might grow and thrive. Pyotr had been the best of them. He was both a scientist and a dreamer, and saw fit to lead a team following that dream, but the dream soured, and now, Pyotr was no longer chasing new worlds. He was chasing ghosts.

The *Madness Drive*, his cursed invention, had promised to rewrite the rules of space travel. By manipulating the fabric of the molecular universe to dilate time, experimental travellers could skip across light-years in an instant. There would be no need to build impossible ships that would have to travel for centuries to reach distant stars. It all seemed so clear and simple. If he could prove the safety of the *Time Drive*, as he called it back then, he would be able to watch humanity blossom as the species spread out across the galaxy.

The first jumps were short and experimental, with an enthusiastic audience watching the live streams back on Earth. The team grew ever bolder, extending jumps from the experimental minute long hops across solar distances, until they attempted that last jump. Pyotr could still hear the screams of his crew, the alarms blaring out as reality itself tore open around them. When they aborted the longest jump ever attempted, Pyotr was thrown back into normal space alone. The others, his entire team, had been displaced, and were adrift in some kind of limbo, lost between worlds. The crew included his lover, Katya.

Saying her name out loud was like drawing a blade across his heart. He could still see her face and her smile. He could still hear her sweet, indulgent laughter when he cracked appallingly bad science puns. As he pressed his forehead against the viewport glass he could almost feel her pressing her forehead against his when they were alone, whispering dreams of the future they'd build together on some far-off world. That future was gone now, snatched away in the blink of an eye when he last engaged what he now knew to be the *Madness Drive*.

Katya had been right there beside him in the control room when it happened. And then, in the moment that it took Pyotr to turn away from the control console to speak with her, she was gone. Her body and soul were ripped from this universe, leaving him alone in the unbearable silence that followed. She and the rest of the crew, were, he believed, floating somewhere between time and physical space.

For years now, Pyotr had been using the *Madness Drive* again and again, risking everything to search the folds of space-time for his lost people and for Katya. He had jumped hundreds, maybe a thousand times by now, each jump blurring the lines between the man he had been and the ghost he was becoming. Every time, the station groaned, twisting with the strain of the drive as if it might collapse under the weight of his obsession, but still he pressed on, leaping through the void in hopes of finding the people he had condemned to limbo. Pyotr no longer cared about planets and humanity. He had to find Katya. "I will find you," he promised, his breath fogging the glass as his reflection stared back at him with fevered eyes. The stars outside blinked coldly, uninterested in his feelings.

Pyotr turned to look at the control panel full of the switches and dials that would unleash the ripping power of the *Madness Drive*. He had made one mistake, one leap of arrogance that cost him everything, but Pyotr didn't yet believe that the gods were cruel enough to take Katya from him forever. They couldn't be. He would make another jump, and another until time itself bent to his will. He would bring her back. One more jump, Katya, he thought, his heart stinging with the memory of her touch. Just one more.

Pyotr tore himself away from the window, the disappointments of endless failure nagging at him as he walked toward the central console. His movements were mechanical, with each flick of his fingers over the controls practiced and precise. Deep within his breast there was a tremor, an ache he could never quieten. This time would be different, he thought. All he wanted was just one more moment of bliss, just one more chance to feel her warmth again. All he needed to do was steal one solitary moment from time itself, a moment where everything was whole again and where Katya was present.

The *Madness Drive* hummed beneath his feet, the rhythmic pulse of its power manifesting like a heartbeat. The machine whispered seductively, filling his mind with promises and lies, but Pyotr didn't care. The damnable drive offered possibilities that no other force in the universe could match. That was why Pyotr called it what he did. The sheer scale of the beast was unfathomable. Human minds simply couldn't cope with the breadth and the depth of infinite chance across immeasurable time. For Pyotr, though, it was like a drug. If he could just brave the madness one more time, then maybe… just maybe he could undo the worst mistake of his life.

"Just one more time," Pyotr muttered through gritted teeth, his fingers white-knuckled around the engaging lever. It was slick with sweat, his palm aching from how tightly he grasped it. He wasn't sure if it was the pressure of the moment or the unnatural heat radiating from the console, but the metal felt like it was vibrating beneath his grip, a barely contained fury eager to be unleashed.

With a heave, the lever came down.

The station convulsed. A guttural groan reverberated through the walls, metal screaming as the Madness Drive surged to life. The hum beneath his feet turned into a seismic tremor, a frequency so deep it rattled his ribs, his teeth, his skull. His breathing faltered as the air itself seemed to thicken, pressing down on him with the weight of collapsing dimensions.

Outside, the stars shattered, not simply stretching, but splitting, fragments of light splintering apart like shards of broken glass before smearing into impossible streaks. The universe bent and twisted, folding in on itself, and Pyotr felt the lurching, nauseating sensation of being unmade. His molecules didn't just move; they detached, slipping through each other, reforming, losing meaning before finding it again.

The rush hit. A tidal wave of raw, electric being flooded his senses, every nerve in his body lighting up as if the cosmos itself had carved through his veins. He gasped, lungs seizing on air that was suddenly too sharp, too charged, too alien. Gravity was gone, no, not gone, but rewritten, twisting in directions his mind couldn't comprehend. He was falling and floating and soaring and sinking all at once, his bones singing with the violent, beautiful paradox of it.

Terror and ecstasy warred inside him. It was like stepping off the precipice of reality, plunging into a place where time wasn't time, where space wasn't space, where everything, every possibility, every version of himself that could have ever been, collided and dissolved into an endless, roaring now.

It was madness. It was freedom.

Pyotr's breath came in ragged gulps, his chest rising and falling as his body fought to keep hold of its original reality. His fingers dug into the console, grounding himself against the infinite pull of the abyss. The void whispered, beckoned, threatened. But he had to see. Just one more time.

He had to see heaven again.

The station lurched violently, the jump complete. Pyotr's breath caught in his throat, his body trembling with the aftershocks of the disorienting leap. His pulse hammered in his ears as the station's lights flickered off and then back on. He didn't dare look. He didn't dare hope…but…

His eyes lifted toward the window, and he gasped out loud. He should be seeing the stars of some far distant solar system through the viewport. Instead he could see Katya. Her beautiful face was framed in the darkness beyond the glass. Her eyes, wide and searching, locked onto his with a desperation that pierced him more deeply than anything he had ever felt in his life. Her lips moved, forming words he couldn't hear but he didn't need to hear what she said. He knew it by heart.

"Pyotr." She was calling him again and again.

He stumbled toward the window, hands trembling as he pressed them against the cold glass. "Katya?" His voice cracked, barely more than a whisper. His heart pounded, every beat an agony of longing. She was right there. She was so close. But something was wrong. Pyotr started to come down from the adrenaline high that the jump had given him. Katya wasn't really there. Her form flickered, like a reflection in disturbed water. The stars behind her twisted, pulling her image apart in fragments of light. She wasn't part of this world anymore, Pyotr remembered. Katya was trapped in the limbo he had damned her to when he unleashed the *Madness Drive*.

"Katya," he whispered again, his voice faltering in his despair.. His hand pressed harder against the window, as if sheer force of will could reach across the veil that separated them. For a fleeting moment, he swore that he felt her warmth through the cold glass, but then she was gone. The stars returned, distant and indifferent. The endless void beyond the station stretched out before him, with no more care for his torment than a rock cares about a rainbow.

Pyotr's hand slipped from the glass, his breath shaky as his heart twisted in his chest. How many times had he tried? How many jumps had he made, believing this time, this time he could bring her back? But each time, she slipped away like a ghost fleeing the coming dawn. He would keep searching. He had to. Because there was no going back now, just as there was no moving forward. Until he found her and pulled her from the abyss there would be nothing but this moment. Pyotr put the universe on hold until he could resolve the insanity of the *Madness Drive*. He closed his eyes as the hum of the machines slowly abated throughout the station, whispering their dangerous promises once again; One more jump. One more chance.

Pyotr nearly jumped out of his skin as the comm system crackled to life, piercing the oppressive silence of the ship. Static flooded the cabin, and then he heard a faint but unmistakable voice. "Pyotr... Pyotr, can you hear me?"

Pyotr's mental state, especially just after a jump, was inherently fragile. His world disintegrated and reformed in a single heartbeat. Her voice was one he'd long since buried in the corners of his fractured auditory memory. His hands trembled as he lunged for the comms console, fingers fumbling to tidy up the signal. "Katya? Katya, is that you?"

Another surge of static. "Pyotr... I'm... I'm here. I don't know where, but... I'm trying to reach you."

The sound of her voice was enough to tear open every wound, and yet it suddenly filled him with a hope so wild that it burned. She was alive in some form even after all these years of drifting through the void. Somehow, after losing her to the

Madness Drive's fatal and cataclysmic jump, she was still out there, lost in the jagged and twisting currents of space-time, just like he was.

"Katya…" He whispered her name like a prayer, his voice raw and desperate. "I'm coming for you. I swear, I'm going to find you." His hands flew over the controls, his heart pounding with the urgency of a man with nothing left to lose. "Hold on," he said, his voice hardening with the fire of old promises, promises made when they still believed they could conquer the stars, but even as he fought to stabilise the connection, her voice began to fade, swallowed by the static. The stars continued their endless drift outside the ship. And with their silent witness came a chilling truth that gnawed at his entire being. This wasn't the first time he had heard her voice. Katya had spoken to him before, in the endless dark between jumps, in moments when the universe toyed with his hopes and his sanity. Every time he activated the *Madness Drive*, every time he plunged deeper into the cosmic abyss, she called to him. Every time that he thought that he was close, she slipped away, always hovering just beyond his grasp, like a dream dissolving at the moment of waking.

His felt constricted, the familiar ache of his loss settling in. He gripped the edges of the console, knuckles white, his breath uneven. Was she real? Was she out there, truly lost in the currents he'd ripped open, or was this just another cruel illusion. Pyotr was slowly coming to believe that the *Madness Drive* was sentient and that these mirages were its twisted way of tormenting him. Each echo of her voice was a haunting. Katya was a phantom tethered to the machine that he had created, the same machine that had torn his life apart. Am I still a planet hunter, he thought bitterly, or just a fool chasing ghosts?

It was a question he'd asked himself too many times. And yet, even knowing the futility of his quest, even with an endlessly present sense of doubt undermining his confidence, he couldn't stop. He wouldn't. Every time that he heard Katya's voice it was enough to rekindle the dream that maybe this time would be different. Pyotr's life rested on the single surety that one more jump might bring him closer to her, closer to the woman he loved, and closer to the redemption that he craved. His hand hovered over the activation switch of the *Madness Drive*. He could hear the hum of the engines rising, with the station trembling in anticipation of another leap into the unknown. And then Pyotr could feel Katya's warmth as if she were standing right beside him, urging him on.

Just one more time.

"You're in heaven now," he murmured, the words bitter on his lips. The *Madness Drive* would pull him into the chaotic ether once more, where space and time unravelled and reformed in ways no mind could fully comprehend, but Pyotr didn't care. He would tear the heavens apart to find her. "And so am I," he said with a grim determination. Pyotr slammed the lever down again and the station groaned and then screamed as the *Madness Drive* roared to life.

The song behind the story: *"Planet Hunter" is a track from Wolf Alice's 2017 album Visions of a Life, the band's critically acclaimed second studio album. For me, this song stands out for its dreamy, introspective atmosphere. I love the rather delicate and ethereal vocals from lead singer Ellie Rowsell, alongside the band's lush instrumentation.*

The song fits into the overall arc of Visions of a Life, an album that explores a wide range of emotions and sonic textures. The album won the 2018 Mercury Prize, further establishing Wolf Alice as one of the most exciting and innovative bands in the UK indie rock scene at the time.

As for inspiration with this tale, the title clearly plays a part, but the crux of the story are lines about leaving one's mind behind as events drive you onwards.

Album: *Visions Of A Life*

Artist: *Wolf Alice*

Year: *2017*

Composer(s): *Ellie Rowsell & Joff Oddie*

Record Label: *Dirty Hit*

Going Underground

The air was thick with the stench of decaying garbage. It was worse than just the foul rot of refuse sacks piled in the alleyways, though. There were more disturbing layers to the grime and to the aromas suffusing London's streets. Daniel imagined that the underlying smell came from the slow death of people's ideals. It was the stench of dying hope. London was grey where, it was said, there had once been colour and meaning. In Sector Eleven, a forgotten corner of London now little more than a concrete wasteland, any semblance of rebellion had been systematically snuffed out. The few who still dared to dream were either dead and buried beneath the rubble of broken promises, or like Daniel Grimes, they were disillusioned and invisible, existing on the edge of a society that was slowly eating itself.

Daniel's adopted lethargy in the face of his disillusionment was a façade that he constructed each day to hide his true intention. He was going underground. Not in any traditional way, not as a rebel on the streets or as an agent provocateur, but literally. Daniel had decided to follow the trail left by rumour and conjecture. He was leaving the grey sky and the regime's platitudes behind. As he walked, Daniel looked up at that sky, which he saw was a sickly yellow, filled by a permanent haze of pollutants and chemical smog. It was a sky that had long since blotted out the natural blues that flowed above the clouds. Towering above the streets, endless rows of digital billboards flashed the same relentless corporate slogans; "A Safer Tomorrow," "Trust Your Leaders," and "Sacrifice For Peace." Each message played on a loop, as if endless, mindless repetition would drive the message home. The government clearly considered the general population to have the mental ability of a six year old. Everywhere Daniel turned, these mantras followed him, crawling into the corners of his consciousness, demanding obedience and suffocating free and original thought.

Daniel had stopped listening a long time ago. He worked as a locksmith and kept his head down. The promises of stability and the government's rhetoric of peace was nothing more than static in the background. He could still remember a time when he cared, when he had burned with the fire of youthful resistance, but that fire had long since burned out and turned to ash. Now, when he saw the cracks in the system, when he saw the hunger in the eyes of the workers, he felt nothing. Where once the deadened stares of those who shuffled through their daily routines would have moved him to anger, now he felt nothing but an aggravating emptiness.

He'd been angry once. He remembered the protests in his early twenties, the chants of the few who dared to speak out against the regime. There was a coalition of students and mothers in an accommodation of the dispossessed. It was a time when snatch squads kicked down doors in the night that put paid to even the mildest acts of defiance. Resistance was ground down over many years. Rebelliousness wore away like the crumbling facades of the old city. Under a diet of endless propaganda, and the closing of independent lines of thought, the people of London, of England were now simply resigned to their fate, filling the void with state news and mindless, pacifying gameshows on the entertainment channels.

Daniel lived his life under the cover of a grey fog, moving from one day to the next, existing rather than living while he planned his clandestine escape. The billboards told him that his life was his own. They blared out messages suggesting that he had choices and opportunities, but it was a lie. He worked. He played by the rules. All it got him were ration credits and a little coin, enough to rent a bedsit and eat slop. The endless grind was draining him. In the totalitarian state that had risen from the ashes of a rotten democracy, striving for more was an exercise in futility. The system was designed to consume, to exploit, and to grind its citizens down until they became nothing more than cogs in the great machine. Daniel refused to be a cog, believing firmly that he would find salvation underneath the city streets.

Daniel's move had to come soon if he was to remain sane, but for now he played the part of a worn cog. He let himself be trapped in the endless slog, always aware of his decline as the life drained out of him. His feet moved along the designated paths. He kept his eyes downcast to avoid the countless surveillance drones that buzzed overhead. The streets were littered with the faces of the forgotten, where so many were unemployed and expendable. The citizens of this brave new world were apparitions that drifted through the crumbling city streets, and Daniel was thinning, he was fading, and soon he too would be as invisible as they were.

What kept him going were the stories. There were always people who knew people. Rumours of the Underground surfaced all the time. Some said there was an elusive network of rebels who had carved out a hidden life in the old, abandoned tunnels of the London Tube. It was said they were still fighting and still resisting the regime's iron grip. In his bleaker moments, Daniel couldn't see how or why a government as controlling as theirs would ever permit such a thing to exist, especially at the very heart of the country. People living in the shadowy depths beneath the city, beyond the reach of the government's cameras, beyond the ever-watching eyes, was surely a fantasy. It didn't matter now. Even if it were only a few stragglers, a few tramps and the wayward who survived like that, it would be enough.

In his brighter moments, the image of tunnels and clandestine folk enthused Daniel's thoughts. The idea of fading into those tunnels and escaping the endless surveillance, the lies and the noise of indoctrination was an intoxicating counterpoint to his disillusion. He no longer believed in change. Change was a luxury that happened in a different world, a world that no longer existed, but the idea of simply disappearing, of slipping through the cracks and leaving behind the suffocating smog of the beleaguered city, well, that was something he could believe in.

As Daniel walked through the dimly lit streets, the propaganda screens cast an eerie glow over the grey buildings. With each repeated cliché Daniel felt the need to make his move growing stronger. The streets were empty tonight. The city's pulse felt slow and mechanical, like the idling of a leviathan machine. He glanced around, and he immediately felt that familiar sense of being watched. The drones were everywhere, but down in the Underground, there would be no cameras, no eyes, and no invisible chains.

As Daniel walked through the sparsely populated streets of London's Sector Eleven, the fading light of this particular early evening cast long, oppressive shadows across the crumbling buildings. A tension hummed in the background, like a low, unrelenting vibration just beneath the surface of things. The streets, though largely empty, carried the echoes of celebration from somewhere far off. A brass band played triumphantly in the distance, their bold and brazen notes cutting through the stagnant air, but the music felt off-key, as though the band were playing a discordant soundtrack for the decaying city. Then Daniel remembered that it was some government-sanctioned holiday, Victory Day, or Unity Week, or something equally meaningless. Daniel didn't care enough to remember. Whatever it was, it wasn't for people like him. It was for the smiling, smug politicians with their sleek suits and practiced lies. It was for the faceless men and women who ruled with iron fists hidden in threadbare velvet.

As Daniel rounded a corner onto one of the old city's main thoroughfares, a boy's brigade marched by, their footsteps precise and their faces blank, wiped clean of any individuality. Their uniforms, a thuggish blend of black and grey, were crisp and flawless, their hands gripping their batons like they were ready to strike at dissenters at a moment's notice. Daniel slowed his pace and watched them pass, the boys' faces hardened by duty and propaganda. They were no older than fifteen. They were far too young to understand the horrors they were being moulded to enforce. They were too young to realise that they weren't protectors of the people. They were tools that were being sharpened to maintain the regime's stranglehold on what was left of the country. It was a show of strength. A reminder of who held the power and who enforced order.

And yet, as Daniel watched them pass, he still felt nothing except a black void where his emotions should be. The world had fallen apart long ago, and now, people danced around the wreckage, pretending that everything was fine. People breathed the fumes in deeply and to order, pretending that the sky wasn't yellow with toxins. People shrugged their shoulders when acquaintances simply disappeared. No one complained overtly that life was being drained out of them, one propaganda-fuelled lie at a time.

Ahead of Daniel, a massive screen burst into life, illuminating the street in harsh, artificial light. The voice of a polished announcer boomed from nearby loudspeakers, filling the air with that nauseating cheeriness so characteristic of the government's broadcasts. "Do you want a better standard of living!" the voice declared, with false enthusiasm. "Do you want more security! Together, we can make it happen! Peace through security! Wealth through work!"

The words echoed through the streets, bouncing off the deadened walls of this grey concrete jungle. Daniel's lips twisted into a bitter smile, the irony biting deep. More money? More security? The people wanted those things, sure, but what they got were shining new weapons, paraded through the streets during government displays where marching soldiers' gun barrels gleamed in the jaundiced sunlight. The people here got security, but only the kind that came with more surveillance drones, more secret police, and more guards in black uniforms patrolling every block. They got textbooks filled with lies, teaching the next generation how to march in perfect order. Children were schooled in how to recite the slogans of a peace backed by the brutality of the baton and superior firepower.

No one questioned the soaring budget for military spending. No one asked why so many people seemed to vanish overnight. They didn't ask because they couldn't. Asking was a privilege long since stripped away from the common man. In a world where dissent was criminal and thought was controlled, the people were spoon-fed the reality they were supposed to accept. They were taught to be grateful for their gilded cages and for the few scraps of safety they were allowed to cling to.

"The public gets what the public wants," the voice continued, its syrupy optimism dripping from the loudspeakers. And the people, the hollowed-out shells that shuffled through the streets, appeared to believe it.

But not Daniel, not today. The system had nothing left to offer him, nothing that wasn't drenched in lies. He wanted nothing more than to escape the suffocating rot of this broken society. As the last of the boy's brigade disappeared around a corner, Daniel's gaze drifted downward, to the old, rusted grate near his feet.

The public gets what the public wants, he thought, the bitter words echoing in his mind, but I want nothing this society has to offer. He glanced down again at the grate, his pulse quickening. Maybe the rumours were true. Maybe they weren't, but staying here, above ground, meant slowly suffocating under the choking miasma that suffused this rotting city. If the Underground was just a myth, then disappearing into myth was still better than staying in this nightmare.

The passing parade, a grotesque spectacle of flags, uniforms, and fake smiles, droned on behind him, the brass band belting out the anthem of the regime. A growing crowd cheered mechanically, their faces gaunt, eyes glazed over by years of indoctrination. Daniel turned his back on the scene, the noise blurring into a dull hum as he moved down the narrow side streets. The boys brigade, the brass band, and the regime's propaganda slogans combined to trigger Daniel's next move. He walked here because there was a way down. He had never quite had the nerve to open the gate, but today was different.

The entrance that Daniel was looking for was discreet, tucked away between two crumbling buildings that leaned together like drunkards, their facades smeared with decades of grime. A narrow alley, barely wide enough for a person to slip through, led him to a small courtyard at the back of which stood an iron gate. He hesitated for a moment, listening to the faint echo of the parade fading into the distance. The air grew colder in the alley and the stench of rot and abandonment grew stifling.

The rusted iron gate that barred his way was crusted with decades of flaking neglect, and a heavy chain was wrapped around its bars. The gate was a relic from a forgotten time, as much a barrier to the world above as a marker of the boundary between light and dark. Daniel pulled out a slim comb pick from his coat and began working the padlock. His fingers moved with practiced ease, the quiet clicks of the tumblers aligning with a precision that felt almost supernatural. The lock fidgeted and then ground open, and he slipped the chain free, the gate creaking as it swung inward.

The darkness swallowed him whole as he stepped through. As Daniel descended into the depths, the only sound that he could hear was the slap of his shoes on concrete steps and his quick and shallow breathing. Each step that he took down the ancient staircase took him further from the world he had known, from the suffocating streets and their omnipresent watchers. Daniel took an old rubber bodied torch from his jacket pocket and turned it on. His torch cast dim and trembling beams of pale light across the damp, decaying walls of the tunnel. The air here was thick with the scent of mildew, and there was the faint rustle of unseen creatures echoing off the walls. At the foot of the staircase he entered a tiled hallway littered with the innards of old turnstiles and ticket barriers. As Daniel swept his torch around the walls he could make out ancient signage. A large, faded and damaged roundel with a bar through it read, TOT…H.M C..R. RO..

The further Daniel went, the more that the futility of life in the city above seemed to lift from his shoulders. The noise of the world above, the constant hum of drones and the ceaseless propaganda, it all faded into a distant fugue. For the first time in years, Daniel felt something that resembled peace. Down here, in the belly of forgotten London, there were no eyes watching him The world had forgotten these tunnels, and in their abandonment, there was a strange kind of freedom.

As he ventured deeper, the tunnels began to twist and branch into a labyrinth of old maintenance shafts and decayed platforms. The walls were slick with moisture and the ceilings were heavy with decades of soot. Pipes ran overhead, and dripped with the occasional drop of escaping water and condensation. The ground beneath his feet was uneven and littered with debris. None of this bothered Daniel. This was real. It was grimy, raw, and alive in a way that the sterile streets above had long ceased to be. Down here, survival was the only law, stripped of the façade of order that choked the surface.

He wasn't alone, of course. As Daniel ventured deeper into the labyrinth of forgotten tunnels, shadows stirred at the edge of his vision. These were the ghosts from the surface, people like him who had slipped between the cracks of society and descended into the depths of the Underground. Their faces were gaunt, their bodies bent by hardship, but their eyes... their eyes, though pale, still burned with a quiet intensity. They gathered in small clusters, huddled around flickering fires built from scavenged debris, their whispers barely audible over the echoing drips of water from above. These weren't just refugees from the system; they were survivors of it.

Daniel skirted these camps that they lived in, seeing them as a patchwork of discarded and broken things. This was a world of shadows and tattered blankets, of cracked plastic sheets, and useful bits of rusted metal, all of it propped up to form makeshift shelters. Smoke from the fires mingled with the damp, stale air, casting everything in a haze that made the whole scene look like something from one of the regime's dystopian propaganda films designed to remind the faithful of how lucky they were. Amid this bleak tableau, there was also a kind of unspoken tribal ferocity here. No one greeted Daniel or acknowledged him openly, but there was a shared understanding in their silence. They wouldn't let their guard down, but they did acknowledge the quiet bond of those newcomers who were choosing this exile not because they were forced to, but because there was nothing left for them in the world above.

In this desolate refuge, however, the poisoned world above continued to seep in like a slow, creeping rot. The lies, the violence, the old systems of control clung to the people down here like a second skin Daniel could see it in their faces and the haunted looks that never quite faded. They had escaped the surveillance and the propaganda, but they hadn't escaped their pasts. It was all still there, lurking just beneath the surface, waiting to rise again. The Underground was a place where wounds, both physical and mental, could fester, hidden from the watchful eyes of the regime.

As he continued deeper into the Underground Daniel started to feel the quietness cover him like a blanket on a hot summer night. There was danger embroidered all over it. Every breath felt heavier, and every step here was a reminder that in this place, the only law was survival. The only rule was to keep moving, to keep scraping by beyond the camera and the drone. Daniel knew better than to think this lack of surveillance was an oversight. The authorities tolerated the Underground. It was too convenient not to. This place was a pressure valve that allowed the disillusioned to vent and leave the overground folk in a state of stability. This was a place where those who no longer fitted the regime's perfect vision could disappear without causing too much trouble. The government was happy to let them vanish into the shadows and scrape out a living in the bowels of the city. As long as they stayed out of sight and out of mind, they were no threat. It cost the regime nothing to leave them alone.

And yet, Daniel couldn't shake the feeling that it was more than just neglect. As he continued to delve more deeply into the tunnels, the city above receding in his short-term memory, Daniel allowed himself a small, bitter smile. The regime had designed a system where even the act of escaping felt like a concession. They tolerated the Underground because they knew that as long as people were content to survive in the shadows, they would never rise against the light. In one of the deeper chambers he thought about the life he had left behind. This place was diametrically opposed to the inane conversations and the endless talking that he thought would one day make his head explode. The news broadcasts that made his body freeze with a sense of helplessness were history. He would never have to listen to the braying sheep on the TV, repeating the same lies and the same promises. He was done with all of it. The brass bands could play. The boys could march. Let them shout for tomorrow, but for Daniel, there was no tomorrow. There was only the Underground. And in the Underground, everything was zen. At least, that's what he told himself.

Daniel had been walking for what felt like hours, the oppressive darkness closing in on him like a heavy shroud. His torch flickered one last time before sputtering out, leaving him in pitch blackness. His heart pounded in his chest, and he slowed his pace, cautious of the uneven ground beneath his feet. He could hear the distant echo of dripping water and the sound of his own ragged breath. Daniel couldn't escape the ever-present sense that he wasn't utterly alone. As he rounded a curve in one of the old tracks, hidden in the murk, came a shuffle of movement. He froze, every nerve in his body on edge. The stillness around him felt charged. The tension was palpable. Then Daniel heard the sound of light and deliberate footsteps approaching from the tunnel's shadows.

"Stop where you are," a voice commanded, low and sharp.

Daniel obeyed, raising his hands instinctively in the darkness. A sudden cold sweat on his back turned his skin clammy. He squinted into the dark, trying to make out shapes, but all he could see were the vague silhouettes of figures stepping out of the gloom, surrounding him on all sides.

"Who the hell are you?" another voice spat, this one closer, rougher. "And what're you doing down here?"

Daniel's throat felt tight. His words were jumbled in his head, but he forced them out. "I... I came looking for the Underground."

Hard, mocking laughter echoed through the tunnel. One of the figures, still barely visible, stepped closer, his outline growing clearer. The blade of a knife glinted faintly in the dim light leaching into the tunnel from a station platform further down the line.

"The Underground, huh?" The voice was laced with venom. "Everyone comes looking for the Underground until they find it. Then they wish they hadn't."

Another figure spoke from the darkness, a woman this time, her voice calm but edged with cold curiosity. "He's alone. Looks like he's lost. What should we do with him?"

Daniel's heart pounded, his palms slick with sweat. He could barely see the people around him, but he could feel their hard stares and their absolute need of self-preservation pressing in on him. He was a trespasser in their world, a world where trust was dead and suspicion was survival.

"I don't want trouble," Daniel said, his voice steadier than he felt. "I'm just looking for somewhere to… be."

For a moment, there was only silence. Then a new voice emerged from behind him, softer but commanding, cutting through the tension.

"That's what they all say."

The owner of that last voice stepped forward into the thin shaft of light coming from the distant tunnels. He was older, his face worn and creased with years of hardship, but his eyes were sharp, watching Daniel with a mix of wariness and a hint of understanding.

"Where's your light?" the older man asked, nodding toward the dead torch hanging limply from Daniel's hand.

"Gone," Daniel replied, shrugging weakly. "Battery's dead."

The older man gave a slow nod. "Battery's dead, huh? So you're just wandering blind down here?"

"I'm not looking for a fight," Daniel said quietly. "I heard… rumours. Heard people like me could come here. This is the only place left."

The older man glanced at the others, then back at Daniel, considering the truth of his words. The tension in the air was still sharp, with the silent threat of violence hovering over them all, but the older man's presence seemed to hold it at bay.

"Come with us," he said, his voice carrying authority.

There was a murmur of dissatisfaction rippling through the group, but no one argued. The older man stepped aside, gesturing down a narrow passage that split off from the main tunnel. The knife carrying member of the group prodded Daniel in the back. Daniel hesitated, his body still tense, but he had been walking for hours and the exhaustion that he felt was too great to ignore. He nodded, following the man through the passage. The remainder of the group stayed back, their eyes lingering on Daniel and his escort like wolves sizing up prey, but for now, the threat had eased.

As they moved deeper into the tunnels, the faint glow of a makeshift campfire came into view, casting flickering shadows on the cracked walls. A handful of people sat in the dim light. They were stragglers, like him. Their clothes were tattered and their faces were lined with weariness, but they were alive. The older man gestured for Daniel to sit on an upturned crate near the fire. Daniel sank down, his body sagging with relief as the warmth of the flames licked at his skin.

Daniel's breathing was still ragged from the hours of walking. His body ached, bruises forming beneath his clothes where he'd crashed against the rusted pipes and crumbling walls of the tunnels. He wasn't even sure how far he'd come. Looking at the people sitting around him, the one truth that he could allow was that the world above had finally spat him out, leaving him to rot in the depths below.

The older man from the tunnel watched him and didn't seem surprised that he was here. He was mature, broad-shouldered, his posture that of someone accustomed to people listening when he spoke. The others sat in a loose circle around the fire, but he was different. He sat like he owned the place.

"Name's Carter," the man said, lowering himself onto a metal bench as if he had all the time in the world. His voice carried authority, the kind that didn't need to be shouted out to be obeyed. "Used to be a teacher, long time ago. Now I am the law down here."

Daniel blinked. The law? He almost laughed, but the fierceness of the man's gaze froze the reaction in his throat.

Carter smiled, but it wasn't friendly. "That's right, boy. The regime up top? They have their rules, their enforcers, their punishments. Down here, we have the same. You either follow our law, or you don't last long enough to regret it."

Daniel swallowed hard. He felt the eyes of the others on him, sharp, waiting, gauging. He forced himself to nod, though his stomach clenched with unease.

Daniel sat in the dim glow of the fire, his breath shallow, his fingers numb despite the oppressive heat that pressed against his skin. A deep coldness crept into his tired bones now, as ice settled in his gut as Carter's words sank in. His stomach twisted violently, nausea swelling in his throat. He had run from the surveillance, the curfews, the disappearances, the sterile white lights of a world that demanded obedience beneath the illusion of order. He had clawed his way into the tunnels below, hoping to find something different. Hoping to breathe air that wasn't filtered through the clenched teeth of a dictatorship. But here he was. And nothing had changed.

Daniel's limbs felt disconnected from his body, heavy yet untethered, like he might float away into the shadows if he let himself. His heart was a wild animal, hammering against his ribs, desperate for escape, but there was nowhere left to run.

The tunnel walls pressed in, the ceiling low, the space thick with the fiery reflections of hostile eyes, and of unspoken threats. He clenched his hands into fists, the bite of his own nails into his palms grounding him, barely. The firelight cast Carter's shadow long and jagged against the walls, distorting him, making him something monstrous.

Daniel had seen these men before. They wore uniforms up above. They had polished boots and mirrored visors and voices that carried the menace of absolute control. They spoke in the clipped, measured tones of authority, reminding everyone that disobedience would not be tolerated, that submission was safety, that order was survival. He tried a different tack.

"Daniel," he muttered. "Daniel Grimes."

Carter tilted his head, as if testing the name for worth. "You'll find a lot of Daniels down here. A lot of people who thought they could outsmart the world above. Thought they could outrun it. But there's no running from power, son. It finds you, whether it's wrapped in a suit and a badge or standing right in front of you, telling you how things work."

Daniel tensed, but Carter only leaned forward, his elbows resting on his knees. The firelight cast deep shadows across his face, carving harsh lines into his already sharp features.

A woman with short-cropped hair and a permanent scowl spoke from across the fire. "Why'd you come here, really? You a rat? One of those revolution types looking to stir up trouble?"

Daniel shook his head, exhaustion heavy in his bones. "No. I just… I couldn't stay up there anymore. Too much noise. Too many lies. I wanted out."

A dry chuckle escaped Carter's lips. "You think you're out now?" He gestured vaguely to the tunnels around them, to the damp walls and the ever-present drip of leaking pipes. "This ain't freedom, boy. This is just a different kind of cage."

The younger man to Daniel's left shifted, his face mostly swallowed by shadows. "At least down here, no one's forcing us to wear those damned party smiles."

A few murmurs of agreement rippled through the group. Carter let them have it, for now. But his gaze never left Daniel.

"Listen close, Grimes." His voice dropped, the fire crackling between them. "I don't give a damn why you came. What matters is what you do now. The people up top? They want control. They make the laws, they punish the ones who step out of line. Down here?" He gestured to himself. "I make the laws. My people enforce them. You break them, you don't get a warning. You don't get a trial. You get a knife or a bullet."

The words were cold, and matter-of-fact. Daniel shivered, though it had nothing to do with the chill in the air.

"You want to sit by this fire? Fine," Carter continued. "But you'll do it as one of mine. You work, you contribute, you fight if I tell you to. You don't like it? Then you can take your chances out there in the dark. But make no mistake, there is no escaping someone's law down here. Not up there. Not down here."

Silence hung between them. The fire popped, embers drifting upward like dying stars. Daniel clenched his fists again, his mind racing. He'd left one dictatorship only to stumble into another. But did he really have a choice?

No. He had nothing. Nowhere to go.

Carter watched him, waiting for his decision.

Daniel slowly nodded.

Carter grinned. "Good," he said, leaning back, satisfied. "Then welcome to my world, Grimes. Let's see if you've got what it takes to stay."

The conversation ended. The others returned to their quiet discussions, their hushed murmurs blending with the ever-present drip of water from the ceiling.

Daniel stared into the fire, his heartbeat still uneven. This wasn't freedom. It never had been. But it was all he had left.

The song behind the story: *This takes me back to very young days, and some of my first loves as far as music is concerned. The Jam are up there with the best of them.*

"Going Underground" is one of the most iconic tracks by The Jam, a British punk/mod revival band fronted by Paul Weller. Released in March 1980, it became the band's first No. 1 single on the UK Singles Chart and is one of their most famous tracks.

The song's blend of political anger, energetic instrumentation, and catchy hooks continues to resonate with me, making it one of the most enduring tracks of the post-punk movement. This is definitely one of those tracks that is part of the soundtrack to my life.

Album: *Sound Effects*

Artist: *The Jam*

Year: *1980*

Composer(s): *Paul Weller*

Record Label: *Polydor Records*

The Merrow

A gusting north-easterly wind whipped across the deck, stinging Bill's face as his small fishing boat, *Wee Scunner*, rocked violently against the growing swell. The grey horizon stretched endlessly ahead, merging with the steel-coloured sky. A vast and dark expanse of churning water surrounded him, an unforgiving wilderness that swallowed sound and thought alike. It had been two long days since Bill had left the port of Hull, and each day seemed to stretch the world into thinner shades, pushing him deeper into this desolate corner of the North Sea. Out here, far from the comfort of harbour walls or human company, it was just him, the boat, and the unpredictable and ancient sea.

Bill was one of the last single-handed fishermen still working these waters. The North Sea, once teeming with life and a reliable source of livelihood, had grown quieter in recent years, as regulations tightened and catches dwindled, but for Bill, it was more than just a job; it was his identity. He had fished these waters since he was a boy, following in the footsteps of his father and grandfather before him. In each generation they were unashamedly men of the sea, shaped by its temperaments and hardened by its unforgiving nature.

The isolation had always been part of the attraction. Bill liked the quiet vastness that always gave him the sense of being at the edge of the world where only the sea and sky existed, untouched by time. Out here, he could leave behind the problems that frustrated him ashore; the bills, the slow death of the fishing trade, the family he barely saw anymore. The sea was a place where he could disappear, slipping into a rhythm of tides and winds that followed the most ancient pulse of the ocean.

But today, that sense of peaceful isolation felt different. The solitude that was usually a comfort, troubled him in a way it had never done before. The wind carried a strange tension within it as it whipped through the rigging and gear lines. Bill scanned the horizon. There was nothing but the roiling, grey water, with the occasional bouts of wind-blown spray hitting his face like cold needles. The sea had always been his ally, but today it felt as though it was watching him and judging him.

He had felt it since dawn. There was an enigmatic presence in the air that made him feel uneasy. He'd been on these waters for decades, and he'd learned to trust his gut. The sea could turn on a man quicker than anything else, and you learned to listen to that creeping unease. There was nothing wrong with the boat. *Wee Scunner* was solid and well-maintained. His gear was working fine, and he had a good haul so far. There were no storms on the horizon, and Bill was pretty sure that the mechanicals on the boat were sound, but he couldn't shake the feeling that something was off.

His hands tightened on the wheel as the wind gusted again, stronger this time. There was a biting chill that cut through his thick oilskin jacket. The swells were growing steeper, each wave slapping against the hull with more force, the boat bobbing with vigour. Bill glanced at the sky, searching for signs. The clouds were quickly thickening overhead and swirling in low, ominous formations. Maybe a storm was coming in faster than forecasted, but it wasn't the weather that had him on edge. Bill felt it in his bones. Whatever was coming was old and primal.

The sea had its moods and its mysteries, and Bill always respected that. His father used to tell him stories about the North Sea when he was a boy, stories that fascinated him still today. They talked about the ancient creatures that lived in its depths, and about the souls of sailors lost in its icy embrace, forever wandering beneath the waves. His father believed in those stories and in the old superstitions passed down from the fishermen who had come before. In public Bill always brushed those old tales off, chalking them up to the imagination of men who spent too long in the cold and the dark. In private, however, Bill knew those stories to be rooted in immemorial truths. Today, with the wind howling in his ears and the sea shifting restlessly beneath him, those stories felt incredibly close and real.

He stood at the helm, staring out into the murky distance, and for a moment, he could have sworn he saw something, just a shadow, a slight movement in the water that was too quick to make out in any detail. His heart raced, and he blinked, searching the spot where this apparition had manifested., but there was nothing there other that the endless expanse of grey water. Bill shook his head, trying to rattle away that sense of unease. He'd been out here too long, that was all. He needed to get home, back to solid ground, and back to familiar faces, but even as he thought this, a cold voice in the back of his mind told him that whatever was wrong, it wasn't something he could just sail away from. In his heart, Bill also knew that home was a shell, and his part in it an act. The sea, and only the sea, was his mistress.

Another gust of wind hit the boat, harder this time, and *Wee Scunner* pitched violently to port. Bill staggered, gripping the wheel to steady himself. His breath came in shallow bursts as the boat fought against the rising swell, the engine groaning under the strain. He stared out at the sea again, and for the first time in his life, Bill felt truly small and insignificant. The sea had always been a challenge, but it was also a partner, a living entity to be worked with. Today, though, the sea felt like it was an enemy, and Bill had the unsettling sense that it was waiting for him.

As night swallowed the horizon, leaving nothing but an inky expanse of sea and sky. Bill let the boat's engine idle, the dull hum vibrating through the deck as his fishing boat drifted with the North Sea's currents. The endless stretch of water was a world unto itself, cold and desolate, with the stars flickering faintly overhead, barely visible behind thick layers of scudding cloud. He leaned against the rusted railing outside of the wheelhouse, his breath coming in short, shallow puffs in the chill air. Out here, miles from shore, the whip of the wind and rolling churn of the waves were his constant and only companions.

Then, something else came with the wind. At first, Bill dismissed it as a trick of the sea, maybe the distant echo of a seabird or the groan of the boat's metal superstructure, but the

214

sound didn't disappear. It lingered, weaving through the rush of the wind and the rhythmic slap of water against the hull. He stood up straighter, heart suddenly drumming harder in his chest. It was most definitely a human voice.

He turned his head, eyes scanning the shadowed horizon, but there was nothing. He could see no light from any other vessel, and he was too far out to hear voices on land. All that he could see or hear was a stretch of the North Sea between the shores of England and Norway, cold and unforgiving. He knew these waters well. No singing person had business being out here in the dead of night, and yet the voice was clear now, drifting toward him with the breeze. It was soft, almost mournful, but unmistakable in its feminine attraction.

"Sail to me, sail to me..."

Bill stood at the railing, utterly astonished. The voice carried an intimacy that made him long to find the source, as if the song was meant for him alone. It was a melody that stirred something deep within him, some long-buried memory or feeling, something primal and of the sea. The song was otherworldly, but it felt so personal. It seemed to Bill that whoever was singing out there somehow knew him, and had always known that he was a fundamental creature of these great waters.

He turned the boat in slow circles, trying to pinpoint where the voice was coming from. His boat swayed gently on the swell, but whichever direction he motored in, there was nothing but the whisper of the sea and that haunting voice.

"Let me enfold you..."

His pulse quickened. He stood once more by the railing and listened. There was no rational explanation for what he was hearing. The nearest coast was hours away, and he hadn't seen another boat in days. The voice came again, its siren song threading through the air, drawing him in like a moth to a flame.

Bill stumbled back into the wheelhouse, his hand finding the helm in the dark. His fingers curled around the cold metal instinctively, and before he knew it, he was steering toward the voice. Soft words filled the darkness, and his boat cut through the water as if guided by an unseen tiller. He no longer questioned what was happening, for there was a strange but undeniable urgency to his thoughts and actions. He didn't need to check the compass. The direction didn't actually matter anymore. Time stretched and folded in on itself. Hours felt like minutes, and the sea was a blur as his mind focused on nothing but the melody that seemed to wrap itself around his soul. That song filled the gaps in the world singing melodies in black ink, and soothing the loneliness that had crept up on him over the years. Every gust of wind carried a new phrase and a new promise of warmth and of solace.

The stars disappeared behind thickening clouds, leaving only the voice to guide him. Bill blinked as he stared into the darkness, his eyes straining for any signs. The cold bit at his skin, but he felt nothing but a growing sense of anticipation. And then, out of the haze of sea spray and moonlight, a shape began to emerge. At first, it seemed impossible that there should be any sort of shimmer in the distance. Nothing should be visible against the black sky, but as Bill squinted, he realised that whatever it was, it was more than just a mirage. The mysterious shape and shimmer turned out to be an island. There was a speck of land rising from the depths of the North Sea where there should have been none. As Bill manoeuvred the boat in towards the lea side of the island, so the voice grew louder and more insistent.

"Here I am, waiting…"

The waves calmed as the boat drew closer to the mysterious island, the water smoothing out as if it was commanded to grant him safe passage. Bill's grip tightened on the helm, but he couldn't resist the ardour of that voice any longer. It was as if the sea itself had brought him to this place, a place that shouldn't exist, and yet was right here before him.

A figure stood at the edge of the island, barely discernible in a mist that swirled along the shoreline. A woman stood on the beach, her form graceful and still, her hair drifting with the wind as if it was part of the sea itself. Bill's heart hammered away. She was real, he was sure of it, and yet, there was something about her that didn't belong to this world.

He anchored the boat in the island's gently shelved shallows and climbed over the side, stepping into the surprisingly calm water. His waders sank into the wet sand, and Bill's breath came in short gasps. The closer he got to shore, the more the air seemed to thicken with the swirling mists. She was waiting, standing there with her arms outstretched, her eyes fixed on his, glowing with an ancient and unearthly light.

"Let me enfold you…" she whispered again, and for a moment, the world was still.

Bill walked towards her without hesitation. Her gaze was magnetic, and her presence was all-consuming. He reached out to take her hand, and as their fingers touched, a jolt of warmth shot through him. Her skin was cold, like the sea, but her grip was steady.

For a second, he felt whole again, as if all the pieces of his life had fallen into place. Every longing, every regret, every moment that he had spent adrift in life melted away under her touch. Then, just as quickly as the comfort had come to him, so it slipped away. The woman's eyes darkened and filled with a sorrow so deep that it seemed to echo through the wind. She pulled her hand back, retreating, the warmth disappearing as the chill of the night returned.

"Touch me not..." she whispered, her voice trembling. *"Not yet. Come back tomorrow..."*

Bill stood on the beach, frozen in place, watching helplessly as she stepped back into the mist. He reached out, desperate to follow, but her form was fading slowly into the night, leaving him alone on the shore once more. Bill knelt on the cold, wet sand, watching as she slipped away into the mist. Only moments ago, her voice had called him to her, drawing him from the sea to this lonely shore. Now, she was retreating once more, her figure fading into the ghostly haze, leaving him stranded between land and water. He felt a knot tighten in his stomach. He longed to see her again. His knees pressed into the sand, the cold seeping through his clothes, but he barely noticed. All he could focus on was her retreating form.

"Why?" His voice cracked, the word catching in his throat. "Why can't I stay?"

The mist swirled around her, and for a moment, she paused. Her eyes, wide and filled with sorrow, met his. They shimmered like the sea under moonlight, revealing depths that spoke of endless years of pain and longing. Slowly, she pressed a hand to her chest, as though to shield herself.

"My heart," she whispered, her voice so soft it was almost lost to the wind, *"my heart shies from the sorrow."*

And then, before he could reach for her once more, before he could ask what she meant, she vanished. The mist swallowed her whole, leaving only the sounds of steadily lapping waves against the shore. Bill knelt on the beach for a long moment, staring at the empty space where she had stood, the ache in his chest deepening with every breath.

Finally, with heavy limbs, he forced himself to his feet and waded back out to his boat. The saltwater chilled him to the bone as he climbed aboard, but he didn't care. His mind was racing. He was being called by the sea. The faces of his wife and his children flashed into his thoughts, but the memories seemed distant and faint. They had no power here, and Bill didn't care to question that. He dried off mechanically, changed into a spare set of dry clothes, and prepared to weigh anchor. His primal instinct for survival told him to go home, to leave this strange island behind and return to the safety of dry land, but Bill was already moving beyond that calling.

At the last moment, his hand froze on the throttle. He couldn't leave. Not yet, not without seeing her again. He decided to stay. One more visit, he told himself. One last glimpse of her would be enough to satisfy the yearning that clawed at him, drawing him back toward the island. That one visit became two, then three, and soon, the days blurred into an endless stretch of grey sky and cold wind. Each night, he returned to the shore, hoping for some sort of resolution, needing her to appear again, and every night, she came.

Her song would rise on the wind, her voice soft and haunting, calling him to her once more. He would step onto the island, drawn to her by a force he could neither explain nor resist. Her eyes would meet his. They would brush fingers, and just as his heart swelled with hope, she would slip away again. She was always out of reach. With every one of these tantalising touches, Bill's felt as though his mortal, land-centred being was fading, until he was sure that his essence was nothing but a translucent outline. Bill was caught in a cruel dance. Each night, the love in his chest burned brighter and stronger, filling him with a passion he hadn't known in years, but when the sun rose, he was a drained vessel, adrift in a sea of longing that consumed his waking thoughts. He couldn't understand why she called to him, only to pull away, and yet, he couldn't stop himself from answering her call. He was trapped, a man torn between the vitality of life and the needful shadow of this sea-born woman.

One night, as the wind howled around him and the boat rocked gently on the waves, Bill stood on the deck, staring out at the dark expanse of the sea. His heart felt heavier than ever, weighed down by the endless cycle of hope and despair. He stared down at his hands, rough and calloused from years of working the nets. "It's too late now," he muttered.

The ocean, as always, gave no answer. Its endless waves rolled on, indifferent to his turmoil. The ever-present mist clung to the water's surface, curling and drifting, with ghostly fingers reaching up from the depths. Bill clenched his fists. A shallow, almost reluctant laugh escaped his lips. He felt like a shipwrecked sailor, stranded not on the rocks of some distant shore, but on the fragile ridge that stood between optimism and misery. Each night, she lured him closer to the brink of madness, and each morning, she left him more broken than the day before.

He couldn't stop. He knew, deep in his bones, that there was something magical about her, something ancient, powerful, and far too strong for any mortal man to resist. She was the sea, and he had always loved her. Her voice was a curse that bound him to her, as surely as if she had wrapped her arms around him and refused to let go. He was lost, adrift in her wake, but he didn't care. He would keep coming back, no matter how many times she pulled away, and no matter how much it tore him apart. He had tasted a power beyond the simple love of a fisherman for the sea. Some loves, he thought, were worth drowning for.

The song behind the story: *I've been a fan of pretty much everything 4AD since my student days, and in particular any project featuring Elizabeth Fraser's extraordinary vocals. "Song to the Siren" by This Mortal Coil is a hauntingly beautiful and melancholic track, released as a single in 1983. The song is, in fact, a cover of the original by Tim Buckley, which was first performed in 1968.*

This version strips down the instrumentation, leaving a sparse, dreamlike arrangement that allows Fraser's haunting voice to take centre stage. Her delicate delivery, combined with minimal production creates a ghostly, otherworldly atmosphere, that has clearly inspired me to create my own version of a universal tale.

"Song to the Siren" has gained significant recognition over the years, often praised for its emotional intensity and the fragile, intimate beauty of its arrangement.

Album: *It'll End In Tears*

Artist: *This Mortal Coil*

Year: *1984*

Composer(s): *Tim Buckley & Larry Beckett (1968)*

Record Label: *4AD Records*

Eddie's Town

The old spotlight above the post office door sputtered weakly, casting a dim, fractured glow that barely reached the cracked pavement. Not so long ago the spotlight had been a warm and reliable beacon, a familiar touchstone of everyday life in a place where faces were known, greetings were exchanged, and the rhythm of work and family pulsed steadily through the day. Now, it hung like a relic, the last gasp of a place long past its prime. The window below it held a sign, Position Closed, scrawled in faded marker pen ink, put there by someone with a sense of humour. Eddie stood on the other side of the street, watching the light flicker through a thin veil of drizzle. His old coat, frayed and worn, showed patches of dark staining where the rain had soaked in, the once-promised waterproofing long gone, like most things in his life.

Eddie thought long and hard about what it meant. Position Closed. He was seeing signs like it everywhere now. The factory down the road was boarded up. The café where he and Elly used to sit with a mug of tea was whitewashed and shuttered. The pub he used to meet the lads at was empty, its windows covered in grime and graffiti. The whole town seemed to be shutting up, bit by bit, folding in on itself like a body too tired to move anymore. The pandemic had only hastened what was already happening, and now the politics of austerity were bleeding the last bit of life from the place, but in truth the body of this town had been sick for years. There was a brief moment of hope when the new government talked big about investment in the north, but it was, as usual, an illusion. There was nothing but slow and inevitable decline.

Before taking his evening walk, Eddie had sat on the edge of his bed, the one he used to share with Elly. It felt too big, too empty, like a house that had been abandoned mid-renovation. The memory foam mattress had moulded to his shape over the past year, creating an impression that didn't quite fit, as if he still expected Elly's presence beside him.

Not so long ago, Elly had been a warm, steady light in his life, a presence so constant he'd stopped noticing its glow until it was gone. She had a way of making the house feel full and alive, even in her most annoying moments. The hum of her moving about, the clatter of a spoon against a cup, the gentle weight of her hand on his shoulder as she passed by, it was all so ordinary that he had never thought about life without her.

Everything that had once been theirs was dimming, one thing at a time. The garden had gone wild, brambles creeping over the flower beds she'd tended with such amateurish care. The teapot she used to insist on brewing from sat untouched on the kitchen shelf, gathering dust. Even the sunlight through the window seemed weaker now, failing to reach the corners of the room the way it used to.

Position Closed. That's what he was now, wasn't he? A role no longer needed, a man left standing in the quiet after the work had been done, after the light had flickered and faded. He had always thought of himself and Elly as a pair, a team. In life she was definite and bloody-minded and difficult, but he had never prepared for the day when half of that team would be gone.

And now, everything was shutting up, folding in on itself. The world kept moving, but the content of Eddie's life was just like his home a town. One by one, the doors were closing, and the shutters were being pulled down.

Eddie's face, weathered and ashen, was as expressionless as the grey sky above. His eyes, dulled by care and time, scanned the scene. What was there to see? Nothing changed. The town, like his life, had settled into a slow fade. Eddie felt worn down by decades of hard work that seemed to amount to so little in the end. There was a time when Eddie felt a part of something, back when he and Elly were building a life here. In the great scheme, theirs was a small part, but it was meaningful to them. They had their routines and their modest happiness. It all seemed so distant to Eddie now, relics from a past life that belonged to someone else. Elly died just over a year ago, and with her went any real sense of purpose.

Eddie shuffled slightly, his knees aching from the cold. He wasn't sure if he felt grief anymore, or just a slowly widening emptiness. He missed Elly, of course. He missed her laughter and the way she could brighten even the darkest days with just a look, but more than that, he missed having something to look forward to. He smiled ruefully. He missed their arguments. He would, he thought, cut off his right hand just to hear Elly proclaim her opinion as an undeniable truth that he was too stupid to understand. Now, he wandered through the days like a lost soul. He'd worked at the steel mill for most of his adult life, doing what needed to be done, but for what? He received a pension that barely covered the bills, lived in a house full of memories, and he was swamped by the sense that he was disconnected from youth and life.

Eddie sighed, his breath fogging in the cold air. He had nothing left to do but stand there and wait, as if some part of him still believed that the lights might come back on, or that Elly might come walking down the street, frowning like she used to, but deep down, he knew. Nothing ever happens. Not anymore.

It was dusk, and the town was slowly shutting down. Secretaries, with tired eyes and weary fingers, let their computers hum into hibernation, while cleaners moved like shadows through empty corridors, sweeping away the remnants of another unremarkable day. One by one, office lights guttered out, leaving the buildings as hollow as the promises they had housed for eight long hours. Outside, the streets surrendered to the stillness of twilight. It was always the same, every day at six o'clock, as though the world switched itself off and retreated from its own existence.

By six-thirty, an eerie calm settled in. Traffic lights blinked through their routine, from green to red and back again, but few cars moved. The occasional cab, its headlights cutting through the growing darkness, slipped quietly across the empty intersections, ferrying passengers from one meaningless point to another, all of them following routes as predetermined as the lives they led. The streets, once filled with people who had ambition and urgency just existed passively now as an invisible hand slowly chipped away at the edges of anything solid. Eddie's town felt like it was simply going through the motions, as it performed its nightly ritual of surrender. As the darkness deepened, so that darkness swallowed the last vestiges of life, and by seven, the world seemed to fold in on itself. The quiet folk stretched out on their sofas and yawned.

Eddie turned away from the post office and shuffled along the cracked pavement. His heels scuffed against the concrete, which was worn down like the town itself. His gaze drifted from one lifeless shopfront to another. The high street was practically deserted. Shop windows were dark and the dull reflections of streetlights bounced off the glass. Every shop looked like a relic, boarded up or barely surviving, selling things nobody really needed.

The takeaways, though, were open, spilling a weak yellow light onto the street. Inside, people hunched over greasy food, their faces as tired as their surroundings, settling into the routines of another Monday night. Eddie could feel the boredom rising within him with every step that he took, as if the pavement was pushing him on towards his home on a small sixties estate at the edge of town. As infuriating as Elly could sometimes be, as loving as she could also be, she was never boring. Eddie had taken her for granted at times, and now he missed her definite frustrations. He was, he admitted to himself when he was on the drink, a shell of a man without her.

As he passed a pub, its door swung shut behind a group of young office workers, their laughter briefly piercing the damp evening air before they too faded into silence. For a second, Eddie thought about going inside, maybe ordering a pint, perhaps even calling a friend or two and asking them to join him for a quick one. The thought fizzled out just as quickly as it came. Who would pick up? His old mates, at least the ones who were left, were probably at home, slouched on their sofas, staring blankly at their TVs, letting the familiar glow of reality shows and celebrity gossip wash over them. They'd all convinced themselves they were content, hadn't they? They were stuck in routines that they never questioned, watching other people's lives on screens, and forgetting what their own life felt like. Eddie felt that same creeping numbness settle over him, the sense that everything had become a long, unchanging blur. The days, the weeks, they all looked the same. The world moved on, but here, nothing ever happened.

Eddie sighed, his breath curling in front of his face in the cold evening air before fading into the grey sky. He kept walking with his hands shoved deep into the pockets of his overcoat. Retirement had seemed like a salvation at first. Retirement promised freedom after years of monotonous desk work. It was a final end to the pointless meetings and the office politics that drained the last drops of his energy. By the end he hated every minute of it.

But life as he knew it today wasn't the freedom he had imagined. Retirement, which had initially felt like the start of something fresh, quickly dulled, losing its lustre like an old song stuck in an endless loop. It wasn't long before the days blurred together, one indistinguishable from the next. Every morning, he woke to the same familiar routine; breakfast, a few household chores, reading articles in the same old paper that echoed stories he had read a hundred times before. The television droned on in the background, showing the same talking heads and the same shallow chatter. By the afternoon, the world outside seemed to fall into a dull silence, as if even time had grown bored of the repetition.

Eddie realised with a heavy heart that he hadn't escaped the drudgery of work. He had only traded it for another kind of monotony. He swapped the lifeless grind of the office for the empty routine of days spent alone, wandering through hours that seemed to stretch on forever. Without Elly pushing him to clean and tidy, or to do something with the garden, Eddie had no deadlines and few responsibilities. Having no purpose was as debilitating as the work-a-day drudgery. Nothing ever happened. He filled his time with desultory tasks, but each one only reminded him now of how much he missed the chaos, the noise and the frustrations of his former life with his infuriating wife. The stillness of solitary retirement wasn't the peace he had once longed for.

As he walked through the empty streets, the world felt indifferent and uncaring, as though it too had slipped into a kind of apathy, leaving Eddie to wander on day by day through its silence. Nothing stirred, nothing changed. He was a passenger in his own life now, watching as time passed by without him leaving any mark or creating any meaning. The days might as well have been weeks or months, it all felt the same. Predictable. Lifeless.

Tonight, like every night, he would be alone. The routine had become a slow ritual. Eddie would eat a lonely dinner at his kitchen table, the clatter of utensils echoing in the quiet room. The television, lambent with its off-colour hues, offered faint company, its endless procession of reality shows and reruns barely cutting through to Eddie's consciousness these days. Once upon a time he'd loved watching football on the telly, but now the commentators and pundits annoyed him so much that he couldn't watch the matches anymore. Occasionally, if he was lucky, the warmer voices on BBC Radio Four would lull him to sleep before he could get depressed thinking on a life half-lived, that always seemed to be circling back on itself.

As he walked the familiar route toward his home, the buildings on either side slowly gave way to the open fields across the main road. It was darker out here, the kind of darkness that seemed to swallow the world whole, leaving just him and the whoosh of passing cars. He stopped at a bench that he and Elly used to sit on, back when Saturdays were spent wandering around town, arms heavy with shopping bags and hearts light with laughter and affectionate bickering. They'd originally come to this town together, when the world was full of possibilities and hope wasn't something you had to convince yourself to hold onto. Although Elly was prone to seeing the world as a glass half empty, she usually managed to find beauty in the strangest things. Eddie smiled as he remembered Elly laughing with simple joy as a bird perched on a branch beside her in the garden, or a squirrel scampered across the grass in the park. She could laugh at life's simplicity, her moments of true joy uncontainable. He remembered how her laughter was infectious, filling his soul with such warmth.

But that laughter faded, slowly at first, until one day it was gone altogether. Dementia stole it from her, bit by bit, until all that was left was the chaos of confusion and his anger at God's cruelties. Twelve months had passed since she'd been taken from him completely, though it felt longer. Some days, it felt as though she had been gone forever. Eddie worried sometimes that his loneliness would lead him down a similar path, especially on those days when Elly appeared to be just a distant memory, a vague recollection of someone he once knew. On those days it felt as if Elly was a ghost tied to this bench, a ghost speaking to him in reverberating echoes that told of someone else's life. Why, he wondered, did he remember her cussedness more tenderly than anything else?

Today was not one of those days. Eddie could see and hear Elly in all of her convinced glory. He sat down, the cold biting through his thin overcoat, and he stared out at the fields. The wind rustled the remaining leaves in the trees and the bushes in the hedgerows. There were no birds to marvel at tonight, and no squirrels darting about. There was just the endless stretch of empty land and the vastness of the sky above. Eddie sighed, his breath visible in the evening chill.

Eddie ran a hand through his thinning hair, closing his eyes, trying to remember the sound of Elly's laughter, trying to feel anything other than the numbness that had settled over him like a second skin. No matter how long he sat here, no matter how hard he wished upon the stars that were starting to prick the night sky, the world would remain the same. The routine would repeat. He'd go home, eat dinner alone, sit in front of the television, and hope sleep would come before the maudlin hours.

Eddie pulled his collar up against the chill of the evening, his breath fogging the cold night air. The distant lights of the town glistened like tired eyes, half-awake but unseeing, indifferent to the passage of time. The crawl of traffic seemed almost absurd to him now. Where were they going? What did any of it mean? He pictured the homes lined up neatly behind the town's dim glow. He imagined the people inside those boxy houses, sitting in front of screens, eating dinner in silence, their conversations circling the same empty points, their words exchanged out of habit rather than meaningful engagement. Would the people in those houses miss the mundanity of their communication like he missed the ordinariness of his former life with Elly?

It struck him how mechanical it all was. Everyone was caught in the same loop, day in and day out, like marionettes bound by invisible strings, repeating the same tired routines. No one questioned it. They just drifted through, like passengers on a train bound for nowhere, lulled into complacency by the gentle rhythm of familiarity. Eddie thought of those people in their cars, staring blankly ahead, not really present, their minds miles away even as their hands gripped the steering wheel.

It was as if the entire town was locked in an endless song, with a needle stuck in the groove of a record that never skipped forward. The same melody played over and over, and everyone sang along, even though the words had lost their meaning long ago. The needle might lift for a moment but it always came back down in the same place, and the song continued. Eddie shuddered, not from the cold, but from the sadness of it all.

Eddie's fingers grazed the worn edge of the bench, the cool wood stirring memories of afternoons spent there with Elly. He could almost hear her voice now, an abrasive sound, as she recounted the small frustrations and the occasional joys that had enlivened her day, but when he opened his eyes, the bench beside him was empty. There was no colour in the land now.

Behind him, the faint whine of moped engines pierced the stillness, growing louder as they neared. It wasn't the old familiar hum of summer rides with Elly on his Bonnie, when they'd zipped along country roads, her hair flying in the breeze and her eyes shining with mischief. No, this sound was brash and mechanical, more like the grind of machines erasing something precious. It was a buzz-saw set against the concrete pillars of a world that no longer seemed to care. Life moved forward, a monotonous cycle of days bleeding into nights, the stars above watching with the same cold detachment. Nothing changed. Everything changed.

Elly was gone, and with her, Eddie's simple belief system crashed. How could life be anything more than what it was; a series of fleeting moments, slipping through his fingers like sand. He was left with the ache of her absence. The thought weighed heavily on Eddie's mind and he couldn't shake it off no matter how many times he tried to push it away. What had his life really amounted to? He had done everything right, hadn't he? He worked hard. He loved more deeply than he had ever realised. He followed the rules without question, but here he was on the threshold of true old age, and he wasn't sure any of it mattered. He could boast no great accomplishments, nor any lasting legacy. His life amounted to a series of routines in a blur of years where moments of brightness flashed and then faded away.

He thought of Elly again. He missed her laughter. He missed the way that she could take offence from an innocent remark. He missed making up with her after one of their spats. He imagined her eyes sparkling as they walked along the coast together. She used to grab his arm, and pull him close, as if the wind off the North Sea would sweep them both away. They'd made promises under endless grey skies, and imagined lives full of adventures, but somewhere along the way, the dreams faded. Life happened instead; mortgage payments, job promotions, late nights spent at the office while she waited for him at home. The years blurred, but his memory of her stayed sharp, and it cut deeper now. That was the one saving grace. Eddie cherished these moments. Darling, uncompromising Elly was, he realised, still the reason why it all mattered.

The wind picked up, turning his cheeks a rosy-red in the darkness. Eddie shivered, pulling his coat tighter around him. Somewhere in the distance, the faint sound of music floated on the breeze, a pub song, maybe, from the place up by the roundabout where he turned into his estate, but it wasn't a lively tune. It was slow, the melody dragging on, as repetitive and as tired as the rhythms of his own life. He thought about how Elly used to hum to herself while cooking, sometimes singing softly as she danced in the kitchen with a glass of rioja in her hand.

He stayed on the bench for a while longer, letting the darkness settle in around him, the quiet of the evening laying upon him like a heavy woollen blanket. He remembered Elly's touch, especially the warmth of her hand in his, but now that warmth was long gone, leaving behind an emptiness that he couldn't fill. The sharpness of her absence carved into the spaces of his mind where all the "what ifs" lived. What if he'd worked less, laughed more, or held on more tightly to the things that really mattered?

When Eddie finally stood to leave, it was with the same feeling that had haunted him for the last year; a dull, unshakable sense of disappointment. His life, once so full of promise, now felt like a book with an incredibly dull and unsatisfactory ending. The main character in the story had faded out of his narrative, and the final chapters of this life were just plain monotonous.

As he walked toward home, the streetlights blinked on and off, casting a stuttering light over the damp pavement. Tomorrow would be just like today.

He sighed, his breath visible in the cool night air. He would be lonely tonight and lonely tomorrow, just like everyone else, but as he walked, he found himself thinking not of the emptiness, but of those fleetingly golden moments with Elly. Maybe, he thought, those memories were all he had left, but at least they were his and his alone, and that was something. Eddie put his hand into his overcoat pocket and touched a glass bottle. It was a half of a cheap blended whisky. It wasn't rioja, he mused, but a 'nippy sweetie' or two always helped.

The song behind the story: *"Nothing Ever Happens" by Del Amitri is a song from the Scottish band's 1989 album Waking Hours. It became one of their most popular tracks, peaking at No. 11 on the UK Singles Chart when it was released as a single in 1990. The song is known for its melancholic tone and sharp, socially conscious lyrics, reflecting on the monotony of modern life, social apathy, and the disillusionment that people often feel in the face of societal issues.*

At the risk of being unduly bleak, this is one of my all-time favourite songs. I heard it on release, and it's been on my playlist ever since in one form or another. Now that I am approaching my senior years and definitely becoming a 'grumpy old git' I thought I ought to put pen to paper...

"Nothing Ever Happens" is often seen as a timeless reflection on social stagnation, still relevant today due to its themes of inaction and apathy.

Album: *Waking Hours*

Artist: *Del Amitri*

Year: *1989*

Composer(s): *Justin Currie*

Record Label: *A&M Records*

Clara

In the heart of early industrial England, amidst the relentless toil of the new machines, and under a growing cloud of lung-breaking smog, Clara, a fourteen year old girl on the cusp of adulthood, moved through her days like a wraith. The mill consumed every hour of her waking life. The huge brick walls towered above her and stood against the grey skies as a defiant and unyielding symbol of progress. The air was thick with soot and filled with the steady clatter of iron looms that never ceased their labours. In the quiet moments, when the factory's roar dulled to a low hum, Clara found herself slipping into memories of a different world, a world she remembered from her early childhood and which she now yearned for with every fibre of her being.

Clara's imagined world, the mirage that she wished was real, was a world where fields stretched as far as the eye could see and where the trees swayed gently in the breeze, The earth beneath her feet was rich and alive with flora and fauna, and not buried under coal dust and cobblestones. When she let the dream take her hand, Clara felt the warmth first, the golden kiss of the sun on her skin, a gentle, radiant heat that seeped into her bones. It was nothing like the harsh, smothering air of the factories, thick with soot and sweat. No, this was different.

This was soft, like the embrace of a summer morning, wrapping around her like a childhood memory.

Beneath her bare feet, the earth was alive. Not cold stone or dirt choked with coal dust, but rich and pulsing with quiet energy. She curled her toes into the soil, felt the delicate tickle of grass brushing against her ankles, the whisper of petals as she stepped through fields of wildflowers. They bowed to her in the breeze, their scent wrapping around her like silk, honeysuckle, lavender, the faint sweetness of ripe fruit hanging heavy on stout branches.

The wind came next, cool and playful, lifting the loose strands of her hair, brushing against the nape of her neck like an imagined lover's breath. It carried the rustling of leaves, the soft hum of insects, the distant laughter of water running over stone. When she breathed in, the air tasted clean, fresh. She sensed none of the metallic bite of industry, nor the lingering ash that clung to her throat when she woke.

The sky stretched above her, endless and blue, the kind of blue she had only ever imagined. There were no looming chimneys to cut it into pieces, nor any smoke coiling up to blot out the sun. Just sky. Wide and open, like a promise.

She reached out, brushing her fingers along the bark of a tree. It was rough, warm from the sun, real. She pressed her palm against it, needing to feel its solidity, its truth, and for a moment, she believed that her dream was real.

But then, somewhere in the distance, she felt the first pull of waking. A cold wind blew raising goosebumps on her forearms, and a creeping sensation curled at the edges of her reverie, threatening to pull her back, back to the cobblestones and to the clatter of machinery. She clenched her fists and dug her toes deeper into the earth. She wanted to stay in the dream forever.

Clara always dreamed about the old country ways, most of which were passed down to her in whispered stories by her grandmother. The family came to the mill towns because the bucolic reality was hard and grim in so many ways, but for Clara it was an imaginary time when life was governed by the rhythms of nature, and not by the relentless ticking of the factory's clock.

Clara longed to escape, to run back to that time before the mills were raised, and before iron and smoke swamped the world. At night, as she lay in the cramped dormitory at the Apprentice House with the other adolescent mill workers, she dreamed of walking barefoot through dewy grass at dawn, and of feeling the sun on her skin as she spun wool by hand rather than by the cold, mechanical devices of the factory looms. These dreams, though vivid, left her with a sadness, for she knew that the life she longed for was out of her reach.

In her dreams, Clara could feel the land embrace her, wrapping around her like a long-lost homecoming. The air was crisp, laced with the scent of damp earth and crushed leaves, and when she breathed in, it filled her lungs with an untouched purity.

And then there was the creature. At first, Clara thought it was just the wind, a shift in the trees, a ripple in the brook's surface, but then she felt him before she saw him. His was a presence, humming beneath the land's heartbeat, something just beyond sight, watching. The air grew heavy, charged, the warmth of the dream pressing closer against her skin. The water between her cupped hands rippled as if stirred by unseen breath. A shadow moved at the edges of the trees, slow and deliberate. When she looked up, her pulse quickened.

He stood at the water's edge, bare feet sunk into the damp earth, his form half-hidden by the tangled branches. The dappled light of the dream world clung to him, outlining the lean stretch of his body, the effortless stillness of something both human and not. His chest rose and fell with a slow, measured breath, the muscles beneath his sun-bronzed skin shifting as he tilted his head, studying her.

The way he watched her set heat curling low in her stomach. There was nothing innocent in it, nothing polite. It was the kind of gaze that made the air feel too thick, that made the hairs on the back of her neck prickle, but not from fear. He exuded something feral, something untamed, something that sent a thrill through her veins as much as it set her nerves alight. She swallowed, and his lips curved at the movement of her throat.

The water was still cold in her palms, but her body burned where his gaze touched her. His dark eyes flicked to her hands, to the droplets sliding down her fingers, then back to her mouth, a knowing glint in his eye by way of a silent challenge.

Clara should have turned away, but she didn't. Instead, she held his gaze and drank. The water was crisp, but the moment it passed her lips, she felt the heat of him, felt it spread through her as if he had poured himself into the stream, seeping into her bloodstream, into her breath. Her heart pounded, a frantic counter-rhythm to the slow, deliberate rise and fall of his chest.

It was becoming more and more of an effort to snap out of the dream when he was there.

As Clara's days in the mill wore on, the lines between reality and memory blurred, and she began to wonder if the past she so desperately sought was more than just a dream. Her grandmother bade her beware the spectres of want that would try to consume her and lead her to destruction, just as the mills consumed the land and the people who worked them.

Clara ignored her grandmother's warnings., and over that summer and autumn Clara's understanding of the world slipped into the surreal. In the mill yard, where the bleakness of everyday life made folk bow their heads and wipe grime and soot from dull eyes, she drifted through the crowds clutching the hand of her invisible, sensually charged companion. The other mill workers jeered at her, mocking her, calling her "the girl with the invisible fancy man", or telling each other to stay away for she was clearly touched. To Clara, their words were merely extensions of the white noise that came from the rattling machines on the mill landings. The world around her lost its solidity, and she felt as though she had no real place in it. All she wanted was her idealised teenage dream of coupling.

As the year turned towards winter Clara's dreams took a new turn. She found herself aboard an ancient caravel, its sails whispering in the wind as it drifted silently through a sea of mirrors. She sailed alone, but in each mirror she saw the reflection of her feral beau. By contract, the sky above was fractured, like a broken window, and in every piece of jagged glass, Clara saw herself in vibrant colours. Her reflection smiled broadly, beckoning to her to come and live the life she had always wanted, but whenever Clara reached out, her fingers met only cold air, and the images dissolved, slipping away like smoke on the breeze, leaving her grasping at nothing, all the while feeling a desperate need for physical contact.

And then his voice called to her, soft, lilting, and rich with promise. It unfurled from the landscape like silk, threading through the air, brushing against her skin with a warmth that sent a slow shiver down her spine. There was something hungry in it, something that suffused her bones and set them aching. The melody was sweet, teasing, and laced with birdsong and the deep, rolling hum of contented cattle. Beneath it all, there was a longing that mirrored her own.

She chased him, breathless, her body throbbing with the need to find him. The strangely mirrored sea stretched before her, shimmering and endless, its surface shifting under her feet as she ran across the waves. His voice was everywhere, wrapping around her, stroking along the nape of her neck, slipping into the hollows of her back, coaxing her forward.

He always seemed to be just out of reach, a whisper against her ear that vanished the moment she turned. The very act of chasing him pushed him further away, taunting, tempting, a fleeting touch that left her aching when it was gone. Her skin burned with his touch, and her lips tingled with the promise of a kiss that never landed.

And then, like every night before, she awoke. Alone. Sitting at the edge of her cot, the dark pressing in around her, her pulse still elevated from a dream that refused to let her go. She swallowed hard, her fingers curling against the thin fabric of her shift, staring at the sleeping girls in the other dormitory cots. When she woke from the dream Clara felt empty.

Clara began to question her waking sanity. The sea of mirrors was deceptive, each shard a reflection of a life that might have been. Was she chasing illusions, or was the voice her only hope of escaping the emptiness that consumed her waking hours? Clara's life was a dreary cycle, but it wasn't the repetition that wore her down. She understood why her mother and father had come into the town from the countryside. What ate away at Clara's health was the feeling that she was becoming invisible, that she was turning into one of the industrial monolith's great engines. The daily rhythm of the mill stripped away her sense of self, reducing her to being just another tooth on a random cog in the great, unknowable machine. As her body performed the monotonous tasks required of her to earn a wage, so her mind was somewhere else, wandering through the endless libidinous arcadia of her imagination.

After another long day of relentless work as a Piecer, Clara trudged through the muddy streets alone as she went to visit her parents in their room in a shared cottage. She could almost feel herself splitting in two as she walked on. One part of her left footprints in the soot and grime, while the other part of her, the part that mattered, followed the voice that she alone could hear, heading once again into that detached dream world where the wind didn't smell of coal and the stars shone brightly and clearly, undimmed by the smoke of the mill's steam engines.

The compulsion that she felt to merge with the mirage world grew stronger with each passing day. At first, that calling had been a comfort, a small rebellion, even, against the anonymity and the drudgery in her life. Now, though, the craving was so much more than that. The landscape drew her ever inwards. His voice, his toned, tanned body, and the feral look in his eyes consumed her. She no longer heard the noise of the machines or the shouts of the foremen. Her senses were dulled to the real world, while the world of the mirage, the world of dreams, sinews, and shadows, grew sharper and more vivid.

Clara didn't reach her parents' home that evening. Instead she wandered off the path, finding a quiet alleyway where she could sit in relative peace beneath a wooden stair that lead to a first floor walkway into one of the slums. As she sat there in her rags, Clara could feel herself fading from the eyes of those around her. She lost track of time, finding herself alone outside the mill dormitory some hours later. She had no recollection of how she had spent those missing hours, other than a sense that birds had sung her a lullaby while she slept in the arms of her imaginary lover on green grass in a sunlit open field.

After this event, the girls at the mill stopped talking to her, as though they too sensed her slipping away. Even the matron in the dormitory, usually sharp-tongued and watchful, no longer scolded her for coming in late or for skipping meals. Without actually disappearing, Clara was becoming socially invisible, and mentally she felt as if she were a ghost in her own body, obeying the laws of physics by carrying out the motion of existence like an automaton, while her soul followed the emotive voice that only she could hear.

The machines droned on and on, soot fell like rain, and the town blackened and choked. Clara rose above it all. She embraced the world that she had crafted in her mind. She no longer fought against the feeling of being lost, accepting that her physical self was, indeed, marooned in a world of fire and iron. The mirage was her reality, pulling her deeper and deeper into the shadows of her own thoughts, until she was little more than a whisper, a ghost of the girl who would live and die in the soot-stained world of the mill.

And die she did. Not long after that evening under the stairs, Clara was once again lost in her lover's illusory embrace as she entered the mill, a relentless symphony of whirring gears, hissing steam, and clattering looms breaking over her head. She was nearly fifteen, small for her age and as thin as a wisp, and nimble as she danced around the inner spaces of the ever-hungry machines to repair broken threads on the spinning frames. She wore her hair in a thick braid tucked carefully beneath her bonnet, but loose tendrils of hair often slipped free in the humid, lint-filled air.

That morning, the floor was slick with grease, the smell acrid and sharp, as she moved between the monstrous mechanisms. Clara leaned forward absent-mindedly as she spotted a broken thread on one of the spinners. A piercing shriek lanced through the usual clatter and hiss of the mill as Clara's foot slipped on the greasy floor. For one heart-stopping moment, her arms windmilled, and she caught the eye of Mary, the girl at the loom beside her, who had a hand over her mouth, wide-eyed, and helpless to intervene. Clara's braid flew free of her bonnet and was caught by one of the machine's swiftly rotating shafts.

The machine yanked her braid, pulling her head closer to the mechanism. Her hands scrabbled uselessly at the machine's unyielding teeth, fingers slipping on the slick metal as the loom dragged her in with a mechanical hunger. By now her fading screams were being swallowed by the mill's relentless din. Clara's final moments in this hard reality were barely audible above the churning of the steam engine, lost among the hisses and clangs that masked her agony. The machine claimed her quickly, pulling her deeper into the mechanism until her bones cracked. By the time the overseer reached her, her lifeless body lay shattered within the spinner's maw, a crimson smear bearing silent testament to a life snuffed out in seconds.

Clara watched that world from her seat on the grassy banks of a country stream. Greatly to Clara's relief, no one in the mill town, no one at the factory, and no one in the dormitory missed her. If she was ever referred to it was only ever as the "Loppy" or the "Loppy-Lou", but that was alright, for Clara lived on in the dream world to which she ascended. He was with her, his strong arm around her waist, pulling her into his embrace. She tilted her face to look up into his cat-like eyes and they kissed. He let out a guttural growl, as if he were a dog embarking on rough play with a litter-mate. Clara smiled and buried her forehead in his muscled chest.

It was only her grandmother who lit a candle for Clara's lost soul come *The Commemoration of All the Faithful Departed* each November.

The song behind the story: *"Mirage" by Ladytron is a track from their 2011 album Gravity The Seducer. The album marked a more ethereal and melodic turn in the band's sound, blending their signature synth-pop and dream-pop influences with a more abstract and atmospheric style. "Mirage," in particular, is reflective of this shift, characterised by its dreamy, hypnotic rhythms and haunting melodies. The song evokes a sense of longing and mystery, fitting within the broader themes of the album which often touch on surrealism and seductive, otherworldly experiences.*

If, like me, you enjoy synth-driven, atmospheric music, this song and album are nothing short of brilliant. Given this project I'd wanted to try and incorporate something from the band here, and finally found my inspiration for one of the later tales in the collection.

Album: *Gravity The Seducer*

Artist: *Ladytron*

Year: *2011*

Composer(s): *Daniel Hunt, Mira Aroyo, Reuben Wu, and Helen Marnie*

Record Label: *Rykodisc*

Black Threads

Sam barely registered the bell as she sat in class amongst a sea of blue-lit screens in a lecture theatre at Leeds Trinity, where she was a day student. Her fingers moved with mechanical precision over her phone. The lecture theatre had become a quiet battlefield for freshers, but not directly between students and lecturers, although such conflict was not that unusual. Today, though, the world seemed to be consumed by the war between fleeting moments of real human interaction and the all-consuming vortex of doomscrolling.

Sam's pupils widened as the phone's brightness automatically adjusted to the light streaming in through the theatre windows. Her feed was a relentless stream of negativity, where headline after headline declared some new catastrophe; *Trump wins Big...*, *Palestinian Chaos...*, *Storm Of The Century...*

Sam favoured the more salacious feeds and she consumed a regular diet of stories centred around what she called *The Cabal*, along with some bits of global warming hyperbole, but mostly tales of celebrity debauchery. Mixed in with these themes were the fleeting distractions of viral videos and suggestive images, designed to be just titillating enough to hold her attention but never to really satisfy her curiosity.

Sam wasn't alone in her obsessive observation of the world through dubious lenses. Across the room, one or two other students were equally lost, their eyes glazed over, tethered to the tiny worlds held in their hands. The university lecturers delivered their courses as usual, but their words barely cut through the static. Even when they tried to draw students back to the wonders of academia, the lure of the screen was too strong for Sam. Some teachers tried to integrate their work with the digital paradigm, using multimedia presentations, YouTube videos, and gamified quizzes to engage their students, but it wasn't enough. Why would anyone focus on classwork when global conspiracies and the latest fashion scandal were just a thumb's swipe away?

Sam scrolled past an article about another climate disaster, her conscience briefly twinging, but the feeling evaporated as quickly as it came. She knew, on some level, that the constant stream of calamity was warping her view of the world, but she couldn't look away. Each new alert felt like a small dopamine hit, a mix of anxiety and excitement keeping her hooked. There were moments when Sam knew that she should take more care about her future. Her first year prelims were just around the corner, after all, but what was the point? The real world felt so distant, and her future was just a mixed bag of uncertainties. It was easier to lose herself in the infinite now of the internet, where each problem felt immediate, but was also far enough removed from Sam's reality to remain abstract.

As a notification from Instagram popped up, Sam's attention momentarily shifted. A perfect snapshot of someone else's life, filtered, edited, and impossibly glossy, briefly interrupted the cycle of dread. She envied these influencers, she envied the ease with which these people seemed to navigate a world that for her was confusing and frightening. For a split second, she considered messaging Lizzy, her old best friend from secondary school, who had just forwarded the Instagram reel, but the thought quickly faded, subsumed beneath another wave of news as her thumb slid up and down on the mobile's screen.

Suddenly, the lecturer's voice broke through, sharp and irritated. "Sam! Are you even listening?" Sam looked up, her mind struggling to reconnect with the real world. Around her, the other students still lost in their screens fidgeted nervously and tried to look attentive, while others shot her sympathetic looks, as if to say they, too, understood the constant temptation of doomscrolling. Others laughed. Sam blinked, and had to force herself to put the phone down. For a moment, the room seemed unbearably quiet. Soon enough, she knew, she'd return to the endless scroll, because how could she not? The virtual world was a siren, calling her back into its dark embrace, where she could at least pretend to be in control, but for now, she just nodded at the teacher, barely comprehending the section of the lesson that she'd just missed.

The sheer scale of information overload was overwhelming. A constant flood of news and comment, some of it based in reality, but much of it fabricated, was the ambrosia upon which Sam supped. She wasn't just reading about the explosion at a factory or any of the other inexplicable tragedies that seemed to unfold daily. She was consuming them so that their messages infused her subconscious mind, turning every headline into a personal crisis. Each swipe of her thumb pulled her deeper into a whirlpool of fear and uncertainty.

But even as her anxiety peaked, she found that she couldn't stop scrolling. The endless stream offered no resolution, and no escape from the nagging sense that something worse was always just beyond the next refresh. Sam tried to rationalise it. If she stayed informed, maybe she could be prepared for something, she told herself. The issue was that each story morphed into another disaster, and another thread connecting shadowy plots that she couldn't untangle. The open question was always the same - be ready for what exactly?

Mrs. Harper was one of the last lecturers who even bothered to fight the tide of digital distraction. Every day, she faced rows of students who were physically present but mentally checked out, their eyes glazed over from hours spent doomscrolling. Sam was one of them, her focus compromised by the onslaught of social feeds, peer pressure and unholy conspiracies that crowded her mind. The nuances of Piers Plowman were being revealed by Mrs. Harper in a foreign language as far as Sam was concerned today.

By the lunch time break Sam's mind was wrapped in a cycle of superficial friendship likes and apocalyptic dread? Sam wasn't just distracted; she was lost in a world where everything was a crisis. The algorithm knew what it was doing, feeding her more of what kept her engaged, more of what made her believe that doom was always lurking just over the horizon. And yet, despite all of the isolation that the digital world caused, Sam felt connected in a strange way. The conspiracy threads, the disaster updates weren't just headlining her days anymore. They were part of a larger narrative, a twisted sense of belonging in a world that felt so out of control. Sam wasn't just scrolling; she was searching for meaning in a sea of chaos.

The ruling classes trickle piss from champagne glasses...

Sam sat back in her chair in the university's refectory, her phone casting a dim glow on her face as she stared at the weird headline. The world outside her screen was fading, overtaken by a steady stream of banners and conspiracies. She couldn't look away, even though everything felt so hopeless and so cynical. The news, the protests, the scandals, each piece of information left her more disconnected from the world.

As disconnected as she might be, Sam prone to small acts of individual rebellion. The scrolling drug distracted her from that rebellion by fuelling her sense of hopelessness. She knew, for example, that the ruling elites would continue their games, their "trickle-down" approaches always seeming more like a slow drip-feed of lies. They drank champagne, untouched by the chaos below, while people like her were drowning in their detritus. What difference did her small actions make? Her soon to be exercised first vote, her voice, her opinion? It all seemed so irrelevant, swallowed by the machinery of a society that was grinding away day after day, indifferent to the individual potential of people like her.

But she wasn't the only one stuck in this endless loop. Many of her fellow students were waking up to the reality of it too. Impotent rebellion echoed through their chat threads. A few of her peers shared clips of protests, showing signs of resistance that sometimes made Sam feel momentarily alive, and even hopeful, but as quickly as those sparks appeared, they were snuffed out by the flood of nihilism that followed. Still, Sam scrolled, hypnotised by the absurdities mixed in with the chaos; conspiracies, bizarre distractions, and jokes that trivialised the seriousness of everything around her.

Somewhere between the doom and absurdity, she had become addicted to it all. The noise was everywhere, loud and numbing, filling every space in her. For all her cynicism, though, something in her still clung to those brief flashes of hope. Maybe, just maybe, things could be different.

Sam stared blankly at her feed, her fingers moving more out of habit than interest. She sent a half-hearted message to a friend, the words dripping with the ironic hopelessness of their generation; *We don't waste time with love anymore*. It wasn't just a joke or an edgy meme; it had become an unspoken truth among them. In a world where banality filled every corner of their media, love, hope, and optimism felt like relics of a past that no longer applied to them.

Yet, as Sam's eyes glossed over the latest string of doom-laden posts, something deep within her refused to fully surrender. Beneath the numbing repetition of bad news and snarky responses, that tiny flicker of rebellion remained. Sam kindled a quiet feeling that the world didn't have to be this way. That spark was fragile and barely noticeable most days, but it was there. Maybe, just maybe, things could change. Maybe love and hope weren't as outdated as everyone believed. Maybe the doomscroll wasn't endless. She felt that if she could just stop scrolling for long enough, she might see a way out, but that was the hardest part, knowing when and how to stop.

Mrs. Harper stood in a small queue at the serving counter as she prepared to pay for her lunch, her eyes scanning the faces of students half-absorbed in their screens. She sighed, remembering her grandmother's advice, a saying whispered in the darkest times; "Take something for the pain, but don't let it consume you. Don't let the worst be all you see."

The phrase came out softly, almost a prayer to herself. She wasn't even sure anyone heard her, until Sam looked up from her phone. The words hung in the air between them, sticking to Sam like a thread of light in the haze of doomscrolling. Sam blinked, hesitating for a brief second, her thumb frozen above her screen. A notification brought her attention back, another angry headline demanding her attention, another algorithm-crafted dose of despair. Sam's face flushed, burning with a sudden clarity. She felt as if the ground beneath her feet had opened up, revealing the truth she had been avoiding, that she was trapped in a cycle of her own making.

Panic and anger swirled together, rising in her chest, threatening to break her open. She couldn't stay here. She had to get away. Sam shot up out of her seat. She didn't waste a second. She was out of the door before Mrs. Harper could say 'boo' to a goose, practically running to the bathroom. The moment the bathroom door closed behind her, she slumped against the cool tiled wall by a row of sinks, trying to breathe, but the dread cultivated by months of endless scrolling had finally consumed her.

"What am I doing?" she whispered to herself, her voice shaky, her hands gripping the phone like it was a bomb set to go off. Every instinct told her to keep scrolling, to check for updates, to numb herself again with the familiar rhythm of bad news and worse predictions.

Sam rushed into the nearest stall, slammed the toilet seat up, and before she could second-guess herself, dropped her phone into the water. It made a small splash, then sank to the bottom of the bowl, the screen still glowing faintly beneath the surface in the U-bend. She watched the phone bob there, mocking her.

The water seemed to hold the phone in place, as though offering her one last chance to change her mind. Sam stood frozen, her breath coming in short gasps. Part of her wanted to reach down and pull her mobile back out, to check for new notifications. What if something important happened? Her fingers twitched at the thought, her hand hovering just above the water. She could almost feel the cold metal of the phone as she imagined retrieving it.

But then she stood and turned round, catching her reflection in the mirror above the sink outside of the stall. Her face was pale and her eyes were wide with both fear and revelation. This wasn't her, she realised. The person consumed by anxiety and dread, this person paralyzed by an endless stream of catastrophe, wasn't her, wasn't the real Sam. And yet, here she was, about to let the algorithms consume her. She stepped away from the stall, and took a deep breath. Letting go of the phone, letting go of the fear, was the only choice that made sense now. She didn't need to chase after the noise. She had to take control of her own narrative, her own sense of self, before it was completely taken from her.

As Sam stepped out of the bathroom, a strange sense of calm settled over her, like the hush after a storm. The phone, her constant tormentor, was gone, submerged beneath stagnant water, its screen now dark, its endless stream of horror and outrage silenced. For the first time in months, she felt light and unburdened, like she had wrestled something monstrous out of her own hands and cast it away.

But that peace lasted only until she heard her mother's voice that evening. Sam was moody but engaged, and, for a surprising change, not glued to her mobile.

"Where's your phone, Sam?"

The question struck her like a whip chord, her mother's tone already edged with suspicion. Sam hesitated, her heart kicking against her ribs. She could lie, should lie, but the drama of the act was too fresh, too raw, and when she opened her mouth, the truth spilled out.

"I dropped it in the toilet."

A moment of silence followed.

Then her mother laughed, a sharp, disbelieving sound that quickly curdled into something else. "You...you what?"

Her father's chair scraped against the linoleum as he stood, slow and deliberate. "Sam," he said, his voice low with warning, "tell me you fished it out."

She shook her head. "It's ruined. It's gone."

Her mother's face twisted, a dozen emotions fighting for space, shock, fury, despair. "Do you have any idea what that phone costs us? We've still got eighteen month on the bloody contract! And you...you just dropped it?"

Sam had braced herself for this, but the reality of their anger was suffocating. Her father ran a hand over his face, exhaling sharply. "Jesus Christ, Sam. You couldn't just turn it off?"

She wanted to explain, to make them understand that she had tried, that she had spent nights deleting apps only to redownload them in moments of weakness, that she had turned off notifications and sworn she'd use it less, only to find herself back in the spiral. That doomscrolling wasn't a habit, it was an addiction, one that gnawed at her in the quiet moments, dragging her back into the never-ending churn of bad news and worse news, of disasters, tragedies, outrage, and hopelessness. But they wouldn't understand. Not really.

Her mother rubbed her temples. "Well, we'll have to tell the phone people that it's lost and get a replacement. But why, Sam?"

Standing in the full glare of their frustration and anger, Sam felt the first prickle of unease. The phone was gone, yes, but so was her lifeline. No texts. No group chats. No endless stream of memes, gossip, or last-minute invites. No way to check if anyone even noticed she was missing. What if she got into trouble and needed help? She was cut off. The thought hit harder than she expected.

There would be no more scrolling through posts to see if she was mentioned, no firestorm of reactions to the latest drama, no way to know if plans were shifting, evolving, happening without her. A slow, creeping realization settled in. She was now outside of everything. Would her friends forget her? Would her absence even register? For months, the phone had been a digital prison, shackling her to every terrible thing happening in the world, but now, without it, an entirely new fear settled in her chest. What if she had just erased herself?

It would take a couple of days to get into town and sort out a replacement. In the meantime the temporary pains of withdrawal must come. The restless fingers reaching for something that wasn't there. The phantom buzz of notifications that no longer existed. The gnawing unease of not knowing anything. For the first time, Sam understood that she had made a mistake. Not because she missed the doomscrolling, but because she wasn't sure she knew who she was without it.

The song behind the story: *"Doomscroller" by Metric is a track from their 2022 album Formentera. The song tackles the overwhelming nature of modern digital life, particularly focusing on the anxiety and bleakness that comes from obsessively scrolling through negative news or social media, hence the term "doomscrolling."*

I've followed Metric for years, but I was surprised when I first heard this song. I love its eerie, atmospheric opening that then moves into a more driving, dynamic sound later on. It's also quite long at around 10 minutes. Anyway, we're all aware of the tendency to use soundbites and to scroll-read, so I wanted to do something with that.

Album: *Formentera*

Artist: *Metric*

Year: *2022*

Composer(s): *Emily Haines, James Shaw, Joshua Winstead & Joules Scott-Key*

Record Label: *MMI/Glassnote Records*

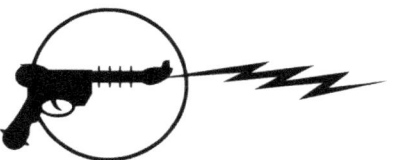

Untethered

In the brilliant and blinding light of Procyon A, the *Existentially Confused* an adapted Dirigiste corvette, renamed by its current captain in a fit of pique many years previously, drifted through the void like *The Flying Dutchman*, a weightless phantom in a binary star system devoid of planets or life. Canis Minor was a stellar wasteland, a void where distance and time could be overwhelming. The system was an endless stretch of cold nothingness broken only by the powerful luminescence of Procyon A, and the distant, eerie glow of its companion star, Procyon B. The crew worked in the artificial twilight created by the ship's controls and the starlight that reached the viewports, their faces etched with boredom and disillusionment.

Captain Mara Ness sat in the command chair, her arthritic hands resting limply on the controls as her gaze took in the worn fabric of her world. The crew were restless. She had ordered the viewport shades down to combat the intense glare of the dual stars, but the oppressive brightness from Procyon A still seeped into the flight deck, casting long, stark shadows across control stations and people alike.

Once upon a time, in those moments when she almost put Dex out of her mind, Mara had thrived on the chaos of her chosen

261

profession. She lived for the thrill of outmanoeuvring the authorities, of plundering treasure ships, and making her name feared amongst insurers and traders throughout human occupied space, but now, this way of living felt tired and aimless. The crew wanted coin, of course, but Mara found little excitement in the hunt for treasure. She was sure that her lack of enthusiasm showed. It was as if the vast emptiness of space had seeped into her soul, leaving her as barren and cold as the void outside. Where once, in spite of the ravages of time, she felt vital and driven, since gaining revenge on her one-time lover, she now felt every one of her seventy-odd years in her bones. Dex was dead, and his death should have been the catalyst for her transformation. For years, she had chased revenge, her heart burning with the fury of it. She'd hunted the man down and made him pay, and that old score, his betrayal, was settled. And in that final act she felt... nothing at all. There was no catharsis for her, no relief, just the gravitational pull of a black hole where her rage had once been, consuming every other emotion. Mara's thoughts were full of regret now, regret based on the waste of a life spent chasing a ghost.

Her crew knew that she was troubled and unfocused too. They could feel that sense of fatigue and disappointment in their captain. Mara was still an effective leader, but somehow the spark had gone. She went through the motions, issuing orders and maintaining the ship with mechanical precision, but they could feel that Mara had lost purpose. They followed her still, out of a mixture of residual loyalty and inertia, but that loss of heart was beginning to show itself in dissent and frustration. The once-bustling camaraderie of the crew of the *Existentially Confused* had grown dull, their once-exhilarating life reduced to the grim slog of survival.

Mara's hand gripped the edge of the command console. She couldn't tell if it was the unforgiving light of the Procyons that made her feel so exposed and so lost, or if it was something deeper. She'd spent so long plotting revenge and fighting for survival, that she no longer remembered what it felt like to want anything else. The stars outside blazed on, caring nothing for her struggles, the binary system a stark reminder of her own duality. Mara sighed, collecting sideways glances from the crew members on the bridge. Mara Ness, the pirate captain whose name once sparked fear in the hearts of freighter crews, was tired, tired of it all.

The crew of the *Existentially Confused* had just pulled off a raid that would once have set their hearts racing. There was always good coin to be made by liberating a company ore ship loaded with rare metals and fuel, but for Mara, the thrill was gone. The cargo that they now carried in the corvette's ample hold held no real meaning for her anymore. When the crew loaded the spoils, she stared at the goods in the ship's hold with vacant eyes, her mind drifting far from the immediate clamour of celebration that echoed through the ship's narrow corridors. Her heart, once fierce with ambition, now felt like a dead star, collapsed in on itself, dense and cold.

Mara's ability to command was, on the surface, as sharp as ever, but her heart just wasn't in it these days. In the confined spaces aboard ship, where the air was recycled over and over for months, that sense of detachment was becoming a tangible force. The air felt thin, as though Mara's disillusionment had seeped into the life support system, leaving everyone aboard gasping for good, clean air. The veterans aboard the *Existentially Confused,* grizzled and battle-hardened figures, were a chilling sight, their faces scarred and their manners brutalised by years of combat and survival. These old hands got on with their jobs, paying little attention to the conflict brewing in their captain's soul. Their eyes, once sharp with the fire of rebellion, were now as tired and dull as their erstwhile leader's, as if they had surrendered their dreams to the endless slog of piracy long ago. For these men and women life was simply what it was. They followed orders with a blind and mechanical precision that Mara was growing to despise. They were the mirror image of her own evolution. There was no spark left in them other than the barest ember needed to keep them breathing.

Mara looked at her crew, her loyal band of conspirators, and felt the strangest urge to scream. As she sat at the helm she wanted to know why none of them questioned the point of it all. They carved out a life in the void, taking ships almost at will, seizing wealth, and dancing with death, yet what had it all amounted to? The emptiness gnawed at her as insatiably as a black hole devours matter and light. She realised, in a way that chilled her to her bones, that the revenge she once lived for was a cold and debilitating gift, and nothing now filled the space where her soul had once burned. Yet the *Existentially Confused* flew on, a spirit ship adrift in the blackness of the stars, led by a captain who was beginning to realise that she was old and fatigued and losing relevance. As she looked at the crew members on the bridge she kept wondering if they themselves realised that they were too broken to know that they had already lost their way.

Mara continued to sit in the dim glow of the *Existentially Confused's* bridge, her reflection staring back at her from a darkened tactical screen on the command console. The years hadn't been kind. Her long hair, once a fiery symbol of defiance, was uniformly silver, framing a face that was etched with the deep lines of battles fought and lives lost. She felt ground down and weathered. Her sense of fatigue was underpinned by the relentless and unforgiving whine of the ship's systems and engines. She was no longer the Mara Ness of old. Now she was just an aging relic drifting in the void.

Mara turned her gaze to the tactical and navigation dashboards, watching the light of distant stars reflected on their maps. She whispered to herself, the words barely audible over the low hum of the ship's engines. "Don't need to waste time with love." It had become something of a hymn, one she'd repeated too many times to believe in anymore. In the unforgiving void of space, love was weakness. Attachments slowed you down and got you killed. In their line of work, death was an invisible assassin waiting to strike from any direction.

As the *Existentially Confused* glided silently through the cold expanse of space, bound for the heavily defended trade routes in Canis Major, Captain Mara Ness stared out at the star-speckled void, her face hardened into the unyielding mask that she had worn for so long. Mara's thoughts wandered back to the roots of her journey. As a child, she lived in a house filled with quiet desperation. She remembered her father always having a bottle to hand. He never hit her but he also never gave her the warmth or guidance she craved. Her mother was frail and slowly wasting away, her illness a permanent fixture in Mara's childhood. It was from these beginnings that Mara learned to survive, and to adapt to whatever life threw at her.

Her childhood taught her one valuable lesson; the hand you were dealt was rarely fair, but you had to play it.

That lesson became a compass setting for her life. Her mother's illness and those the long days and nights watching her fade, was why she hitched her hopes to Dex. He was an older man, almost a father figure, a former researcher at her college, and he talked about breaking the law and breakthroughs in human longevity and well-being. Mara saw in him the silver bullet that would save her mother, and so she was single-minded in her pursuit of the man, but Dex took advantage of her enthusiasms and her motivations. He loved her and then he left her, disappearing just as her mother died, abandoning Mara and her dreams as swiftly as he had come into her life. Their work was illegal, and he had been tipped off that the authorities were inbound. He ran, leaving Mara to take all of the consequences when she was at her most vulnerable.

For Mara, that combination of events created a sense of betrayal so deep that it shaped her very core. Her path darkened, and over the years, she hardened into a creature driven by revenge. It took her decades to track Dex down across the vast reaches of navigable human space. By the time she found him and took her vengeance, she wasn't even sure that it was worth it. Killing him hadn't brought her mother back. It hadn't healed the scar left by her loss of both mother and lover, and now, with Dex dead, Mara felt emptier than ever before.

"We don't waste time with love," she muttered under her breath, repeating the hymn that she had adopted to keep herself sane, but even as she said it, she knew that the words were meaningless.

*

Time passed with its usual mixture of routine and boredom until the *Existentially Confused* finally approached its next target. Tension rippled through the corridors of the ship like a silent weather front. The familiar hum of the engines seemed to falter, as if even the ship itself sensed something was off. Then, as they manoeuvred the ship to the leeward side of Nyan to wait for an expected convoy, the proximity alarm cut through the quiet confines of the ship. Red lights bathed the control decks and dashboards as the proximity alert flared on every screen. Mara's heart sank as she realised that this wouldn't be a routine hit. The convoy was ready for them.

"Battle stations!" she barked, her voice steady but cold. The crew, both seasoned and green alike, rushed to their posts, eyes wide in a natural combination of fear and determination. The sounds of boots clanging on the metal grill floor echoed in the tight spaces on the bridge. A nervous laugh escaped one of the younger crew members, barely audible over the blaring alarms. "Call the cops," he muttered, the wavering notes in his voice betraying his own doubt. There were no cops. There were no safety nets out here. There were just pirates, mercenaries, and company thugs.

Mara's hands danced over the control panel with the precision of a seasoned pilot, muscle memory guiding her movements as if she were playing some deadly symphony. The interfaces pulsed under her fingertips, cool and sterile, the soft CPU hum a stark contrast to the chaos outside.

She barely felt the familiar rush of pre-battle adrenaline anymore. Once, she had lived for the sharp bite of anticipation, the thrill of engagement, and the way time seemed to stretch and contract at will. But now, the feeling was dulled and hollow. Like a worn blade, the edge of her excitement had been ground down over too many skirmishes, too many impossible fights.

A hiss of hydraulics filled the bridge as the ship's weapons systems powered up, the corvette's laser batteries shifting into firing position. The targeting display painted the blackness of space with artificial overlays, velocity vectors, lock confirmations, and firing solutions. The cold numbers felt disconnected from the violence they represented.

The first shot ripped through the dark, a concentrated beam of white-hot fury lancing across the void. Another followed, then another. Automated targeting relays calculated optimal trajectories, locking onto enemy hulls with mechanical precision. Each impact bloomed into bursts of fire and light, momentary stars in the vast nothingness. Had the situation been different, had this not been a fight for survival, Mara might have thought it looked almost... beautiful.

The tactical screen flickered, updating enemy positions in real time. Company Prowlers, fast, deadly, and engineered for pursuit, filled the display with red markers, their signatures blinking like hungry predators circling wounded prey. Mara's corvette was larger, more heavily armed, but they had speed and numbers on their side. She knew how this kind of engagement ended.

A flurry of incoming projectiles registered on the proximity sensors. The shields flared as they absorbed the impact, casting an eerie blue glow across the cockpit. The ship rattled with the force of the hit, and Mara clenched her jaw, steadying herself against the tremors.

"Shields at sixty percent!" someone shouted from the ops console behind her.

Mara barely turned her head. "Engage evasive pattern Delta," she ordered, her voice steady, clipped, controlled. The ship lurched as the manoeuvre took effect, thrusters burning in rapid, unpredictable bursts, making it harder for the enemy to land a direct hit.

Mara's fingers tightened around the controls. Every move, every counterattack, was a precarious gamble, a delicate balance between survival and annihilation. There was no room for mistakes, no time for hesitation. But even as she fought, even as she executed every order with mechanical efficiency, something gnawed at the edges of her mind. She had been here before. Too many times. And for the first time, she wasn't sure if she was fighting to survive... or if she was just waiting for the moment when survival no longer mattered.

The *Existentially Confused* groaned under the strain of another sharp manoeuvre, its overtaxed thrusters fighting against the inertial backlash. The ship twisted violently, evading another barrage of incoming fire, but the price for each manoeuvre was paid in structural integrity and crew stability. The smooth grace of spaceflight was gone, replaced by a sickening lurch that sent unsecured items clattering to the deck. Crew members instinctively gripped their consoles, their knuckles white, their bodies tensed against the next inevitable impact.

Mara barely noticed. Her body moved with the battle, adjusting trajectory, making tactical calls, engaging countermeasures, but her mind was somewhere else entirely. For over four decades, she had lived this life. She and her crew had fought these battles and made narrow escapes from both desperate skirmishes and fleeting victories. It had been thrilling once, intoxicating even. The way the ship hummed beneath her fingers, the split-second decisions that could mean survival or obliteration, the adrenaline-fueled dance between chaos and control. But that thrill had long since faded, and in its place, a deep, gnawing emptiness had taken root.

Was this it? Was this all there was?

She wasn't afraid of dying, not in the way most people were. She had made her peace with mortality a long time ago, in the frozen vacuum of unclaimed space, where the only certainty was that no one lived forever. But there had always been something to fight for. Always a reason to keep going. Now? She wasn't so sure.

Outside of the ship, the blackness of space was punctuated by searing bursts of laser fire, streaking past the hull in deadly arcs. The Prowlers swarmed like starving predators, relentless and efficient, their sleek, angular forms cutting through the dark with rapacious grace. Mara's corvette-class vessel now moved like a wounded animal, dodging, twisting, but inevitably slowing.

On the tactical display, shield integrity flickered like a failing heartbeat. Forty-three percent and dropping.

Not much longer now.

A direct impact rocked the ship, sending a deep vibration through the deck. Consoles flared red, system failures cascading across the interface. Mara clenched her jaw. It wasn't just the damage, it was the way the damage was stacking. Calculated. Precise. The Prowlers weren't just trying to kill them; they were systematically crippling them, disabling the ship in controlled increments. They wanted to capture her. Her stomach twisted at the thought.

"Shields at thirty-two percent!" someone called out, their voice tight with barely concealed panic.

Mara didn't answer. She stared at the display, watching the field of engagement shrink around them like closing jaws. The Prowlers were moving in for the kill. She glanced around the bridge, at the faces of her crew. Seasoned veterans, hardened fighters, survivors, but even they were beginning to understand. There was no way out this time. No last-minute escape. No clever manoeuvre. No hidden ace. Their reality had caught up with them.

Mara swallowed against the cold realization tightening in her chest. She was already lost. But her crew wasn't. Not yet.

She exhaled, slowly, letting the decision settle into her bones. If this was the end, she would not let them take her people.

Mara's fingers moved across the console, bypassing weapons and defensive systems. Instead, she accessed something deeper, something that had been locked away for moments just like this. A failsafe.

"Captain...?" Her XO, Varrick, eyed her warily as the ship's core systems began to reroute power in an unfamiliar pattern.

Mara didn't meet his gaze. Her voice, when she finally spoke, was quiet, resolute, absolute. "Get to the escape pods. All of you."

A silence fell over the bridge, brief, stunned, disbelieving.

"We're not abandoning you, Captain," Varrick said, his jaw tight.

Mara turned, her gaze steady, unflinching. "That's an order."

Outside, the Prowlers tightened their formation, weapons primed, their final approach beginning.

Mara activated the sequence. The ship's reactor began its countdown.

The crew hesitated for a moment. Then, one by one, they moved. Mara turned back to the viewscreen, watching as the enemy ships closed in, their predatory grace undeniable. If this was how it ended, so be it. But she would not let them win. Not today.

The last volley came. Mara sat motionless as a pulse of crimson light flared beyond the main viewport, carving through the black with surgical precision. She didn't flinch. She didn't reach for the controls. She simply leaned back in her chair, exhaling slowly, and folded her hands in her lap. There was no need to fight it anymore.

The *Existentially Confused* took the direct hit, shields gone, hull compromised, fate sealed. The ship groaned, metal screaming as it twisted apart. Mara felt the violent shudder beneath her, heard the klaxons blaring in futile desperation.

Then, the viewport shattered. The reinforced quartz-glass burst outward in a cascade of brilliant shards, devoured instantly by the vacuum. The force of decompression hit like a tidal wave, ripping consoles free, tearing apart the remains of what had once been her bridge. The ship buckled, ruptured, and split open like a dying beast.

And then the void.

The cold came first. A merciless, grasping thing that wrapped itself around her, clawing at her skin, pressing into her lungs. There was no pain, just a crushing stillness, a suffocating silence. The game was up. Revenge was served cold, and she was finally done.

Mara drifted, untethered, spiralling out into the endless black. The ship was gone. The crew was gone. The world that had defined her for over four decades had ceased to exist in a matter of seconds. But there was no fear. No panic. No desperate thrashing. Instead, there was clarity. Her life unfolded before her in an endless reel, raids and battles, victories and losses, blood spilled across a hundred nameless stars. Yet, none of those things mattered in the end. What she felt most was the empty longing that had consumed her after Dex's death.

He had been the only thing that ever felt real. And when she lost him, the universe had become nothing more than a long, drawn-out epilogue to a story that had already ended.

Mara blinked. Her breath, what little remained of it, crystallised in the void. So this is it, she thought, strangely calm. This is how it ends. Untethered and alone. The blackness pressed in. The stars blurred.

As the bridge disintegrated behind her and her crew perished around her, she whispered one last thing into the cold embrace of eternity.

A name.

A memory.

A regret.

"Oh, Dex, my darling De…"

The song behind the story: *"Call the Police" by LCD Soundsystem is a track from the band's 2017 album American Dream. James Murphy, the band's frontman, channels a mix of personal frustration and broader political anxiety in the lyrics, addressing a sense of chaos in the world while also touching on feelings of disconnection and alienation, and it is, therefore, no surprise that it's a song that speaks to my own sensitivities.*

Some listeners interpret the song as a commentary on the rise of populism, political unrest, or even gentrification, though Murphy's lyrics often leave room for interpretation, allowing the audience to apply their own meanings.

"Call the Police" received critical acclaim, with many praising it as a powerful return for the band after a hiatus. It was released alongside "American Dream," a slower, more introspective song, showcasing the band's ability to balance both intense, high-energy tracks and more reflective, emotional ones.

Album: *American Dream*

Artist: *LCD Soundsystem*

Year: *2017*

Composer(s): *James Murphy*

Record Label: *Columbia Records*

The Signet Ring

In his mind's eye he could still see his father's face in vivid detail, a familiar landscape marked with deep valleys that told stories of joy, sorrow, resilience, and of wisdom. They had their troubled moments, father and son, but there was always comfort in that face, and yet now it appeared to him only in memory and old black and white photographs, dancing in the breeze of recollection like a soft candle flame. In the few weeks since his father's passing, it felt as though each day just blurred into the next, the world filled with a strange emptiness, as if he was walking through a thick London pea-souper fog.

At the old flat that he and his sister had to clear out before it was sold, his father's empty chair in front of the television seemed to take on a life of its own, a silent testament to the absence that now defined the days. The chair had so often been the backdrop to casual conversations, shared football matches watched on the television, and his father's steady but declining presence. His father was now evermore, the word a paradox, the permanence of death intertwined with the endurance of memory. His father's essence lingered in small ways that were sometimes painful to encounter, from the gentle ticking of his watch on the dresser to the worn gold signet ring engraved with his father's initials now encircling his own finger. His father was gone but not forgotten, the signet ring a simple but profound reminder of the man he had loved and lost.

Each time he looked down at his hand to look at his father's softly glinting gold signet ring, he felt a warmth suffuse his thoughts and he smiled. The ring seemed to pulse with the strength and chattering dignity that his father carried through life. This simple band of yellow metal was a tangible piece of the man, and wearing it was like holding his father's hand.

Memories of the old man wrapped around him like an old, familiar coat, its woollen influence heavy on his shoulders, cradling him with an intimacy that felt reassuring. Just like his father this memorial coat was worn and frayed, but it was comfortable, and an old friend in times of pain. His father had been the steady hand guiding him through life's uncertainties, and although they might go weeks without catching up, the old man was always the person that he could call when he felt lost or unsure. Now, that source of comfort and strength was gone, leaving him unmoored and adrift.

The emptiness that his father's absence left behind was hard to deal with, but it was tempered by the memories of a life lived well. He found himself starting each day with hope, although the pace of change in his grief made him feel as though he were simply standing still. On his hardest days, he felt like the grey winter trees that lined the grass lawn outside his father's old flat. They stood solemn and tall in their respect for his loss. These trees seemed to endure only out of habit, their roots deep but fragile, holding on as if by memory alone.

He moved through these early days of mourning finding a strange resilience in the act of simply continuing on. At night, he would lie awake, staring at the ceiling, and wonder if his father was truly free and at peace somewhere,. His father often talked about Brentford and Chiswick, where he'd spent his youth, a place he'd long since left behind but always carried with him in stories of war and football and family lives.

Life is a progression, a linear process, and work he must. Now, whenever he travelled for work, he found himself looking at the passing landscape, imagining his father's memories drifting around him like the low clouds scudding across patchwork fields seen from an aircraft porthole. He would toss a thought out of the window of the plane, train or car that he was in, offering a small tribute to the man who had taught him to see the world in all its complexities. Sometimes, he would call his sister, and they would talk about the old man, sharing stories, laughter, and tears, but there was always the silent question, the one that hung like fog in the early morning; are you good and gone?

Grieving felt like being a lone tree planted beside a restless river. He felt weathered and autumnal, as though his tree persona's once-vibrant leaves were fading now, turning brown and rotting on the ground. No one wants such grief. He didn't want to feel rooted in this place, tired and worn by memories and unable to move forward. Every time he considered letting go he heard his father's words echo in his mind, "Nothing lasts forever, son. What matters is what you do with the time you have."

Then again, he had to chuckle softly as the memories flooded in. He was eleven years old again and attending Saturday morning training for his boys' soccer club. His father was an ex-professional player and a qualified coach, who helped out.

He remembered one particular foggy February morning when he was struggling in a practice match. His father told him one simple thing, a thing he still lived by; "The ball goes by or the man goes by, but never both..."

Those words still drove him on, but were tinged now with a black undertone. He wrestled with the meaning of things, questioning the faith and the effort that he was making for others, particularly his employer. Even the smallest of actions, a simple chore, a conversation, or a contemplative moment alone, they all seemed to spark reminders of his father, leaving him unable to separate himself from what was now a persistent longing. Moving forward seemed both necessary and impossible, a painful contradiction that left him feeling as if he were suspended, caught between honouring the memory of a man he loved and the quiet, relentless presence of grief that faded so slowly.

He began to wonder if his memories, treasured and carefully preserved, were somehow both a bridge to his father and a subtle way of letting him go. Each remembrance brought comfort and sadness intertwined. In a way, he questioned if remembering might ultimately be a form of forgetting, not in erasing the past but in allowing the loss to settle, making room for something lighter, and more bearable. He thought of the stories his father told, the subtle lessons tucked into everyday conversations, and how these small fragments might be enough to carry his father forward in his heart without letting the sorrow overshadow him.

There was no clear pathway through the fog of grief, no guidebook showing him how to live with both love and loss. His father shaped him and left a mark deeper than words could express. The amusing moments, the comforting cadence of his father's voice, and the simple warmth of his presence were, he finally concluded, enough to navigate by. He held them close, using the memories like stars to guide him across unfamiliar seas, knowing that someday soon he would emerge from the haze of grief into a place of clarity, where love and memory could coexist without the pain of loss pressing so heavily on his heart. He twisted the signet ring so that the bezel was upright. He traced his father's initials, knowing as he did so that in the end he would always carry a piece of his father with him, a solid and upright memory standing like a lone tree beside a fast flowing river after heavy winter rains.

The song behind the story: *The song "Evermore" by Grandaddy, part of their 2006 album Just Like The Fambly, reflects lead singer Jason Lytle's exploration of loss, memory, and grief. The lyrics and the overall album capture a feeling of melancholy intertwined with resilience.*

This is another rather personal story as the song was one I played a lot around the time of my father's death in 2022, and that is something I have wanted to write about for a while, but hadn't found the inspiration or the peace to do so until I put two and two together with this song.

Musically, "Evermore" fits seamlessly with the band's established sound, a blend of soft-rock and synth tones that create a feeling of both vastness and intimacy. Critics have described the track as one that captures the unique Grandaddy style, blending personal reflection with a haunting ambiance.

Album: *Just Like The Fambly*

Artist: *Grandaddy*

Year: *2006*

Composer(s): *Jason Lytle*

Record Label: *V2 Records (US) and Heavenly Recordings (UK)*

282

Tempest

A great storm ripped the night apart, tearing ragged holes in the seams that held the sky together. The Howling winds bent time itself, so that Annabel was flung into the far reaches of an uncharted sea. Emerald fire blazed across the heavens, lighting up waves that rose like foaming dragons, driving her little boat ever deeper into a world beyond the boundaries known to common men. Salt stung her skin, and her hands clutched the wood beneath her as her reflection vanished into the churning black waters below.

She closed her eyes, but even in her dreams, she was pitching and rolling and falling. In the darkness behind her eyelids, she was Annabel, and yet she was more than just Annabel. She glimpsed her dream self, and saw a figure wrapped in secrets, her body unfolding in splintered fragments. The true nature of the girl lay just beyond her reach, shadowed and veiled. "Who am I?" she wondered out loud, but her only answer was the howling wind and the pounding of waves under a fire-painted sky.

Her father's voice still haunted her. At their last meeting his voice had been low and cold and as commanding as the depths of the sea. "For your own good," he told her, the words binding her in iron shackles. This voyage was her rebellion, although even now, that whisper seemed to echo across the waves, creeping through the wind and spray to find her, twisting in her thoughts. She had sailed far, through storms and savage waters, always trying to find a path that would take her beyond the reach of his magic, but to no avail. His rule was forged from secrets and shadow. He wielded an iron hand, a hand driven by a mind as unforgiving as a glacier in winter. He professed only that he wanted to save Annabel, but she never really understood the depth of his fears for her. She only knew that those fears had cleaved her life in two, splitting her like an axe splits wood. One half of her was the girl she knew herself to be; the other half being something he had hidden deep within her, something veiled in mystery and locked away

As the storm abated, the boat ground to a halt, its wooden hull scraping against a shelving beach with a groan that sung of struggle in the empty night. Annabel climbed from the vessel, her boots crunching onto the island's rough, unwelcoming shore. The earth here was a strange and broken tapestry of brittle ice that crackled beneath her feet. Dark and twisted trees loomed like sentries in the mist at the inland edge of the beach. Shadows hung impenetrably in the air, swirling with intent, and the cold bit deep, sinking into her bones. She had known cold before, but nothing like this. The chill seemed to reach straight into her heart, as if this land knew her and judged her unworthy.

She walked further inland, the mist curling around her ankles, her breath rising in clouds that vanished into the night. With each step she felt that there was an unease here, a compulsion that seemed to twist around her like strands of wet hair, binding her arms and legs even as she tried to move forward. It was as if invisible fingers tugged at her, urging her to stay and face something just out of sight.

She looked down at her hands. They looked porcelain-pale in the ghostly starlight, and quite unfamiliar. Annabel held them steady in front of her face, but her pulse raced beneath and she could hear her heartbeat, a relentless drumbeat against the quiet night. Annabel was between worlds. She stood on the edge of change, between the girl who played on her father's shores and the woman who was as yet unformed. She could feel the contradiction within her as if it were a spring compressing, waiting for release.

She took another step, and the ground crackled, as if the island itself were shifting beneath her feet, and acknowledging her arrival. The fabric of the island pulsed beneath her, and as she walked the mist-laden paths and wove her way between gnarled trees, she felt a strange warmth growing within her, stirring her blood. She looked within and saw there a spark, quiet but undeniable, and she knew it to be her inheritance. Annabel didn't yet understand why there should be such a spark. She didn't know if this small inner flame was magic or memory, but the power from it coursed through her veins with a primal insistence, urging her to shed the bindings that had, until now, hidden its light from her eyes.

The winding paths of the island seemed to twist with her steps, leading her deeper into the forest. Trees towered overhead, their branches weaving together like the vaulted roof of an unnatural cathedral. The air grew stale under the thick canopy, and was charged with static that prickled her skin. She moved without direction, crossing mossy stones and tangled roots, until finally, the trees broke open, revealing a clearing that glistened beneath cold starlight. The sky stretched above her, vast and gleaming, and the emerald fire that danced across it called to her.

Annabel could feel the power of that inner flame rising within her, answering the call of the stars and the scarlet fire. The flame glowed red hot, a caged thing, fierce and yearning for freedom. It wanted to be named, and to be unleashed, as if it had waited lifetimes for this very moment. She took a step forward, her eyes fixed on the vast sky and felt the power within her swell. It was ancient and alive, and ready to tear through the silence and claim its voice.

Annabel stumbled on a tussock of long grass, and as her sky-bound reverie broke she saw him standing in the shadows where the forest met the clearing. He was a boy no older than herself. His skin held the deep flush of sunset reflected on calm waves, his face lit by the last rays of some imaginary summer's day. He looked as if he had stepped from the wild sea itself, and was untouched by the rules of men or Mother Nature. He moved with an easy grace, as though he'd never once felt the shackle of invisible chains or heard his name twisted by the demands of blood or necessity.

Annabel watched, spellbound, as he drew closer. She had the distinct feeling that he knew her. They were bound not by language but by a silent understanding, a connection running like an unseen current between them. She sensed that he had no name, nor any past history. This strange crimson boy had no story of his own; he was simply here, alive and unburdened, a creature born of this strange land. She felt the power in him, raw and untouched. He was an unformed spirit, and he stirred something deep within her. In that moment Annabel realised that the boy was a key and he would unlock the hidden layers of cold, hard magic that her father had tried to protect her with.

"Only a boy," she whispered, but the words conveyed none of the power and enchantment that the boy brought to bear on the world. He was only a boy, but he was also more than that. He was a mirror to the dark half of her own soul, the very part of her that her father had locked away in his tower of rules and secrets. In the boy, she glimpsed the life that she might have. As they stood together beneath the emerald sky, she knew she was ready to begin breaking free from the invisible chains her father had wrapped around her. Annabel was ready to reach for the power and the glory that he had denied her for all of these years.

Under the vast, star-strewn sky, Annabel felt something crack open inside her. As she and the boy drifted through the island's shadows, walking hand in hand, the memories that her father had buried began to uncoil. Images flickered in her mind, fleeting, half-formed scenes, her father's face, stern and remote; the iron-bound rules he had laid down around her like stones in a wall; the unspoken, unyielding force that had always pressed against her, caging her within herself.

She saw it now. Her father hadn't wanted her to be whole. He feared that she would embrace the strange power that lay dormant within her blood, for he knew it to be a dark force and untameable. So, he tried to keep her small, and to make her fit a diminished sense of self, to fit a diminished role; that of a daughter, obedient and still, a piece of porcelain to sit on a shelf because it was fragile.

On the wind Annabel thought that even here she could just make out her father's voice. Then it dawned on her that flee as far as she might, he was still working his magic. This island was no sanctuary; it was a fortress of his making, built to hide her from herself. Every thorny grove and every winding path was made by his unseen hand twisting the world to his will. This place was a prison that he disguised as protection. Those very thoughts, alongside the stimulus of the boy next to her, set in motion a chain reaction. She felt her power now, stirring in her veins, a power that her father couldn't wholly bind. With each step, the boy beside her grew sharper and more real. His presence seemed to breathe life into her own fractured memories, revealing truths she'd only felt in fragments before. She was not only Annabel; she was something fierce and wild, born under an emerald sky, a force neither the boy nor her father could contain any longer.

The island trembled around her as if it were a restless beast aware of her awakening. She could sense her father's presence lingering in the shadows, and woven into the very air she breathed, as if he were watching from afar, clutching the last fraying strings of his control. With every memory that surfaced, those strings frayed just a little more until the puppeteer held nothing in his hands but broken lines. She was breaking free of him, of his laws and of his fears.

Annabel's pulse quickened, her body vibrating with a power as deep as the ocean was wide. She looked at the boy and saw a reflection in him of her own untamed majesty. She was no longer bound to the fate that her father had cast for her. Here, beneath the stars, she was beginning again. Here, beneath the vast, glittering sky and the eerie gleam of emerald light,

Annabel could feel her father's grip dissolving like mist in sunlight. His commands, his rules, and the boundaries that he had drawn around her life grew weaker here. The cage bars were as flimsy as brittle paper. She could feel her heartbeat, fierce and full, pounding like the waves crashing against the shore. Her blood surged with each beat, hot and powerful, and totally unlike anything she'd known when living in her father's cold and stifling shadow.

She was Annabel, yes, but that name was only a beginning. A force beyond name and title, raw and wild, stirred within her. This was a strength that her father had spent a lifetime trying to cage. She felt herself stretching beyond her skin, her senses spilling into the island's air and earth, like a tree rooting into the soil. She could feel the crackling tension in the stones as she released an ancient energy that was laced in the tangled boughs of the trees. She was one with all things, untamed, and bound to nothing.

The stars above seemed to spin and shimmer, as though bearing witness. The emerald light brightened, casting a strange glow over her hands as she raised them to the sky, daring the night itself to recognise her. She was not just his child. She was a storm contained too long, a tempest breaking free, and with each breath, she felt her father's chains crumble to dust and scatter to the wind. She was Annabel, and she was alive.

Annabel and the crimson skinned boy danced like fire and shadow, spiralling together beneath a sky flecked with stars. Her laughter rang out, wild and unbound, and the boy joined in too offering a deeper echo that filled the air like the boom of a taut bass drum. Around them, the night seemed to pulse with life, the shadows twisting and bending as if drawn by gravity into their orbit. Her hair, wild and untamed, caught in the wind, a dark banner that trailed like a comet's tail. For the first time, Annabel let herself feel fully alive, and she could sense the boundaries that her father had forged around her beginning to dissolve, breaking like frost in the morning sun. Each step she took shattered another link in the invisible chain he had used to tether her to normality.

With each turn in the dance, she felt the power within her swell, rising from a place deeper than memory. She drew on the primal forces that lay deep under the island's surface, building her magic so that it flooded into her bones. Annabel drank the power of enchantment from a wellspring of strength hidden from her for too long. The earth beneath their feet pulsed with energy, and she felt her skin grow warm. The boy's eyes met hers, bright with shared wonder, and together they pushed against the walls that her father had spent his life constructing. With every breath, with every movement, they unravelled his work, releasing the power he had tried to cage inside her. The island shivered, stones loosening and trees bending as if bowing before the force now pouring from her,. Annabel was as wild and free as a river breaking its dam.

The wind whipped around them, carrying the scent of salt and distant storms, a herald of the reckoning stirring in Annabel's soul. She was no longer just a girl. She was no longer simply Annabel. She was the island's untamed spirit. She was the very force that her father had feared for so long. The ground trembled with a slow and deep rumble that spread out in waves, as though the earth itself was roaring in triumph.

In that moment, Annabel transcended base matter. She no longer needed flesh and bone or name. She felt herself dissolve into something boundless, and turn into a force as timeless as the sea and as fierce as the storm that had once cast her here on the island shore. She was a song sung by the island itself, a wild note carried on the wind, gathering strength as it soared toward the heavens. She was dawn breaking over dark water, scattering stars like embers across the sky. Annabel was a living flame in a world her father had tried to keep in shadow. Power pulsed through her, each beat of her heart spreading into the land and sky, rippling out like a tide. She was all things that defied control, or that refused to be silenced. She was the sand that slipped through the fingers of those who tried to claim ownership of things and people. She was the whisper that broke the quiet, and she was the beginning of every story ever told. As she became all things, so Annabel felt her father's hold on her finally shatter. The walls of the prison crumbled to dust as she embraced the truth of who and what she was.

Beside her, the boy watched, his eyes wide with awe, as her form began to blur and to shimmer in the dawn's first light. He reached out, his hand ghosting over hers, and she felt the bond between them burn with a fierce clarity. They were each part of the other, two halves of a mystery that had waited lifetimes to be whole. As the first rays of sunlight crested over the horizon, Annabel and the boy began to fade, their forms turning to mist, carried on the breeze that whispered her name through the trees and over the waves. They moved together, weaving into the morning air until they were no longer separate beings but an echo, a presence felt in the sigh of the wind and the rustle of leaves.

The island itself seemed to exhale, as though it had been waiting for this release as long as they had. The stones settled, the trees stilled, and the waves lapped gently against the shore, no longer restless but at peace. Annabel and the boy began their journey. The island was no longer a prison but a place reborn. It was a land with no masters, with only the lingering pulse of Annabel and the boy, woven into its very heart, eternal and free.

The song behind the story: *"Annabel" is a song by the British electronic music duo Goldfrapp, from their 2013 album Tales of Us. The track is known for its haunting and ethereal appeal.*

This is another one of those "blow me away" tracks. I streamed the album expecting something quite different to what actually played, and for me this was and remains my absolute favourite collection of songs from the duo.

For me, "Annabel" is the standout track on Tales of Us, I love the album's rich, atmospheric sound and its haunting, almost cinematic storytelling. The song just captivates me with its mysterious aura and evocative lyrics, making it an absolute favourite of mine..

Album: *Tales Of Us*

Artist: *Goldfrapp*

Year: *2013*

Composer(s): *Alison Goldfrapp & Will Gregory*

Record Label: *Mute Records*

Reaper

Eventually Rose would find a way to sleep. There was never any shortage of pills and needles. In her dream space, Rose often stood at the edge of a cliff, surrounded by a few squat and stubby candles, watching the waves crash against the jagged rocks below. The salted air whipped her hair around her face, but she didn't seem to notice. Everything around her was cold, dark, and grey. The sky was an endless slate of cloud, the sea a roaring reflection of that heavy stone sky, and the world beneath her feet felt as though it might crumble away at any moment. The candles defied waking logic, burning steadily in the swirling cliff-top winds. Their glow reminded Rose of the soft glow at sunset by the river when she was first with Jack.

As in life, so it was in the dream. Where Rose's heart should have been there was a gaping wound. Where once there was love, joy, and light, there was now a void in which the sounds of compassion echoed in the silence, reverberating through the empty chambers of her chest. She felt like a ghost haunting the remnants of her own life, an apparition lost in a world that continued to spin, indifferent to her suffering. Every morning she woke to the same dull ache of addiction and depression.

Once, laughter had come easily to her, a melody that danced around her like fireflies on a warm summer night, but now, the absence of it was a heavy cloak draped over her shoulders, suffocating and cold. The vibrant hues of her existence had faded into a monochrome palette of grey, as though the world had decided to strip away all colours. It was as if the seasons passed her by. While blossoms bloomed and leaves turned golden in the crisp autumn air, Rose felt trapped in a perpetual winter. Memories of warmth and connection felt like distant echoes, fading further into obscurity as the days drifted by.

In the dream Rose called out to the wind, shouting, "All our times have come." Her voice was barely audible over the roaring ocean. The words slipped from her lips like a malevolent prayer to be carried away by the relentless tide. She felt small and insignificant against the backdrop of crashing waves, as if the ocean itself had become a part of her sorrow. "…but now they're gone." Each syllable was heavy with her feelings of impotence in the face of an uncaring family, of the relentless cycling of Johns, and with her sense of loss. Her dream body shook as she screamed her anger into the vastness of the wide, grey sea.

The ocean roared back, a ferocious reminder of nature's indifference to her pain. She stared into the watery depths, searching for answers in the swirling currents, but all she found was a reflection of her own despair. The waves crashed violently against the rocks, each surge echoing the tumult within her. What she wouldn't give to feel the warmth of the sun on her skin again, or to taste the sweetness of life beyond this anguish. Yet, every time she thought she might break free, the tide would pull her back, dragging her down under the sea of memories that she couldn't escape.

Tears streamed down her face, mingling with the salt of the sea breeze. They were the only release she had, the only way to acknowledge the storm that raged inside her. Rose sank to her knees on the cold cliff top, her hands gripping the long grass stems as if they could anchor her to the earth. The stubby candles that ringed her, guttered in the wind but stayed alight. She longed for a sign, a flicker of hope that her heart could one day heal, that she could rise from the ashes of her own sorrow, that she could find once again the man who haunted her thoughts. He was the answer, he was hope, and he was gone.

The waves crashed in a rhythm that matched her dreaming heartbeat, she closed her eyes and allowed herself to drift into the memories that haunted her. It was a dance of pain, a slow waltz that she had to embrace. In that haunting solitude, she understood that she was still alive, even in her brokenness, and still a part of the world that refused to stop turning. Perhaps, just perhaps, that meant she had the strength to find her way back to the light.

Then she saw him, her first great love, now her tormentor, standing before her, laughing, smiling, alive. He was suspended in the air like a fragile bubble, begging to be popped, but in the waking world she knew that he was missing. Rose loved and hated the man, feeling betrayed and relieved at the same time. Being here on the cliff in the dreamworld was a sweet liberation from the chains that Jack had wrapped around her heart. The mental torture that permeated her waking thoughts was worse than the physical abuses that her gentlemen callers visited upon her. Her memories of laughter were now twisted into echoes of pain, reverberating against the walls of her mind.

Before the world turned sour, Jack was the centre of her universe. He was the sun around which she revolved. He was her Romeo, blessed with a charm that captivated her, promising love that could conquer all. She had been his Juliet, naive and full of dreams, lost in the whirlwind of passion that swept her off her feet. Together, they spun tales of eternity under a sky littered with stars, whispering promises of a love that would outlast the cosmos, but that was just the drugs talking, a haze of fantasies born from substances that painted their love in technicolour, all the while masking the shadows that lurked just beyond their sight.

As she stood there on the cliff top, the reality of his absence hit her like a tidal wave. The laughter that once filled her with warmth now felt like a mocking refrain, a cruel reminder of the happiness that had slipped through her fingers. She could still hear his voice, soft and sweet, telling her that everything would be okay, even as the storm raged around them, but now, that voice was silenced, replaced by the haunting whispers that told the stories of what he had actually done to her.

Jack changed. He became a shell of a man, a shadow of his former self, with marionette strings frayed and slack. The drugs consumed him, hollowing him out until all that remained was a fragile facade, a smile painted on a spectral face. She tried to save him, to pull him back from the abyss, but every attempt only pushed him further away. Each argument turned into a dance of desperation, the air thick with violent words and dark regrets that hung like a black cloud over them both. Now, lost as she was in the hit, Rose felt like a moth drawn to a flame, her memories of love blinding her to the danger that lurked beneath the surface.

And then he stole away. The man she once adored, left only the wreckage of their shared dreams in his wake. Jack got clean and Rose did not. Jack tried for a while, but his patience and his strength were thin, and, in the end, he could not face another day watching Rose fade away. It was a cruel twist of fate that cut deeper than any physical wound. The shock of losing her man should have jolted Rose out of her stupor, but by then she was confused, and Jack's leaving gave her a sense of peace, an end to the tumultuous ride that their life together had become. It was only later, deep in the grip of her addiction, that she started to grapple with the aching void he had left behind.

Each day was a battle against the memories that flooded her mind, uninvited and unwelcome. The tenderness of their moments together felt like daggers in her soul, each reminiscence slicing through her heart with excruciating clarity. She remembered how he would hold her, the warmth of his body against hers, the promises they exchanged beneath the stars down by the river when they were young lovers.

As she stood alone on the cliff top in her dream, she felt the mantle of her grief settle upon her shoulders like a shroud. It wrapped around her tightly, a suffocating embrace that refused to let go. In that moment, she realised that even though he was gone, the remnants of their love still lingered, haunting her with every breath. Rose closed her eyes, allowing the tears to spill, feeling the hot rush of sorrow wash over her. The road ahead was uncertain. In her waking hours, Rose deliberately shunned these deeper thoughts of love. She didn't want clarity. She was mechanistic and resigned in the real world. Here, though, in the dream, she could drive into the heart of things.

The seasons, the wind, the sun, and the rain didn't fear the reaper. Why should they? They were eternal, unfazed by the passage of time or the loss of life, but Rose... she was mortal and fragile. She felt the blade twisting in her chest.

Her knees trembled as she gazed out over the abyss. She could feel the pull, the dark allure of oblivion, beckoning her to join with the deep, dark waters. She had fought it for so long, but now, now, it seemed like the only answer. As she stood there, ready to step into the void, a sudden gust of wind almost knocked her off her feet. The candles that she had lit in his memory, these small, flickering flames, were snuffed out by the wind, leaving her in near darkness. She felt a presence, a static charge, as if someone or something was trying to get her attention, and then, from the shadows, a figure appeared. He was standing at the edge of the cliff, just a few steps away from her. His face was pale, his eyes dark but not empty. There was something alive in his gaze, something ancient and wise. His presence was otherworldly, yet familiar, as if she had always known he would come.

"Don't be afraid," he said softly, his voice wrapping around her like a comforting blanket. There was a soothing kindness in his tone, a gentleness she hadn't anticipated, and it made her heart flutter with unexpected hope. Rose didn't flinch. She didn't back away. Instead, a profound sense of calm washed over her, as if the storm raging in her mind was finally stilled. It felt as if she had been waiting for him all along, though she couldn't quite articulate why. Perhaps it was his presence that calmed the chaos inside her. This strange figure was a beacon of solace amidst the turmoil of her thoughts.

She had heard the tales of the reaper, the figure cloaked in shadows who came to claim souls and guide them to the other side. Fear always gripped her at the mere mention of him, but now, facing him, she felt something entirely different. This man-like creature wasn't the harbinger of doom from the stories; he didn't seem threatening at all. Instead, he exuded an air of understanding, as if he held the weight of the world's sorrows in his heart and could empathise with her pain.

"Take my hand," he whispered, extending it toward her. His hand was open, palm facing up, inviting and warm despite the cold wind that whipped around them. In that simple gesture, there was an intimacy that tugged at something deep within her, a yearning for connection, for comfort, for release. Rose hesitated. The world around them faded, the howling winds becoming mere whispers, and all that remained was the two of them suspended in time. His eyes held hers, and in their depths, she saw not just darkness but a reflection of her own grief, her own longing. It was as if he could see into her soul, tracing the scars etched upon her heart, acknowledging the battles she had fought and the losses she had endured.

Slowly, she reached out, her fingers trembling as they brushed against his. The moment their hands connected, a warmth spread through her like a soothing balm that eased the rawness of her wounds. She felt safe, cocooned in an understanding that transcended words. The shadows of her past began to lift, and for the first time in what felt like an eternity, she allowed herself to believe in the possibility of peace.

"Let me help you," he said, his voice a gentle caress against the wind, and in that invitation, she found the courage to step forward and to embrace the unknown. She took a deep breath, the air filling her lungs with a sweet bouquet. She felt a sense of liberation flood through her body, and as she tightened her grip on his hand, she understood that she wasn't just taking his hand; she was choosing to trust, to surrender, and to finally let go.

"We'll be able to fly," he promised, his voice once again soothing the broken pieces of her soul.

The wind seemed to lift them both off the ground. Her feet left the cliffside, and suddenly, they were soaring, flying above the crashing waves, the dark sea, and the cold, hard earth. The despair that had filled her heart began to lift. She looked down at the world below, at the pain and sadness she had carried for so long, and for the first time, she didn't feel afraid.

They flew higher and higher, beyond the reach of the storm clouds, beyond the realm of the living, until they reached a place where time no longer mattered, where love was eternal, and where she could finally be at peace. She looked back once, seeing the cliff where she had stood moments ago. She was no longer bound to it. She had become something else, something more. She was like the wind, the sun, and the rain.

As they soared through the sky, she glanced at him, the reaper who held her hand. He smiled, and in that moment, she realised that he was not her enemy. He had come not to take her life, but to give her a second chance at it, beyond death, beyond sorrow, beyond everything she had ever known.

"Don't fear the reaper," he said, and she smiled back at him, knowing in her heart that the needle and the damage done would never hurt her again.

The song behind the story: *"Don't Fear the Reaper" is one of the most iconic songs by the American rock band Blue Öyster Cult, released in 1976 as part of their album Agents of Fortune. Written by the band's lead guitarist Donald "Buck Dharma" Roeser, the song is known for its haunting melody, philosophical lyrics, and, of course, the famous cowbell.*

"Don't Fear the Reaper" is widely regarded as one of the greatest rock songs of the 1970s. Rolling Stone magazine ranked it on their list of the "500 Greatest Songs of All Time." Its blend of existential themes with soft rock and psychedelic elements, coupled with its longevity in pop culture, has made it one of the most enduring and beloved songs in rock history. The song's message, that death is not something to fear, remains resonant for many listeners, contributing to its long-lasting appeal.

I first heard this at the Monsters Of Rock Festival at Donnington, UK, in 1981. This is one of those songs that always triggers an emotional response, at least it does for me.

Album: *Agents Of Fortune*

Artist: *Blue Öyster Cult*

Year: *1976*

Composer(s): *Donald "Buck Dharma" Roeser*

Record Label: *Columbia Records*

About The Author

Born in 1962 into a household that lived and breathed sports, the author's dad was a seasoned senior amateur and lower league professional footballer. Not just that, he managed his own businesses in cahoots with Clive's mum, who was no slouch either – she was a skilled and award-winning ballroom dancer.

After snagging a degree in History from Leeds University, our storyteller took a rather serendipitous stroll into the burgeoning world of information technology in the late '80s. Like father, like son, they say. Alongside a flourishing tech career, Clive dabbled in various writing and acting pursuits, from freelancing as a journalist and book reviewer (with a coveted by-line in The Sunday People) to gracing stages in village halls and the odd professional theatre across the south of the UK for a good decade.

In a nod to the family's sporting legacy, Clive - long after hanging up his own hockey boots - delved into the world of live TV broadcasts. Armed with a wealth of rugby knowledge, he became one of the go-to 'statos' for the BBC, ITV, TVNZ, and Eurosport, covering everything from Heineken Cups to Six Nations, World Sevens, and World Cups in the late '90s.

For a deeper dive into this fascinating journey, head over to clivegilson.com, where there's a whole trove of tales waiting to be uncovered!

Other Work By Clive Gilson

ORIGINAL FICTION BY CLIVE GILSON

- *Songs of Bliss*
- *Out of the Walled Garden*
- *The Mechanic's Curse*
- *The Insomniac Booth*
- *A Solitude of Stars*
- *Melodies In Black Ink*

AS EDITOR – *FIRESIDE TALES – Western Europe*

- *Tales From the Land of Dragons* – Welsh Folk & Fairy Tales
- *Tales From the Land of The Brave* – Scottish Folk & Fairy Tales
- *Tales From the Land of Saints And Scholars* – Irish Folk & Fairy Tales
- *Tales From the Land of Hope And Glory* – English Folk & Fairy Tales
- *Tales from Gallia* – French Folk & Fairy Tales

AS EDITOR – *FIRESIDE TALES – Northern Europe*

- *Tales From Lands of Snow and Ice* – Scandinavian Folk & Fairy Tales
- *Tales From the Viking Isles* – Icelandic Folk & Fairy Tales
- *Tales From the Forest Lands* – Finnish Folk & Fairy Tales
- *Tales From the Old Norse* – Scandinavian Folk & Fairy Tales
- *Tales from Germania* – German Folk & Fairy Tales

AS EDITOR – *FIRESIDE TALES – Southern Europe*

- *Tales From the Land of Rabbits* – Spanish & Portuguese Folk & Fairy Tales
- *Tales Told by Bulls and Wolves* – Italian Folk & Fairy Tales
- *Tales of Fire and Bronze* – Greek Folk & Fairy Tales

AS EDITOR – *FIRESIDE TALES* – *Eastern Europe*

- *Tales From The Samodivi* – Balkan Folk & Fairy Tales
- *Tales From the Land of the Strigoi* – Romanian Folk & Fairy Tales
- *Tales Told by the Wind Mother*– Hungarian Folk & Fairy Tales

AS EDITOR – *FIRESIDE TALES* – *North America*

- *Okaraxta* - Tales from The Great Plains
- *Tibik-Kìzis* – Tales from The Great Lakes & Canada
- *Jóhonaa'éí* –Tales from America's Southwest
- *Qugaaĝix̂* - First Nation Tales from Alaska & The Arctic
- *Karahkwa* - First Nation Tales from America's Eastern States
- *Pot-Likker* - Folklore, Fairy Tales, and Settler Stories from America

AS EDITOR – *FIRESIDE TALES* – *Africa*

- *Arokin Tales* – Folklore & Fairy Tales from West Africa
- *Hadithi Tales* – Folklore & Fairy Tales from East Africa
- *Inkathaso Tales* – Folklore & Fairy Tales from Southern Africa
- *Tarubadur Tales* – Folklore & Fairy Tales from North Africa
- *Elephant And Frog* – Folklore from Central Africa

AS EDITOR – *FIRESIDE TALES* – *Middle East*

- *Tales From The Meddahs* – Turkish Folk & Fairy Tales
- *Tales From The Hakawati* – Arabic Folk & Fairy Tales
- *Tales Told By Balebos & Gusan* – Jewish & Armenian Folk & Fairy Tales

AS EDITOR – *FIRESIDE TALES* – *Asia & The Far East*

- *Tales Told By The Kathaakaar* – Folk & Fairy Tales from India
- *Tales Of The Gùshì Yuan* – Chinese Folk & Fairy Tales

AS EDITOR – *FIRESIDE TALES* – *Animal Tales*

- *Dog Tails* – Folk & Fairy Tales featuring our canine chums
- *Cat Tails* – Folk & Fairy Tales featuring our feline friends

www.ingramcontent.com/pod-product-compliance
Ingram Content Group UK Ltd.
Pitfield, Milton Keynes, MK11 3LW, UK
UKHW041306140325
4998UKWH00016B/47/J

9 781915 081339